Millions of Kids Have Loved Her Books—Now Judy Blume Writes One for Us!

"Remember when you were a curious twelve or thirteen and your mother told you to stay away from the neatest kid on the block because she was a bad influence . . . told you hilarious things about S-E-X that you just *couldn't* believe?

"Well, this neat kid is still around, although in adult form. . . . GET TO KNOW JUDY BLUME. IN HER NOVEL *WIFEY* SHE'S STILL A BAD INFLUENCE, AND SHE IS STILL A LOT OF FUN!"
—*Cincinnati Enquirer*

"ONE FOR THE GROWN-UPS! . . . PATHOS, SLAPSTICK, ROMANCE. . . . My children have been addicted to her for years—now one sees why."
—*Los Angeles Times*

"ADULTEROUS FUN!"
—*Philadelphia Inquirer*

PUBLISHED BY POCKET BOOKS NEW YORK

Judy Blume's
Wifey

PUBLISHED BY POCKET BOOKS NEW YORK

POCKET BOOKS, a Simon & Schuster division of
GULF & WESTERN CORPORATION
1230 Avenue of the Americas, New York, N.Y. 10020

Published by arrangement with G. P. Putnam's Sons
Library of Congress Catalog Card Number: 78-6145

ISBN: 0-671-83531-9

First Pocket Books printing July, 1979

15   14   13   12   11

POCKET and colophon are trademarks of Simon & Schuster.

Printed in the U.S.A.

To Tom, *for loving*
To Claire and Phyllis, *for believing*
To Randy and Larry, *for enduring*

In terms of affluence America in the 60's reached a stage that other societies can only dream of.

from Good Times *by Peter Joseph*

1

SANDY SAT UP in bed and looked at the clock. Quarter to eight. Damn! Last night she'd told Norman she might sleep all day just to catch up. No kids for once, no demands, no responsibilities. But the noise. What was it, a truck, a bus? It sounded so close. And then the empty sound after the engine cut off. She'd never get back to sleep now. She slipped into her robe, the one the children had given her for Mother's Day. "Daddy picked it out," Jen had said. "Do you like it?" "Oh yes, it's perfect," Sandy had answered, hating it. Imagine Norman choosing the same robe for her as she had sent to his mother and her own.

She traipsed across the room to the window, rubbing her eyes to keep them open, spitting her hair out of her face. She looked down into the wooded backyard. He was in front of the crab apple tree, hands on hips, as if waiting for her, dressed in a white bed sheet and a stars and stripes helmet, standing next to a motorcycle. What was this? A kid, playing Halloween? A neighborhood ghost? No . . . look . . . he threw off the bed sheet and stood before her, naked, his penis long and stiff. Sandy dropped to her knees, barely peeking out the window, afraid, but fascinated, not just by the act itself, but by the style. So fast, so hard! Didn't it hurt, handling it that way? She'd always been so careful with Norman's, scared that she might damage it. Who was he? What was he doing in her yard? *Nineteen, twenty, twenty-one,* Sandy counted. He came on twenty-seven, leaving his stuff on her lawn, then jumped on his bike, kicked down with one foot, and started up the engine. But wait. It stalled. Would she have to call Triple A and if so how was she going to explain the problem? *Hello, this is Mrs. Pressman . . . there's a . . . you see . . . well . . . anyway . . . and he's having trouble with his motorcycle . . .* No. No need to worry. The engine caught and he took off, zooming down the street, wearing only the stars and stripes helmet.

She called Norman first, at the plant, and he asked, "Did it make ridges in the lawn?"

"What?"

"The motorcycle, did it make ridges in the lawn?"

"I don't know."

"Well, find out."

"Now?"

"Yes, I'll hold."

She put the phone down and ran outside.

"Yes, there are ridges," she told Norman. "Two of them."

"Okay. First thing, call Rufano, tell him to take care of it."

"Right. Rufano," she repeated, jotting it down. "Should he reseed or what?"

"I can't say. I'm not there, am I? Let him decide, he's the doctor."

"But it doesn't pay to put money into the lawn when we're moving, does it?"

"We haven't sold the house yet. It would be different if we'd already sold."

"Norm . . ."

"What?"

"I'm a little shaky."

"I'll call the police as soon as we hang up."

"I'm not dressed."

"So get dressed."

"Are you coming home?"

"I can't, Sandy. I'm in the middle of a new solution."

"Oh."

"See you tonight."

"Right."

Sandy showered and dressed and waited for the police.

"Okay, Mrs. Pressman, let's have it again." She'd expected, at the very least, Columbo. Instead she got Hubanski, tall and thin, with a missing tooth and an itchy leg. He sat on the sofa and scratched the area above his black anklet sock. Plainfield, New Jersey's, finest.

"My husband told you the whole story, didn't he?"

"Uh huh."

He whipped his notebook out of his pocket and made squiggles with his ballpoint pen. "Doesn't seem to be working today."

"Try blowing in it," Sandy suggested. "Sometimes that helps."

Hubanski blew into the end of his ballpoint and tried again. "Nope, nothing."

"Just a minute." Sandy went into the kitchen and came back with a pen. "Try this one."

"Thanks," he said, printing his name.

3

Sandy sat down on the love seat opposite him, tucking her legs under her.

"Okay, now I want to hear it from you, Mrs. Pressman. You say it was about quarter past eight?"

"No, quarter to."

"You're sure of that?"

"Yes, positive, because as soon as I woke up I looked at the clock."

"And the noise that woke you sounded like a motorcycle?"

"Well, I didn't know it was a motorcycle then. I just knew it was a noise, which is why I went over to the window in the first place."

"Now, we have to be very sure about this, Mrs. Pressman."

"I looked out the window and there he was," Sandy said. "It's very simple."

"He didn't ring the bell or anything, first?"

"Why would he have done that?"

"I'm only trying to set the record straight, Mrs. Pressman, because, you know, this isn't our everyday, ordinary kind of complaint. So just take your time and tell me again."

"He was wearing a sheet and he was looking up at me."

"Now, this here's the important part, Mrs. Pressman, and I want to be sure I've got it one hundred per cent right. You're telling me that this guy rides up on a motorcycle."

"Yes."

"And he's got a bed sheet over him."

"That's right."

"Like your ordinary everyday kind of bed sheet?"

"Yes, plain white, hospital variety."

"Okay, I get the picture. So let's take it from there,

4

Mrs. Pressman. Now, you look down from your bedroom window and he looks up. Is that right so far?"

"Very good, you're doing fine."

"Look, Mrs. Pressman, you might not believe it, but
this is no picnic for me either."

"Sorry."

"Okay, so he takes off the sheet."

"Right."

"And he's stark naked."

"Yes, except for his helmet . . . stars and
stripes . . ."

"Yeah, I already got that. So, go on."

"Well, then he masturbated. And that's about it."

"You say *about*. Is there something else?"

"No, he got on his motorcycle and rode off. That's
it."

"Naked?"

"Yes, I told you that."

"So where's the bed sheet, Mrs. Pressman?" He held
up his hand, a hint of a smile showing on his face for
the first time.

"I don't know."

"You didn't pick it up when you went out to inspect
the lawn?"

"No."

"And you didn't see him pick it up either?"

"No, but he might have. Because I was pretty upset
at the time, as you can imagine. I might have missed
that."

"What I don't get, Mrs. Pressman, is how come you
watched the whole thing. I mean, you could have
called us right off. We might have been able to get
over here in time."

"I was scared, I guess. I just don't know."

"How about a make on the motorcycle?"

"It was chrome."

"Come on, Mrs. Pressman. You can do better than that. Was it this year's model, a 1970? Or would you say it was five to ten years old?"

"I don't know. They all look the same to me."

He clicked the pen closed, stood up, and handed it to Sandy.

"Keep it," she said, "I'm sure you'll need it."

"Thanks. Say listen, what about the dog? Your husband said you have a dog."

"We do, a miniature schnauzer, Banushka. But he slept through it."

"You're sure he was white?"

"Who?"

"The guy—the exhibitionist."

"Oh, yes."

"Because a lot of these mixed races can look almost white."

"No, he was white. Like you."

He sighed. "Well, you haven't given me much to go on, Mrs. Pressman."

"I'm sorry."

"Look, if you remember anything else, no matter how small, give me a call, okay? And in the meantime I'll do my best."

"That's all anyone can ask for, sergeant . . ." Sandy paused. What the hell was his name?

"Hubanski. U-ban-ski. The H is silent."

"I'll remember that. Good-bye . . . and thank you."

As Hubanski was walking down the front steps Sandy called, "Oh, sergeant?"

He turned. "Yeah."

"I just remembered . . . he was left-handed."

"Hubanski didn't believe me," she told Norman

that night, over chicken piquant. She was really pissed about that.

"It is an incredible story, Sandy."

"Don't you think I know that?"

"How come we're having chicken tonight? It's Monday, we always have chicken on Wednesdays."

"I didn't stop to think. I just defrosted the first thing I saw when I opened the freezer. Besides, with the kids away, what's the difference?"

"The difference is that I count on chicken on Wednesdays, the way I count on pot roast on Thursdays and some sort of chopped meat on Tuesdays. I had chicken salad for lunch."

"Oh, I'm sorry."

"Did you get this recipe from your sister?"

"No, from *Elegant but Easy*."

"Not bad. You should have browned it first, though."

"It's a pain to brown chicken. That's why I made this one, you don't need to brown it first."

"It would look more appetizing if you did, next time."

"So close your eyes!"

"I'm just making a suggestion, San. No need to get so touchy about it."

"Who's touchy?"

Norman took off his glasses and wiped them with his dinner napkin. "I think what you need is new interests, especially now, with the kids away for the whole summer."

Was he doubting her story too? "I have plenty to do. There's the new house and besides that, I'm going to read. I'm going to do the classics. I told you that."

"But you need to get out of the house more, to mingle," Norman said.

7

"I don't need to be around people all the time."

"You lack self-confidence."

"What's that supposed to mean?"

"I'm trying to tell you, trying to help you, if only you'll let me."

"Do you want more rice?"

"Yes, thank you. I think The Club is the answer, San."

"Oh, please, Norm, don't start that again."

"I thought we agreed that as soon as the kids left you'd give it another try."

"Look, I told you when you joined that it wasn't my thing . . . that I didn't want any part of it. So don't expect . . . don't ask me to . . ." She got up to clear away the dishes.

"Look at your sister," Norman said.

"You look at her."

"Four years older than you."

"Three and a half, but who's counting?"

"She loves The Club, practically lives there."

"She was always the family athlete."

"Tan and firm, in terrific shape."

"I failed gym in eighth grade, did you know that?" She put a plate of cookies on the table and set two cups of cold water, with tea bags, in the new microwave oven.

"You're not in the eighth grade any more, Sandy." He took a bite of one of the cookies. "Pepperidge Farm?"

"No, Keeblers." The microwave pinged and Sandy carried the teacups to the table. "Myra got straight A's in gym, all the way through school. She won letters. She was a goddamned cheerleader!"

"You ought to learn to do more with the microwave than just heat water."

"I don't like gadgets."

"Because you lack self-confidence."

"What does self-confidence have to do with the microwave?"

"What do gadgets have to do with it?"

"I tried The Club, Norm. I took two golf lessons and two tennis lessons and I was awful. I just don't have the aptitude, the coordination."

"Don't give me that shit, Sandy. You could be as good as most of the girls if you'd make the effort." He crunched another cookie. "Why don't you have your hair done . . . buy yourself something new to wear . . . you used to look terrific yourself."

"Jesus, you sound like my mother now."

"So she's noticed too?"

"I've been sick, Norm!"

"That was months ago. That's no excuse for now."

Sandy went to the sink and turned the water on full blast.

"I guess I'll walk Banushka," Norman said.

"You do that!"

"Oh, San, for God's sake." He tried to put his arms around her but she brushed him away. "You're so damned *touchy* these days," he said. "I can't even talk to you any more."

Any more? Sandy thought. But she didn't say it.

As soon as she heard the back door close she picked up a plate and flung it across the kitchen. It smashed into tiny pieces. She felt better.

tions on your face."

2

OKAY. SO SHE didn't look her best. But that wasn't her fault, was it? She'd had a rough couple of months and was just beginning to feel healthy again. After an illness like hers it could take a year to get back to normal. And it hadn't been a year yet. It had started last Halloween, at the supermarket. She'd felt sick at the checkout counter and had to be helped to the Ladies Room by the cashier. She thought she was going to pass out, but once she got her head down, she was okay. The manager had carried her groceries to the car, even offered to drive her home, but she assured him she was fine, that it was just the combination of the overheated store and her heavy jacket. Too warm for October.

In the car, on the way home, she'd been overcome by a wave of nausea and sharp pains in her head. She'd pulled over, feeling very much the way she had when coming down with mono, years ago. In a few minutes that passed too and she was able to drive the rest of the way home. Jen had greeted her at the door. "Oh, Mom, you look so cute with those Halloween decorations on your face."

11

"What decorations?"

"Those little hearts."

Sandy had run to the mirror. Good God, she did have little heart-shaped marks around her eyes and on her cheeks.

William R. Ackerman, M.D., P.C., Diplomate in Internal Medicine, with a sub-specialty in livers, had seen her late that afternoon. By then, the heart-shaped marks had disappeared. "Scarlet fever," he'd said, relating her condition to Bucky's recent strep infection. He'd taken a throat culture, then prescribed penicillin; one capsule, three times a day.

Within the week she'd improved enough to resume her family responsibilities, although she certainly wasn't feeling great. Ten days later it returned, but much worse. A fever of 105, aches and pains in her joints, a strange rash suddenly covering her body; hivelike on her arms, measlelike on her stomach, blotches on her swollen face. She wanted only to sleep.

She was vaguely aware of routine household activity. Aware, but not caring. Aware of the children. "Is Mom going to die?" asked in the same casual tone as *Is Mom going shopping?* Aware of Norman's anger. She never could understand his anger when she or the children were sick, when life didn't go as planned, as if it were all her fault. Aware of her mother, called in by Norman to take charge, because in eleven and a half years of marriage he had never missed a day of work or a golf or tennis game. "Oh, my God, my God," Mona had cried. "My little girl, my darling Sandy."

This time Dr. Ackerman had stood at the foot of Sandy's bed, not because he made house calls, but because it was Sunday and he lived across the street and it was more convenient for him to see her at home than to drive across town to his office. He stood there, looking down at her, ticking off possibilities on his fingers. ". . . or it could be indicative of thoracic cancer, leprosy, leukemia, lupus, or a severe allergic reaction."

Sandy closed her eyes. She didn't want to hear any more. *Please God, don't let it be leprosy,* she prayed.

"I think we'll go with the allergic reaction theory and start her on steroids right away," Dr. Ackerman said.

"But what exactly is it?" Norman had pressed.

"Erythema multiformi. Debilitating but not fatal."

So, she wasn't going to die this time.

"There must be something she can do to prevent these illnesses," Norman said. "Take vitamins or something. I haven't got the time for all of this."

And later, after the doctor had left, she opened her eyes to find Norman's Nikon pointing at her. "What are you doing?"

"Just a couple of shots," Norman told her.

"But, Norm . . ."

"Just in case."

"In case, what?"

"Medical malpractice, you never know."

Norman read the *AMA Journal* religiously, unusual for a man in the dry-cleaning business. Was he a frustrated physician? Or did his morbid interest stem from Sandy's physical problems? Dr. Ackerman once told her she was the healthiest *sick* person he had ever treated. Healthy, because basically there was nothing wrong. She had been tested and re-tested. Everything was in good shape, although Dr. Ackerman once suspected her stomach of being in her chest cavity because he heard gurglings while listening to her heart. Not an illness, he'd told her, reassuringly, but a condition *we* should know about, for *our* records. He'd sent her to a radiologist who served her a tall glass of

lime-flavored barium. But the X-rays only proved that
her stomach was exactly where it should have been.

Camille, Aunt Lottie had called her as a girl. But
Mona said, "It's not her fault, she has no resistance!"

She had her first important illness at ten. Pilitis, pus
in the kidney. It had burned when she peed. How
comfortable, how warm and safe, to crawl into bed
and have her mother take care of her. Mona was a
somewhat nervous but gentle nurse, catering to Sandy's
every need, every wish. The first few days she'd been
too sick to do anything but just lie there, dozing off
and on. Mona fed her the yucky chocolate-flavored
medicine the doctor had prescribed and when the lab
technician came to the house for a blood sample Sandy
had vomited it all over him. Mona was terribly embarrassed. "Why didn't you ask for the bucket?"

"I didn't know," Sandy had said. "I'm sorry."

She had lain in bed for two weeks that time, listening to soap operas on her radio, doing movie star cut-
out books, reading Nancy Drew mysteries, and
practicing upside-down tunnels with her tongue, learned
during speech class, before Mona had rushed into
school, demanding that Sandy be removed because
"There is nothing wrong with my daughter's speech!"
"It's her *ing* endings," Miss Tobias had explained.
"Her *ing* endings are as good as your *ing* endings,
maybe better," Mona had argued. And won.

In junior high it had been a three-year battle with
atopic dermatitis. Everybody else had plain old acne
but Sandy suffered through eczema like patches all
over her body and had to sleep with white cotton gloves
so that if she scratched during the night she wouldn't
tear her flesh open. In high school she'd been tested
for diabetes because of her fainting spells but the tests
were negative. And then, as a college freshman, mono.

A year later she married Norman, and marriage brought with it a never-ending parade of physical problems. Recurring sore throats, assorted viruses, stomach pains, a ganglian cyst in her right wrist, plantar warts on the bottoms of her feet, combined with two children who had inherited her low resistance, carrying home every available bug, and then, once she'd nursed them back to health, passing each disease on to her. But this, this erythema multiformi, was the most frightening, yet most exotic illness yet.

Sandy responded to the cortisone treatment, without side effects. "Lucky girl," Dr. Ackerman had said, and within two weeks all the symptoms had disappeared, leaving her ten pounds lighter, tired out, and looking like hell.

They'd gone to Jamaica over the Christmas holidays. Myra and Gordon had insisted. "Look at you," Myra had said, "a bird could blow you over. What you need is sunshine, sunshine and rest and besides, if there's any trouble Gordy can look after you."

"Gordon's a gynecologist," Sandy had said. "This isn't a gynecological problem."

"You think just because he's a gynecologist all he knows about are pussies? I'll have him talk to Bill Ackerman. We'll let *him* decide what's best for you."

And Dr. Ackerman had given his blessing.

They had flown down to Montego Bay together. Myra, Gordon, and their twin daughters; Sandy, Norman, Bucky, and Jen. "If this plane should go down, God forbid," Mona had said, seeing them off, "then I'm taking pills . . . maybe gas . . . my whole life's on board!"

"You should be coming with us," Myra said.

"I don't fly, period!" Mona answered. And then she

repeated her story about taking pills or gas to the ticket agent, who smiled and said, "No problem." With what . . . the pills . . . the plane . . . Sandy wondered, taking every word literally. Flying was no joking matter.

She was a nervous flier but she played it cool for the kids. *See how brave Mommy is.* Once on board she prayed every half-hour and tuned in to strange noises, odors, flickering lights, calls for the flight attendants, suspicious-looking characters likely to carry bombs in their luggage, or whatever. And during takeoffs and landings she grabbed Norman's hand and squeezed as hard as she could. He once got an infection because her fingernail pierced his skin.

Her oldest and dearest friend, Lisbeth, who was into psychology, explained it as Sandy's need to control her own destiny. "If you were the pilot," she said, "you wouldn't be afraid. What you really ought to do is take flying lessons."

"Oh, sure," Sandy said, "I don't have enough trouble driving the car. I still don't back into parking spaces."

"And your terror of thunderstorms is the same thing," Lisbeth had said one summer day when the sky turned black and rumbly. "You have no control over nature."

"So who does?" Sandy had asked.

"Nobody, but most people accept that."

"Your explanation is very sensible, but accepting it doesn't help me."

"You've got to fight to overcome your fears, believe me, I know."

And Sandy wanted to overcome her fears, was willing to fight, but not on this particular flight. She was too worn out to try anything new.

They'd landed safely, five minutes early, and were welcomed at the airport by a steel band and complimentary daiquiris. Myra had shipped three hundred dollars' worth of meat with her baggage, packed and frozen in dry ice by her butcher in South Orange. She'd arranged to find the meat broker in front of the Air Jamaica counter but so far he hadn't shown. Without him her meat would be confiscated. Sandy drank two more daiquiris while Myra ran through the airport in a frenzy, searching for him. Bucky and Jen, hot and bored, were chasing each other. The twins, sullen, as usual, complained about the lack of air-conditioning, and fanned themselves with magazines.

After an hour it was clear that the meat broker was not going to show and they lined up to go through customs. "Bastards!" Myra hissed. "It's so unfair. They make it hard on us when we're the ones bringing in the money . . ."

"Relax, lady," the customs official said, "you got tree days to claim it before it's confiscated . . ."

"And I'm supposed to trust you to keep it frozen for three days?"

"Sure lady . . . you come back wit de meat broker . . . you take de meat home wit you . . ."

"You expect me to give up a full day of vacation to come back here, unnecessarily?"

"Yes, lady. Dat's de rule."

"Oh, you people!" Myra shook her frosted head at him. "No wonder it's like . . . you think . . ." She pointed at him. "Someday you'll see."

"Yes, lady."

Myra walked off in a huff, gold bracelets bangling, chains swinging around her neck, and were those really perspiration stains under the arms of her beige silk shirt? Sandy had never seen Myra sweat.

17

The car was there, waiting for them, but even in the Buick Rancho wagon it was tight. Jen fished a piece of wool out of her goody bag and worked a cat's cradle on her fingers, while Bucky polished off the rest of the cookies, melted by now. Connie and Kate sacked out. Sandy had trouble keeping her eyes open too. It took an hour and a half to get to Runaway Bay. At least none of the kids got carsick any more.

Myra and Gordon had bought the house eighteen months ago, after falling in love with the area. It came complete with furnishings, four servants, a Rhodesian Ridgeback, and a name. Sandy had seen endless pictures of it but even they didn't prepare her for the real La Carousella. Round, as its name implied, with a swimming pool in the middle, the roof opened to the sky above it, four bedroom suites around the pool, and a large, glass-walled living room overlooking the golf course, a separate building to house the servants, and a brand new Har-tru tennis court with adjacent thatched-roof bar.

"Hollywooooood . . ." Myra sang, dancing around the pool.

"Mother, please!" her daughters cried.

"Can't I even enjoy my own house?" Myra asked. "So what do you think, San?"

"I can't . . . that is . . . I'm speechless!"

"Can we go swimming, Aunt Myra?" Bucky asked.

"Yes, go and change. Everybody go and change. Last one in's a rotten egg!"

Sandy, exhausted from the trip, said, "I think I'll take a little rest first." She didn't wake up until the next morning.

☙ 3 ❧

BY NEXT HALLOWEEN she was sure she'd be fully recovered. Maybe she'd even encourage the kids to throw a costume party, a good way to help them make new friends once they moved, Sandy thought, sweeping up the broken plate. She finished the kitchen and was sitting in the den, watching the Monday-night movie and wondering how Bucky and Jen were doing at camp when Norman returned with Banushka. "Three sticks and two wees," he said. "Would you mark his chart, San? I've got to make an important phone call."

Sandy waited until the first commercial, then went back to the kitchen and marked Banushka's chart. Banushka's chart had been Norman's idea. He'd recorded every pee and crap the dog had taken since they'd brought him home from the kennel, four years ago. When the children were born Norman had insisted that Sandy keep charts for them too. Careful records of their temperatures and bowel movements, with the appropriate descriptions, exactly as his mother, Enid, had kept for him when he was a boy. Sandy threw away the children's charts three years ago, when Bucky was eight and had checked off seven bowel movements in one day. She'd given him a huge dose of Kaopectate before finding out that it was Bucky's idea of a joke. Norman had never forgiven her. He and Enid still discussed bowel movements and their bathroom cupboards were filled with disposable Fleet enema bottles, just in case.

They got ready for bed without speaking, Sandy brushing her teeth with Crest, making blue spit in her sink, Norman using Colgate, as he had all his life. He got into his bed, wearing striped permanent-press boxer shorts, Sandy got into hers, dressed in peach nylon baby dolls, her hair pinned up with barrettes because lately she'd been perspiring in her sleep, strands of hair sticking to the sides of her face, causing an acnelike rash. An adolescent at thirty-two. Norman turned his back to her, she turned hers to him.

Sandy shivered and rolled herself into a ball, pulling the covers up around her head. Norman kept the house like a goddamned refrigerator, the air-conditioning always turned up too high. But he was never cold. He had body heat. That's what he called it, not that it did Sandy any good. He didn't like sleeping close so they had twin beds, attached to one headboard, a royal pain to make in the mornings, but why should she complain? Florenzia made the beds four mornings a week.

One bed for Norman, with cool, crisp sheets, preferably changed twice a week, not that he didn't want fresh ones daily, but even he knew that was an unreasonable, never mind impractical, request. And one bed for Sandy, where once a week, on Saturday nights, if she didn't have her period, they *did it*. A Jewish nymphomaniac. They fucked in her bed, then Norman went to the bathroom to wash his hands and penis, making Sandy feel dirty and ashamed. He'd climb into his own bed then, into his clean, cool sheets, and he'd fall asleep in seconds, never any tossing, turning, sighing. Never any need to hold hands, cuddle, or laugh quietly with her. Three to five minutes from start to finish. She knew. She'd watched the digital bedside clock often enough. Three to five minutes. Then he'd say, "Very nice, did you get your dessert?"

"Yes, thank you, dessert was fine."

"Well, then, good night."

" 'Night, Norm."

She'd learned to come in minutes, seconds if she had to, and she almost always made it twice. No problem there. She almost always got her main course and her dessert. But usually it was a TV dinner and an Oreo when she craved scampi and mousse au chocolat.

And there was no agonizing itchy pussy for Norman either, to keep him up half the night. It was driving her wild. Scratching, scratching, all night long, reminiscent of her junior high condition but concentrated only in her vaginal area. Digging her nails into the soft delicate flesh of her lower lips, tearing them open and in the morning, when she sat down to pee, the unbearable sting of her urine hitting the open wound. She'd tried creams and lotions and powders and cornstarch and antihistamines and cotton underpants, but so far nothing worked.

"We've ruled out the possibility of a fungus," Gordon told her, "and there's no sign of infection. We're still considering an allergic reaction, to Norm's semen, but at the same time we also have to consider the possibility that it's strictly functional . . ."

"Functional?"

21

"Yes, psychosomatic, relating to your sex life. So how is your sex life, Sandy?"

My sex life? Oh, you mean my *sex* life. Yes. Well. Let's see. Ummm, if you want to judge it strictly on the basis of orgasms it's fine. Terrific. That is, I masturbate like crazy, Gordon. You wouldn't believe how I masturbate. God, I'm always at it. Driving here, for instance, this morning . . . driving, get that, in traffic, no less . . . no, not the Cadillac, Norm took that to work. The Buick . . . driving the Buick, I hear this song on the radio . . . from my youth, Gordy . . . like when I was seventeen or something . . . *Blue velvet, bluer than velvet was the night* . . . it reminds me of Shep . . . and I get this feeling in my cunt . . . this really hot feeling . . . and just a little rubbing with one hand . . . just a little tickle, tickle on the outside of my clothes . . . just one-two-three and that's enough . . . I'm coming and I don't even want to come yet because it feels so good . . . I want it to last. And guess what, Gordy? I never itch after I come that way. I itch only after Norman. So, you see, it must have something to do with him. Maybe I *am* allergic to his semen . . . maybe I'm allergic to his cock . . . maybe I'm allergic to him! Wouldn't that be something?

Oh, you'd rather hear about my sex life *with* Norman? Yes. Of Course. I understand, Gordy. Bearing on the case. Certainly. Well. Every Saturday night, rain or shine, unless I have my period. Variety? You mean like in the books? Well, no . . . Norm isn't one for variety. Changes make him uncomfortable. And I'm not one for making suggestions, Gordy. You think I should? I don't know . . . I'd have to think about that . . . maybe . . .

Oral sex? Oh, Gordy . . . now you're getting so personal. Must we? I mean, really. Well, of course I see that it's part of my sex life. Yes, certainly we've tried . . . but the one time Norm put his face between my legs . . . well, poor Norm . . . he gagged and coughed and spent half an hour in the bathroom gargling with Listerine afterward and I felt terribly guilty. He was like a cat with a hair ball. All that suffering just to please me. And then there's the problem of smell . . . odor, you know . . . Norman hates the smell of fuck. He always complains the morning after, opens all the windows in the bedroom and sprays Lysol. That's why I douche with vinegar . . . cunt vinaigrette . . . to make it more appetizing . . . you know, like browned chicken.

"So how is it, Sandy?"
"What?"
"Your sex life."
"What does that have to do with my problem?"
"It could have a lot to do with it."
"I don't think I can discuss it with you, Gordon."
"Would you like me to send you to someone else?"
"No, I don't think I could discuss the subject at all."

"If you tell them I'm pregnant, they'll underst

"All right, as long as you do your share like mama

4

SHE USED TO look like Jackie Kennedy. Everybody said so. In 1960 she won the Jackie Kennedy look-alike contest sponsored by the Plainfield *Courier-News*. Norman's mother had sent in her photo. She hadn't even known she was a contestant until they'd called her to say she'd won and they were running her picture on the front page, two columns wide. A celebrity. A star.

Of course she'd voted for Jack. It was her first presidential election and there was no way she was going to support Norman's candidate, even though Norm was treasurer of the Plainfield Young Republicans' Club at the time. But Norman didn't know, didn't guess what she was up to. He thought his politics were her politics; his candidate, her candidate. Oh, the thrill of pulling the lever for Kennedy, defying Norman, even secretly!

"You should be out there ringing doorbells with me," he'd told her, during the campaign.

"If you tell them I'm pregnant, they'll understand."

"All right, as long as you do your share like a wife

should." So Norman brought home lists of registered voters and every night during election week Sandy sat at the phone making calls. The Young Republicans' Blitz.

She'd done her share to support her husband. She'd earned the right to celebrate secretly over Jack's election. For the first time Sandy had been touched by politics, by a current event. There had been no depression or world war to affect her life and Mona and Ivan were determined to spare their children the insecurities, the anxieties they had known. She had once asked her mother, after spending two weeks in the country with Aunt Lottie, "How is the war in Korea?" And Mona had answered, "The same, and don't worry your pretty little head about it. It has nothing to do with you."

Until now. Sandy and Jackie. They'd been pregnant together. John-John was born first, in November, and Bucky followed, in December. Sandy didn't watch the delivery in the overhead mirror although Dr. Snyder wanted her to. It was bad enough that he'd placed the baby on her belly fresh out of the oven, all bloody and ugly. She was high on Demerol. "Take him away," she'd cried, "he's a mess."

Dr. Snyder had laughed. "You don't mean that, Sandy. This is the happiest moment of your life."

She'd dozed off. Later, a nurse had carried Bucky to her, clean and wrapped in a soft blanket, all cuddly and warm. And the nurse had undressed him so that Sandy could examine his tiny fingers and toes, his navel, his miniature penis, and acknowledge the fact that she and Norm had produced a perfect baby.

They'd named him Bertram, after her grandfather, but agreed to call him Bucky until he was old enough to handle such a serious name.

"Bucky?" Enid had snickered. "What kind of name is that for a Jewish boy?"

"It's as good as Brett," Sandy had answered, tossing out the name of Enid's other grandson.

"From Miss Piss I expect a name like Brett," Enid had said. "From you I expected something better."

Miss Piss was married to Norman's brother, Fred, a California Casualty agent in Sherman Oaks. Other people called her Arlene. They saw each other only on rare occasions and Sandy always marveled over Arlene's never-ending change of hair color.

Six months later, when Norman's father, Sam, dropped dead while firing a cashier for pocketing cash, Enid had cried to Sandy, "If only you were having the baby now, he could have a proper name. Who knows how long I'll have to wait for Miss Piss to give me another grandchild. Or for that matter, you."

Jen had come along two and a half years later, just months after Jackie had lost her infant, Patrick, to hyaline membrane disease. Sandy had named her Jennifer Patrice. Jennifer because she loved the name; Patrice for Jackie's baby.

"Don't you think we should name her Sarah, after my father?" Norm had asked.

"Sarah can be her Hebrew name," Sandy said, and Norman hadn't argued. After all, she'd done all the work. And they'd both found out, through Bucky, that Norman's idea of *father* meant paying the bills, period.

Enid and Mona had arrived together, for afternoon visiting hours, each bearing a gift for the latest grandchild. A musical giraffe from Mona, a pink and white orlon bunting from Enid. Sandy had a small private room, filled with cards and flowers, the most elaborate a bouquet from Norman. To make up for the fact that he hadn't been around to drive her to the hospital? Sandy wasn't sure. By the time he'd been located on the sixteenth hole she'd already delivered the baby.

She wore the pink satin bed jacket Myra had sent when she'd had Bucky, and she'd pinned her hair up in a French twist, sprayed herself with Chanel, and put on makeup, denying the fact that under the blanket she sat on a rubber doughnut to ease the pain of her stitches and that she was slightly fuzzy from the Darvon Dr. Snyder had prescribed to numb her tender, swollen breasts.

At night the nurse provided ice packs to hold under her arms. "It's always you little girls who fill up that way . . . such a shame to let it all go to waste."

"I don't believe in nursing," Sandy told her. "I was nursed for eight months and I've always been sick."

"You should have told that to your doctor. There are shots, you know."

"I did tell him."

And Dr. Snyder sympathized with Sandy's discomfort. "I thought you'd change your mind this time," he'd said.

"I'll never change my mind about breast-feeding."

"Well, next time we'll give you a shot right after delivery so you won't have to suffer this way."

Next time? Who said anything about next time? She'd been expected to produce two children, preferably one of each sex. She'd fulfilled her obligation.

The first time Norman had been so impressed with the sudden growth of her breasts he'd brought his Nikon to the hospital, snapping pictures of Sandy in her bed jacket, unbuttoned enough to show some cleavage. This time he was less enthusiastic, realizing that the change was only temporary and would leave

28

her as small-breasted as before, unlike her sister, Myra, who had inherited Aunt Lottie's mammoth breasts, and who had, two years ago, undergone a breast reduction operation because "you can't imagine what it's like to carry around a pair of tits like these!"

"Too bad she can't give some to you," Norman had said at the time, adding, "ha ha . . ."

"Yes, too bad," Sandy had answered. "Ha ha ha . . ."

"So, when is my little Sarah going home?" Enid asked, reading the cards lined up on Sandy's dresser.

"Her name is Jennifer," Sandy said, "Jennifer Patrice. Didn't Norman tell you?"

"He said *Sarah*."

"Well, yes, in Hebrew it's Sarah, but we're going to call her Jen."

"I don't believe it!"

"It's true," Sandy said. "I've already signed the birth certificate. Jennifer Patrice."

"Mona, tell me I'm dreaming," Enid said, with one hand to her head, the other to her chest.

"The baby is hers to name," Mona said. "You had your chance with Norman and Fred."

"Oh, God, oh, God." Enid swayed, then sat down. "I feel weak, like I might faint."

Mona poured a cup of water for Enid. "Try to relax," she said, "don't get yourself all worked up for nothing . . ."

"Nothing? You think my son didn't want to name his own baby after his father, may he rest in peace. No, it's her . . ." Enid said, with a nod toward the bed. "She thinks she's too good for a simple, beautiful, biblical name like Sarah." She sipped some water.

"It's not that . . ." Sandy began.

29

"Miss High and Mighty!"

So she'd been christened too.

"Miss High and Mighty is too good to care about her poor old mother-in-law and did I or didn't I once send her picture to the *Courier-News,* making her a celebrity?"

"Please . . ." Sandy said.

"And how much time do I have left? A little happiness is all I ask."

"Stop it . . ." Sandy said, "please, stop it!"

The nurse poked her head in the doorway. "Ladies, could we try to remember we're in a hospital?"

Enid turned to face Mona. "I'll tell you this, my enemies treat me better than my daughter-in-laws. You don't know how lucky you are to have girls instead of boys. With boys you wind up with tsouris . . ."

"At least be happy the baby has the Hebrew name you want," Mona told her.

"To me she'll always be Sarah, no matter what Miss High and Mighty calls her."

"Her name is Jennifer, dammit!" Sandy shouted. "And I've got the birth certificate to prove it!" She could no longer hold back her tears.

"Ladies, ladies." The nurse returned, shaking her head at them. "I'll have to ask you to leave now. Look at our patient."

Sandy was crying hard. "Take care, darling," Mona said, kissing her cheek. "I'd better go too. She shouldn't drive like this."

The nurse gave Sandy a sedative and she slept through feeding time and missed evening visiting hours.

Sandy was filled with guilt. It wasn't just that she liked the name Jennifer, and certainly she didn't dislike the name Sarah. It was that she couldn't, wouldn't name her child after Samuel D. Pressman. Sam Pressman had never addressed Sandy by name. He'd called her *girl* or *you,* not entirely without affection, but without concern. Samuel David Pressman, owner of Pressman's Dry Cleaning Establishment, a chain of four stores in Plainfield, Roselle, and New Brunswick, catering to the *Black is Beautiful in Cleaned and Pressed Clothes* business. And in each store a doberman slept in the front window, a reminder that burglars should take their business elsewhere.

Two months after the funeral Enid decided to give up her organizations, her luncheons, her shopping expeditions to Loehman's and her afternoon Mah-Jongg games for the sake of the business. "I can't expect my boy to do it all by himself, can I?" And she established herself as manager of the Plainfield store, leaving Norman free to expand and improve the business. And he had. He'd opened three new stores that year and four more since then. He was always up to his elbows in a new solution.

Sandy was under the dryer at Coiffures Elegante in downtown Plainfield that gray November afternoon in 1963, her head covered with giant blue rollers, which, after an hour of intense discomfort would turn into the popular bouffant hairstyle of her look-alike. She was flipping the pages of the latest issue of *Vogue* with the stub of her fingers, careful not to mess up the freshly applied Frosted Sherbet on her nails, when the news came over the radio. Sandy didn't know what was happening since she couldn't hear anything but suddenly there was a lot of activity in the shop. She raised the hood of her dryer. "What's wrong?"

"The president's been shot!"

"Is it serious?"

"Looks like it."

"Oh God."

And the other women pulled their dryers back down over their wet heads. But not Sandy. She'd jumped up, knocking over the manicurist's table, tiny bottles of polish crashing to the floor. She ran through the shop to the back room, where her coat hung, and as she tore out the door the last words she heard were spoken by her neighbor, Doris Richter. "Alex . . . could you tease it a little higher on the left because it always drops by the next day . . ."

She drove home quickly, rushed into the house, found Bucky snuggled next to Mazie on the sofa in the den, the baby asleep in her lap, the TV on. "Oh, Mrs. Pressman," Mazie cried, "the president's dead. He's been shot in the head. Lord help us our president's dead."

Bucky made a gun with his finger. "Bang bang, the president's dead!" He studied Sandy for a minute. "You look funny like that, Mommy . . . like a moon-man."

Sandy took him in her arms, cried into his warm, puppy-smelling head, then went to her room, took the rollers out of her hair, laid out her black dress and shoes, dug out the black veil she'd worn to Samuel's funeral, and prepared for mourning.

"What the hell," Norman said, when he got home and found Sandy dressed in black.

"I'm sitting shiveh for the president."

"Are you crazy?"

"No."

"You didn't sit shiveh when my father died."

"That has nothing to do with this."

"And the Kennedys are Catholic!"

"So what?"

"I think you're really going off your rocker this time. I think you're really going bananas."

Sandy shrugged. "I don't expect you to understand . . . you didn't even vote for him."

"And neither did you!"

"That's how much you know." She gathered several sheets from the linen closet and draped one over the mirror in their bedroom.

"Jesus Christ, now you're going Orthodox?"

"This is the way we did it when Grandpa died," Sandy said, "I remember."

"I can't believe this. You're not Jackie, you know, just because you won that fucking contest."

How could Sandy explain? In a way she was Jackie, with blood and brains all over her suit. "I know exactly who I am and exactly what I'm doing."

"We're due at the Levinworths' in two hours. You better do something about your hair. It looks like hell."

"You'll have to call to say we can't make it."

"Not *we*, Sandy. I'm going anyway."

"Don't you have any feelings? Don't you know the whole country's in mourning?"

"So we'll mourn at Lew's house. It's not going to make any difference. It's not going to bring him back."

"No!" Sandy headed for the dining room, to cover the mirror above the sideboard.

"Pardon me, Mrs. Pressman," Mazie said. She'd changed out of her uniform into a green wool suit and she carried a small suitcase. "I'm going to take a few days off to go down to Washington . . . to the funeral . . . you know . . ."

"That is absolutely out of the question, Mazie,"

Norman said. "You can see what condition Mrs. Pressman is in."

"Same as me," Mazie said, "sad and sick." She put down her suitcase and helped Sandy drape the sheet over the mirror. "I don't know just when I'll be back, Mrs. Pressman . . . maybe three or four days . . . after the weekend. I just don't know."

"Maybe you didn't hear me, Mazie," Norm said, raising his voice, "but there's no way you can have time off now. Who's going to take care of the children?"

"Take care of them yourself, Mr. Pressman."

"If you go, you can kiss this job good-bye!"

"Norman!" Sandy came alive. "What are you saying? Mazie loved the president! If she wants to go to his funeral . . ."

"It's just an excuse, Sandy, can't you see that? Every goddamned fucking excuse."

"I won't tolerate no language like that," Mazie said. "I'm sorry, Mrs. Pressman, but I can't work for no Communist!"

She picked up Jen, who was in her infant seat, and carried her down the hall to her room. Bucky followed, wailing, "Mazie . . . Mazie . . ." Sandy followed too. Mazie put the baby into her crib and kissed both children. "Good-bye, sugars, you be good for your mommy, hear?" Then she grabbed her suitcase and marched out the front door. "Goodbye, Mrs. Pressman. I'm really sorry."

"Oh, Mazie," Sandy cried, "I don't know what we're going to do without you." She closed the door, trying to keep out the chill night air, and said to Norman, "I can't believe you did that. I'll never forgive you. Mazie was wonderful." She brushed past him and went to the bedroom. Suddenly she felt very tired. She had to lie down. To contemplate. How did Jackie feel at this moment? A widow, with two young children. And Caroline used to parade around in her pumps, interrupting his meetings . . .

The phone rang. Norman picked it up. "Yes, Lew, how are you? . . . Well, certainly, we were just about to call you . . . No night to celebrate, that's for sure . . . Yes, that's right, Sandy feels especially close to Jackie, always has. I can hear Hannah crying . . . yes, same here, they're very emotional . . . You too, another time. Uh huh . . . Bye . . ." He hung up. "That was Lew."

"Hypocrite!"

"That's the thanks I get for covering for your emotional immaturity?"

"Mommy, I'm hungry," Bucky called.

"Just a minute," Norman called back. "Mommy's coming." He whispered, "Your children are starving. Will you quit this idiot act and take care of them?"

But Sandy wouldn't budge, wouldn't speak, and Norman, unable to cope with the situation, frantic at the idea of feeding the kids supper by himself, and convinced that Sandy was really going off the deep end, phoned Gordon, as if Gordon could look into Sandy's head the way he could look into her cunt. Gordon advised two aspirin and a good night's sleep.

And then, while millions of TV viewers, including Sandy and Norman, watched Jack Ruby shoot Lee Harvey Oswald, the call came from the highway patrol. Sandy's father, Ivan Schaedel, had had a flat tire on the Pulaski Skyway. Mona had sat on the hood of the car, shooing away cars with her scarf, as Ivan attempted to change the tire. But he never finished. He was smashed by a Juniper Moving Van and killed instantly.

And then the shiveh began in earnest.

5

LAST DECEMBER WHILE Sandy was recuperating in Jamaica, Norman was making a name for himself as athlete of the century. He'd jump out of bed at six, jog around the grounds of La Carousella for half an hour, perform Royal Canadian Air Force exercises for twenty minutes, swim a dozen laps, play eighteen holes of golf, rush out to the new court for doubles, followed by singles, followed by mixed doubles, and before dinner, while the others were napping, he was back in the pool, holding his breath under water.

"Daddy can count to one hundred," Jen told Sandy. "How high can you count under water?"

"If I hold my nose I think I can make it to five."

"That's not very good."

"It's good enough. I don't expect to ever have to hold my breath under water."

"But suppose you do?"

"I'll drown, I guess."

"But Daddy says . . ."

"Never mind what Daddy says this time. Go and get ready for lunch."

"Can I eat in the kitchen with Lydia?"

"I guess so, if she doesn't mind."

"She likes me and I like her. She's the best cook. Why don't you ever make fried bananas?"

"I never thought about frying them but I used to feed you mashed bananas when you were a baby."

"Mashed bananas, yuck! Will you fry them when we get home?"

"Maybe, now go and find Bucky and tell him to wash up for lunch."

On the twenty-seventh Myra threw a party for her friends, three couples from The Club who were also vacationing at Runaway Bay, two of them in rented houses, and the third staying at the hotel on the beach. All were thinking seriously about buying a piece of property of their own so that they could continue to vacation together. Besides, it was tax deductible, they reminded each other, daily.

Before the party, while Myra scurried around filling candy dishes, rearranging furniture, and checking the bar, Sandy asked, "Don't you find it boring to be down here with the same people you see all the time at home?"

"Not at all," Myra answered. "We love it."

"But don't you want to meet new people down here?"

Myra dumped a jar of Planters dry-roasted nuts into a silver bowl. "It would be awful." She tilted her head back and dropped a handful of nuts into her mouth.

"I think it would be nice."

"Awful to have to find games, I mean." Myra chewed and swallowed the nuts, then brushed off her hands. "Take golf . . . they could say they're class A players when they're really B's, and if I had to play with beginners, well, frankly, I'd rather not play at all. And then there's tennis," Myra said. "Playing with people who aren't in your class is *horrendous*. There are people who'll tell you they're high intermediates when by your standards they might be low intermediates or, worse yet, high beginners."

"What are you?"

"I'm low advanced, but I can handle any average advanced player and upward. Norman, for instance, is headed for high advanced, but he and I can still have a good game. How do you think the candy looks? Do you like it piled high or spread out in rows?"

"Piled high."

"Me too. Remember how Mona used to spread out the after-dinner mints?"

"Yes."

"Where'd you get that dress?"

"It's not a dress, it's a skirt and top." Sandy fingered the material, an Indian cotton print in bright colors, with elephants marching around it. She enjoyed the comfortable wraparound style. "Do you like it?"

"It's cute."

Sandy felt that Myra was waiting to be admired. "I like yours too."

"I couldn't have worn this in the old days," Myra said, "but now I can go braless if I feel like it." Her dress was a long, clingy, black jersey with a high neck in front, plunging to the waist in back. Her frosted hair hung to her shoulders and framed her face, like a lion's mane. And under the black jersey Sandy could see the outline of Myra's perfect 34-B breasts, of her perfect, rose-colored nipples, each one the circumference of a quarter, where Sandy's were only the size of dimes.

"I wish to hell Gordy could play tennis like Norman," Myra said. "If he could, we'd win all the married couples tournaments at The Club. As it is I'm embarrassed having a shelf full of trophies when Gordy's never won anything."

"Does he mind?"

"He says he doesn't."

"Well, then, don't worry."

"I'll bet Norman's great in bed."

"Myra!"

"Does that embarrass you?"

"Not exactly."

"They say you can tell a lot about how a man performs in bed by watching him play tennis." Myra was at the bar now, arranging brandy glasses on a tray.

"I've always heard you can tell by the way a man dances," Sandy said, "and Norman can't dance at all."

"Are you saying he's no good then?" She looked over at Sandy, raising her eyebrows.

Sandy looked away. "I'm not saying anything, one way or the other."

"You're not having trouble, are you?"

"No, who said anything about trouble?"

Myra sighed. "I remember when Daddy told you that Norman was *phlegmatic* and you left the room in tears. I was shocked myself. Who would have guessed Daddy even knew such a word . . ."

"That was years ago."

"But Mona said he was a good catch," Myra added, "and she turned out to be right, as usual."

"Yes."

"You used to tell me everything, San . . . you used to come to my room with questions, remember? I wish we could be that close now."

"I don't have any more questions."

Myra busied herself with the cocktail napkins, counting out equal piles and distributing them around the room. "Tell me something," she said in a low voice, looking around to make sure no one was in sight or hearing distance. "Do you suck?"

"Myra, please!"

"Oh, come on. You can tell me. Everybody's doing it these days."

"Including you?"

Myra shrugged. "Of course. So how about you and Norm?"

Sandy hesitated. "Certainly."

"Do you swallow?"

"Do you?"

"I asked you first," Myra said, "and anyway, it's pure protein, it can't hurt you."

"I know."

"Mother!" Kate called in her fishwife's voice. "I think your friends are here. I heard a car drive up."

Myra ran her hands over her hair and her tongue across her teeth. "I don't have lipstick on my teeth, do I?" she asked Sandy, making a horse face.

"No, you're fine."

"Why don't you run in and put some on. You could use the color . . ."

"I think I'm getting a herpes . . . I'm using Blistex . . ."

"Hello. . . hello . . . hello . . ."

Barbara and Gish. Lucille and Ben. Phyllis and Mickey. Myra's friends. It was hard for Sandy to keep them straight. She'd watched them on the court each day but dressed in their Head color-coordinated outfits they all looked the same. They'd tried to get her to join them, tried to make friends. "I'd love to play," she'd explained. "But I've been sick and I have to take it easy for a while."

Now here they were, out of their daily uniforms, into their evening ones. The women wore clingy jersey dresses, like Myra's, and the men were all in plaid slacks and Lacoste shirts. During the week, Sandy had given the women code names, to help her remember who was who. Brown, Luscious, and Funky instead of Barbara, Lucille, and Phyllis. Sandy thought she might like Funky, with a bandana tied around her head, loaded down with Indian jewelry, best, until they got into a discussion about Plainfield.

"Plainfield, my God!" Funky said. "I thought Plainfield was all black."

"Not quite."

"You mean not yet! If I were you, I'd get out while the going's good and move up to the Hills. We built our final house in Watchung last year. We can see the lights from our living room, just like stars. It's fantastic . . . you'd love it . . . is your Plainfield house your first house?"

"Yes, we bought it from Norman's mother after his father died."

"Oh. Because I was going to say if it was your final house then I could understand your reluctance to leave it, but with your first house . . ."

"It's very nice," Sandy said, feeling defensive about Enid's house for the first time. "It's in Sleepy Hollow."

"But the schools . . ."

"The children go to private school."

"In Watchung you could send them to public school. We have only two black families in the town and both of them are professional."

"It's really not a racial thing," Brown said, joining them. Brown's nails were filed to squares instead of points and polished in frosty brown, to match her frosty brown eye shadow, her frosty brown hair, her frosty brown suntan, her frosty brown dress. "It's more of a socioeconomic thing, don't you think?"

"Yes and no," Funky said. "Yes, in the sense that the professional ones tend to think more like us and want what's best for their children. No, in the sense that they're still different no matter how hard you try to pretend they're not. I mean, put one in this room, right now, and suddenly we'd all clam up." She took a cheese puff from the tray offered by Elena, the black maid. "Thank you."

Sandy was trying to sort out the men. Ben was the urologist with the vasectomy button on his collar. Had he performed his own vasectomy? No, how could he see over that belly? It might be nice if Norman had a vasectomy. Sandy hated her diaphragm. It was so messy. And the Pill made her sick. She'd have to approach the subject carefully, though, because Norm was very sensitive about his genitals.

Mickey had a lot of hair and some kind of engineering company. Then there was Gish. He practiced law in Newark, specialized in personal injury work and was, according to Myra, cleaning up. He and Brown were neighbors of Myra's in Short Hills. Sandy didn't like the way he looked her up and down every time she crossed the room. It made her uncomfortable.

So much for the men.

"Your husband," Luscious said, settling next to Sandy on the sofa, "is such a tiger! That serve . . . what a smash! I told him, don't let up on me just because I'm a girl, and he didn't . . . aced me every time . . . you must be really proud of him . . ." Luscious, tiny, blonde, and perfect, looked like an aging Barbie Doll.

"Yes," Sandy answered.

"And his backhand is nothing to sneeze at," Brown

said, sitting on Sandy's other side. "Wicked, absolutely wicked!"

"He really enjoys his games," Sandy told them.

"It's not just a question of *enjoy,*" Funky added, leaning over the back of the sofa so that Sandy could feel her breath on her neck. "It's talent. Pure, unadulterated talent."

Pure, unadulterated bullshit, Sandy thought, wishing she were brave enough to say it out loud.

"I should be so lucky!" Brown said, laughing down her vodka and orange juice.

"Normie . . . tiger . . ." Luscious called across the room to where the men had gathered. "Will you play with me tomorrow . . . singles . . . for just a little while?"

"Sure thing," Norman called back. "Let's say, from three-thirty to three forty-five."

And later, after dessert, while they were sitting around sipping brandy, Ben said to Norman, "You should join The Club."

"I've been telling him that all week," Myra said.

"And I've been thinking about it," Norman said.

That was certainly news to Sandy.

"It makes a lot of sense," Norman said.

Gish, who was seated next to Sandy on the small sofa, turned to her and said, "What do you think?"

"What . . . oh, me?" Sandy asked, surprised to find herself in the conversation. "Well, I'm not an athlete so it's hard for me to say if we should invest that much in The Club."

"But Sandy," Myra said, "it's more than a club . . . it's a way of life . . . it's not just golf and tennis . . . you'd make wonderful friends . . . look at us . . ." She smiled and extended her arms.

"And your children will meet the right kinds of young people too," Funky said.

"Playing those public courses is a waste of time," Ben told Norman. "How long do you have to wait to tee off on weekends?"

"I get up at six so I usually don't have to wait."

"Wouldn't you rather sleep till nine?" Funky asked.

"I'm not a late sleeper," Norman said.

"So, you'd have time for a quickie," Ben said.

"We just love our Sunday-morning quickies," Luscious told them all.

Gish put his arm around Sandy's shoulder and whispered, "I'd like to make it with you, quick or slow, your choice."

"And Sandy," Brown said, "once you take lessons you'll love it like everybody else. We're not all born athletes like your husband."

"I'll bet you don't need any lessons in the sack," Gish whispered.

"And on Thanksgiving and Mother's Day and all the other holidays you'll always have a nice place to go," Funky said.

"And The Club does a terrific job on affairs," Brown said.

Affairs? Sandy thought.

Myra stood up. "I think I have a Club booklet somewhere." She went into her bedroom and returned with it. *Green Hollow Country Club. Rules and Regulations.* "Read this, San, it'll give you a better idea."

"Thanks." Sandy stood up too. "It's been very nice," she said, "I hope you'll excuse me . . . I'm really tired . . ." She looked across the room, at Norman.

"Sandy's recuperating, you know," Myra said.

"She's been quite sick. Take care, San. Get a good night's sleep."

"I'll be in soon," Norman told her.

"Yes, see you all tomorrow."

Sandy got into bed with the green booklet. *Had Gish been serious? No, it was just a joke.* She opened the booklet. There were General Rules, Golf Course Rules, Tee Off Procedures, Club House Rules, Guest Rules, Tennis Regulations, Pool Regulations, Rules Pertaining to Children on the Premises, Rules Pertaining to Restaurant Minimums, and Rules Pertaining to Sons of Members Who Wished to Caddy.

Suppose Gish had been serious? He was attractive.

No, it was out of the question. He'd just been kidding around. Flirting, but not seriously.

There were Lessons For All, including but not limited to Private Tennis Instruction (by the hour or half-hour), Golf (by the hour or half-hour), Playing Lessons (nine holes or eighteen), Having the Pro Play in Your Foursome . . .

Sandy dozed off, the bedroom light still on.

6

Two days later Sandy, Myra, and the twins were having their lunch on the patio. "It's just wonderful to be able to share your vacation with your family," Myra said, squeezing Sandy's hand in a sudden burst of enthusiasm. "You're looking so much better, San. How do you feel?"

"Stronger . . . healthier . . . I always feel good with a tan."

Myra inhaled deeply and stretched. "I can't think of any place on earth I'd rather be."

"Well, I can!" Kate said. "And I'd also like to know why we can't ever have anything besides blended salad for lunch?"

"Because blended salad is good for you," Myra said. It was her latest kick in fad foods. She bought romaine lettuce by the crate. Sandy found it hard to take herself, but instead of complaining she just waited until the others left for their afternoon activities, then made herself a peanut butter sandwich.

"Green mush!" Kate moved it around on her plate.

"Seaweed!" Connie added. "And Bucky and Jen

47

are in the kitchen eating hamburgers and fried bananas, is that fair?"

"Bucky and Jen are little children," Myra told them, "but you are young women and need to watch your weight."

"Bullshit!" Kate said, pushing back her chair.

"I thought I told you to watch your language," Myra said, clenching her teeth.

"Oh, come off it, Mother. Aunt Sandy knows we're human. Let's go, Con." She and Connie got up and stalked off.

Myra tried to laugh it off. "Just wait until Bucky and Jen reach adolescence." She sipped her mint iced tea. "It isn't easy." She flicked her hair back. "Did I tell you I made appointments for them with Dr. Saphire?"

Dr. Saphire had performed Myra's breast reduction surgery.

"No, aren't they too young?"

"Nose jobs . . . not the other . . . not yet . . ."

"Oh, I didn't know he did those."

"Yes, he's the best in the business."

"When are they going in?"

"Early July."

She nodded. She was always surprised that Myra had produced such unattractive children. It must be hard on them, having a gorgeous perfectly groomed mother, like Myra, Sandy thought. But no matter how hard she tried to like them, to find some redeeming feature, she couldn't. It was so unpleasant being around them. Bucky and Jen felt it too. Just that morning Jen had said, "I hate Connie and Kate, don't you?"

Bucky answered, "I hate Kate. Connie's just dumb."

"I don't want to hear you talking about your cousins that way," Sandy had said.

48

"Why not? It's true," Bucky told her.

"Yeah," Jen said, "they never laugh or have any fun and they're so ugly."

"But they sure do have huge tits," Bucky said.

"Will mine grow like that, Mommy?" Jen asked.

"I doubt it," Sandy told her. "You're small-boned, like me. The twins are built more like Aunt Lottie."

"I hope mine grow bigger than yours," Jen said. "Yours are so little."

"Big breasts aren't everything," Sandy said.

"Yeah, I'm an ass man myself," Bucky said. "Like Dad."

"Like Dad?" Sandy asked.

"Yeah, he told me the other day when we saw Aunt Myra's ass."

"Bucky!"

"Well, we did and it wasn't our fault either. She was standing there talking on the phone and it was sticking out for everybody to see."

"You should have looked the other way," Sandy said.

"Dad didn't."

Norman, an ass man? He'd never told her that, but she should have guessed, given his fascination with the product of that part of the body.

Bucky and Jen were not happy that afternoon, when Connie and Kate piled into the car with them. They poked each other and whispered but Sandy was determined to make it a pleasant outing.

"Now remember, Mom," Bucky said, "you drive on the *left* here."

"I know, I know."

It was a short ride down the hill to the small, private, homeowners' beach which was adjacent to the long beach belonging to the Runaway Bay Hotel. Often, Sandy and her children were the only ones there. The other homeowners and tenants had their own swimming pools, like Myra, and spent most of their time playing golf or tennis anyway. Norman hated the beach. "All that sand," he'd say. "It gets up my ass and between my toes . . . who needs it?" But Sandy loved the beach. The warm sand, the endless blue-green sea, the salty air. "Isn't the water beautiful down here?" she asked the twins.

"It's all right," Connie said.

More than their looks, it was Connie and Kate's apathy, their lifelessness, that bothered Sandy. The twins took off their beach shirts, revealing bikinis. Their loose flesh hung around their middles and poured out from their bikini bottoms. They weren't fair-skinned like Sandy and Myra. They were more like Gordon's family. Gordon had olive skin and tanned deeply, changing his looks. Otherwise, during the winter months, Gordon appeared to have faintly green skin. He was balding and combed his remaining hair carefully across his head. His eyes were deep-set and his cheeks becoming jowly, but he still had a hard, compact body, although at just under five five, Myra dwarfed him.

How lucky Sandy was to have Bucky and Jen. Lovely little Jen, small and delicate with wispy hair and an almost constant smile. And Bucky, growing up to look like Norman, with a square body and almost no neck, set on broad shoulders. But Bucky would be warmer than Norman, warmer and kinder and unafraid of his feelings.

Jen ran off to hunt for shells and Sandy settled down for her afternoon nap. Just as she was dozing off, Kate screamed. Sandy jumped up and ran to her. "What is it?"

"My belly . . . my belly . . ."

Appendicitis? Would she be able to find Myra or Gordon? Oh, Jesus, she should have left them home. They were nothing but trouble.

"He burned it! It's killing me."

"Burned it . . . who . . . what?"

"Bucky! With his fucking magnifying glass."

"What? He did what?" Sandy looked over at him. He was sitting under a palm tree, holding his magnifying glass, a sheepish look on his face.

"I didn't know it would happen so fast," Bucky said. "It takes a long time for leaves to burn."

"I'm not a leaf, you fucking imbecile!"

"Okay, okay," Sandy said, "let's calm down now. Bucky, apologize to Kate and give me your magnifying glass."

"Do I have to?"

"Yes, and now."

He handed her his magnifying glass. "Can I have it back tomorrow?"

"No."

"Day after?"

"I doubt it."

"When?"

"We'll see."

"You always say that!"

"Apologize to Kate, please."

"Oh, Mom."

"We're waiting, Bucky."

"Okay, I'm sorry."

"I don't think he really means it, Aunt Sandy."

"I do so," Bucky said.

"I'm sure he does," Sandy told Kate.

"What happened?" Jen asked, racing back, her Baggie filled with shells.

"Bucky burned Kate with his magnifying glass," Connie said. "Look at that red mark on her belly."

Jen examined Kate's belly and held back a laugh.

"It hurt like hell," Kate told her. "I thought a snake bit me, or something."

"They don't have snakes on the beach," Bucky said.

"The hell they don't."

"Do they, Mom?"

"I really don't know." Sandy rummaged through her beach bag. "Look, why don't the four of you go over to the hotel and have a drink. Here's five dollars. You can bring me the change."

"Five won't buy us all drinks," Kate said, "not down here."

"Oh, I suppose you're right," Sandy said, fishing out another five. "Take ten then and bring back the change."

"They're having crab races this afternoon," Jen said. "I love crab races. Please, please, can we go?"

"Oh, all right . . . I suppose it can't hurt."

"Thank you, thank you." Jen jumped up and down and planted a kiss on Sandy's cheek. "You're the best mother that ever was."

Sandy laughed. "Go on, have a good time."

She watched as they ran down the beach, Bucky and Jen out front, Kate and Connie behind them. Then she made a pillow out of two beach towels, settled back on her blanket, and closed her eyes, her face lifted to the sun. Ah, the hot sunshine. It felt so good. She began to drift off . . . the sun hot on her face, her belly, her legs. Hot between her legs. Yes, good and hot . . . so nice . . . so long since she'd had that feeling . . . since before she'd been sick. Norman hadn't . . . that is, they hadn't fucked since before. He wanted to, she knew, but she told him she was still too weak. Nice to know it was still working, that the cortisone hadn't affected her that way. She opened her legs a bit more, letting the hot sun warm her there, warming her all over . . . on her nipples . . . erect now . . . she ran her hand across her belly . . . fuck me . . . fuck me, sunshine . . . so delicious, as it crept up her legs, to her thighs, to her cunt . . . kiss me there . . . lick me . . . oh, please . . . oh, hurry . . . She pictured the beachboy, the one at the hotel who set up lounge chairs and handed out towels. A beautiful boy, with white blond hair and deeply tanned skin. A beautiful body too. She could see every muscle in his back. Strong arms. And a line of pale fur extending from his navel to the top of his bathing trunks . . . and beyond? Yes, probably beyond. She could see the outline of his cock, of his balls, through his tight little Speedo suit. Everytime she passed him, as she walked along the beach with the children, everytime she looked, although she promised herself she wouldn't any more . . . she saw his bulge. How nice it would be to feel him against her. If he walked by right now, she would say, *Lie on me,* and he would, rubbing against her. Rubbing, rubbing, but not putting it inside her. It would be exciting enough that way, just rubbing on the outside of her suit, the way Shep used to do because she'd told him, *I can't Shep . . . I promised my mother . . . I can't do it . . . not all the way . . . but we can do this . . . and this . . . yes, Shep, yes . . . I can feel you through my clothes . . . can you feel me? Yes, I can come this way. I'm coming, Shep . . . oh, God . . . I'm coming . . . now now now . . .*

"I think I love you."

Sandy opened her eyes and sat up. A middle-aged man in madras bathing trunks was sitting opposite her, drawing in the sand with a stick. "I'm sorry, did you say something?" Sandy asked, rearranging her bathing suit, hoping she hadn't been squirming, that the man had no idea what she'd been thinking.

"I said I think I love you."

Sandy jumped up, gathered her things in a hurry, and took off, running down the beach.

He called after her. "Don't go, I said I love you and I mean it. Come back. Come swim with me."

Jesus, a pervert on the private beach! She ran until her side ached, until she reached the safety of the crowded hotel grounds. God, he could have killed her. He could have bashed in her head with a coconut. Never again. From now on she was going to make her headquarters on the hotel beach.

She used the Ladies Room near the hotel pool, got herself together, then went up to the crab races and found Bucky and Jen.

"Hi, Mom, what are you doing here?" Bucky asked. He didn't wait for her answer. He was too engrossed in the crab race. "Go little guy . . . go . . . look at that . . . go number three . . . go . . ."

"I lost," Jen said. "I bet on number six and then he turned around and walked the wrong way."

"Maybe that will teach you a lesson about gambling," Sandy said. "Where's Connie and Kate?"

"Oh, they went off with the ganja man," Bucky said.

"The ganja man?"

"The dealer."

"What dealer?"

"You know, Mom, quit acting dumb."

"Bucky, I do not know what you're talking about."

"Ganja . . . it's like grass . . . like dope . . . pot . . ."

"Marijuana?"

"Yeah, down here they call it ganja."

"And they went off with him?"

"Yeah, but they'll be back, don't worry."

"They're just down the beach," Jen said pointing, "but Kate said if I told anybody she'd kill me. She said she'd hold me under water until I turn blue. That's why I have to learn to hold my breath till one hundred, like Daddy."

"Nobody's going to hurt you," Sandy said. "Now, listen . . . you two stay right here and watch the rest of the crab races . . . don't move . . . I'll be back with Kate and Connie and then we're going home."

Just what she needed. Where the hell were they and what was she supposed to do about them? And if they'd used her money, she'd kill them. The bitches!

She found them in a clump of trees, laughing their heads off. "Hi, Aunt Sandy," Kate said. "What are you doing way down here?"

"I was just going to ask you the same question. I thought you were going to stay with Bucky and Jen."

"Bucky and Jen aren't babies. They can take care of themselves."

"Have you been smoking pot?"

They laughed again.

"Do your parents know you smoke?"

"I don't know," Kate said. "We've never discussed it."

"Are you going to tell them?" Connie asked.

"Of course she's not," Kate said. "What purpose would that serve?"

"Look," Sandy said, "I'm not feeling well and I want to get home."

"Gee, that's too bad, Aunt Sandy," Kate said. "Would you like a joint? That might help."

"No, let's just get out of here."

That night Norman asked, "Feeling stronger, San?"

"Yes." She was already in bed, reading.

"You're getting a nice tan. Are you ready for a little something?"

"I think so."

"Got your diaphragm in?"

"No, I forgot."

"Where is it?"

"In the bathroom cabinet."

"I'll get it for you."

"Okay."

He came back and handed her the case, then looked the other way while she reached under the covers and inserted it. "Ready," she said when it was in place. Norman turned out the light and climbed into bed beside her.

Rules and Regulations for a Norman Pressman Fuck.

The room must be dark so they do not have to look at each other. There will be one kiss, with tongue, to get things going. His fingers will pass lightly over her breasts, travel down her belly to her cunt, and stop. He will attempt to find her clitoris. If he succeeds, he will take it between his thumb and forefinger and rub. Too hard. He will roll over on top of her. He will raise himself on his elbows, and then . . .

Norman kissed her. He tasted like Colgate toothpaste. She hated Colgate. Question: Did she also hate Norman? Answer: Yes, sometimes.

Norman's cold tongue was darting in and out of her mouth. One kiss. That was enough for him. Sandy didn't mind. Her lip hurt. Besides, his kisses no longer pleased her, no longer offered any excitement.

"Ready, San?"

"Yes." Sandy raised her hips to catch him. In and Out. In and Out. She closed her eyes and imagined herself with the beachboy. She would be on top, bouncing wildly. Almost thirty-two years old and never been on top. How unfair! Uh oh . . . Norman was beginning his descent. Three more strokes and it would be over. *Hurry, Sandy . . . hurry, or you'll be left out.* She moved with Norman but it was too late. No main course tonight.

"Sorry," he said, "it's been a long time. I couldn't wait. Wake me in twenty minutes and we'll try again."

"It doesn't matter," Sandy said. *Liar. Liar. Of course it mattered.*

Norman used the bathroom. She heard him gargling. Was he afraid that her kisses still bore germs? He returned to his own bed, across the room. In seconds he was asleep, snoring softly. Sandy masturbated, continuing her fantasy with the beachboy. The climax she reached alone was stronger and more satisfying than any she had had with Norman. When she could breathe easily again she said, "Norman, do you love me?"

She knew he was asleep. She didn't really expect him to answer. And he didn't.

7

1970. NOT ONLY a New Year but a New Decade. When they returned from Jamaica Sandy was full of resolutions. She would learn to be a gourmet cook. She would get a slinky dress. She would become an outstanding mother of the year. She would clean out all the closets and organize them. She would make sure the baseboards were as clean as Norman claimed Enid's were. She would read *Time* magazine from cover to cover and make interesting, occasionally startling, comments. She would devour three books a week from the library and only one of them would be fiction. She would be sexy. Yes, she would be very sexy. Always. Looking her best. Never in need of a shampoo. Shaving her legs before it was necessary. Dental floss between her teeth morning and night. Regular douches with vinegar, maybe wine vinegar for variety, and not just the morning after. She would please Norman in every way. If she made him happier, if she concentrated on his every wish, then she would be rewarded. She would become a happier person. A better person.

"Make his interests your interests. Make his friends,

your friends. When he's in the mood, you're in the mood. Dress to please him. Cook to please him. What else matters? A happy husband is the answer to a happy life," Mona Schaedel said to her daughters, Myra Suzanne and Sondra Elaine, December, 1954, upon the former's engagement to Gordon Michael Lefferts, third-year medical student, excellent catch, who the night before had presented Myra Suzanne with a perfect, blue-white, three-carat Marquise cut diamond engagement ring, purchased from his uncle Jerome, who, thank God, was in the business and got him a terrific price, because someday when Gordon was a specialist and Uncle Jerome was old, Gordon would take care of him and there would be no charge. Uncle Jerome never thought to ask about Gordon's future plans. Maybe if he had he wouldn't have been so generous. On the other hand there was Aunt Fanny and her hysterectomy to consider.

Myra let Sandy try on her ring and from that moment on Sandy's goal in life was to become engaged.

They'd been back from Jamaica for two weeks when Sandy bought a pictorial sexual encyclopedia. "I have an idea," she said to Norman. "Let's do it every night for a week."

"Are you serious?"

"Yes, and a different position everytime."

"Starting when?"

"Tonight?"

"You've got yourself a deal!"

But when she tried to explore his body he tensed. "No, not there," he said, when her hands touched the soft patches of hair under his arms. "I don't like to be touched there."

"Oh, sorry." She kissed his neck, then made her way down to his chest.

"No," he said, squirming, as her fingers rested on his nipples. He took her hands in his. "What do you think I am, a fag?"

"I'm just exploring," Sandy said, "like the book says."

"To hell with the book!"

She had planned to work her way down to his feet, where she would bite and kiss his toes, and then, hopefully, he would follow her lead and do to her all the lovely things she had done to him. He would lick her nipples, round and round, and kiss her inner thighs until she was wet, until she had to have him; and only then would he enter her, long and stiff and they would move together for hours, maybe all night.

But she could see now that there was no point in going on. It wasn't going to work. She might as well get on with the different position. She climbed on top of him.

"What are you doing?"

"Let's try it this way."

"No, not with you on top."

"It's a very common position, Norm . . ."

"For dykes, for women's libbers who want to take over."

"No, it has nothing to do with that. It's supposed to feel good this way . . ."

"I'm the man in this family. I get on top."

"That's silly, Norm, it has nothing to do with being the man."

But he was on top of her now, pushing into her. "You're my wife, not some whore."

"I could pretend to be a whore, just for fun."

He pushed harder. "You're my wife . . . there, there . . ." he said, coming into her.

Every night for a week, proving that he was the man.

Every night for a week, and Sandy was sore.

So much for her New Year's resolutions.

Norman joined The Club in early February and was promptly asked to serve as chairman of the Grievance Committee. "That's some honor for a new member!" Myra told Sandy. "You should be very proud."

"Oh, I am. Anything that makes Norm happy."

And he was *very* happy. His enthusiasm for The Club carried over to the children. "Can I learn to play golf?" Bucky asked.

"Of course, there's a practice range and a putting green and you can take lessons this spring."

"What about me, Daddy?" Jen asked. "Can I take lessons too?"

"Certainly, Princess."

"What about Mommy?" Jen and Bucky looked at her.

Sandy shook her head but Norman said, "Mommy's going to learn to play golf and tennis too."

"Come on, Norm . . . don't tell them that . . . you know it's not my thing."

But for her birthday Norman gave her a set of matched clubs in a lemon yellow bag, brown and white golf shoes, reminiscent of her beloved junior high saddles, and a dozen pairs of peds with different color trim.

And for Mother's Day he presented her with a Davis Classic racquet, Tretorn tennis shoes, two Head outfits, a tennis sweater, and three cans of fuchsia balls.

All right. She would try. She'd make an effort. After all, eighth grade was twenty years ago. Her coordination might have improved. She'd had babies since then and masturbation took coordination, didn't it? Especially while driving.

first. She needed something for the carriage suit for

8

THE MAN ON the motorcycle returned on Monday morning, but this time he was dressed in jeans and a T-shirt although he wore the same helmet and rode the same bike. As soon as Sandy looked out the window he unzipped his jeans and dropped them to his ankles. No underwear. Interesting. He worked quickly, making it on the nineteenth stroke. After, he waved to her. She didn't wave back. At least he didn't ride up on the lawn this time.

Sandy didn't call Norman. She didn't call the police either. What was the point? They hadn't believed her before. Besides, he wasn't hurting anyone. But who was he? And why had he singled her out? Or did he go to a different house every day? Yes, last time he had come on a Monday too. Maybe Monday was *her* day. *Some day he'll come along, the man I love . . . and he'll be big and strong, the man I love . . . maybe Monday . . .* Oh, the possibilities were endless.

She had to hurry if she was going to make the nine-thirty-two train. She had a date to meet Lisbeth in New York for lunch and wanted to do some shopping first. She needed something for the Fourth of July for-

65

mal at The Club, something black and slinky like Myra and her friends had worn in Jamaica. Maybe she'd get her hair cut too, if there was time.

The phone was ringing when she stepped out of the shower. She wrapped herself in a towel and answered.

"Mrs. Pressman?"

"Yes."

"This is Hubanski."

"Who?"

"Sergeant Hubanski, Plainfield PD."

"Oh . . . yes . . . of course . . ."

"We found a sheet."

"You did?"

"Yes, plain white, exactly the kind you described."

"Where?"

"The corner of Sunset and Morning Glory."

"That's not far from here."

"We know."

"When?"

"When, what?"

"When did you find it?"

"Oh. Yesterday afternoon. I was off. My boys picked it up, so I didn't know about it until this morning. We're checking out the laundry marks now. When we've got something we'll give you a call."

"Yes, please."

"Just wanted you to know we're hot on his trail."

"Yes. Well, thank you for calling, sergeant."

So, they'd found a sheet. Was it his? Was that why he was dressed differently today, because he'd lost his sheet? Unlikely. He must have more than one sheet. This one that Sergeant Hubanski had come up with probably belonged to some neighborhood child who had been playing tent and left it outside.

"Good morning, Mrs. Pressman," Florenzia called

from downstairs, slamming the front door. "That's just me."

"Good morning, Florenzia," Sandy called back.

"You got some mail . . . You like to see?"

"Yes, please." Sandy met her halfway down the stairs. Florenzia handed it to her. "Thank you."

"It be very hot today."

"You can turn the air-conditioning back on now. I turned it off for my shower."

"I be doing downstairs today in case somebody come looking to buy house?"

"Yes, that's a good idea."

"Mr. Pressman, he tell me to keep house looking good and he be giving me a raise."

"Oh?"

"That's so. He tell me two weeks ago."

"I didn't know, Florenzia, but we're certainly very pleased with the way you keep the house." How like Norman to offer a raise when they were about to move.

Sandy took the mail to her bedroom and closed the door.

Nothing from Bucky yet but there was a card from Jen. The first.

DEAR MOMMY,
Camp sucks! I am starving to death. There is no steak. There is no roast beef. Only one cookie a day. You should see me. I am all bones. Please, please, get me out of here. And hurry!

Your daughter,
JENNIFER P.

That proved it! Jen was too young for camp. She shouldn't have listened to Norman. Just because Enid

67

sent *him* off to camp when he was five didn't mean Jen was ready. Poor little Jen. Sandy had a mental picture of her behind barbed wire, crying. Painfully thin. A concentration camp for overprivileged youngsters.

Oh, God.

But wait. She had visited Camp Wah-Wee-Nah-Kee last summer. Had seen how lovely it was. Across the lake from Bucky's camp. Iris Miller, the director, had shown them around. Pretty little bunks lined up at the crest of the hill. Manicured lawns. Flower beds. Modern bathrooms. Tennis courts. A dining room with a view of the mountains. And certainly no barbed wire. Jen would be all right. She had to be.

Sandy picked up the phone and dialed.

"This is Camp Wah-Wee-Nah-Kee in the heart of the Berkshires." A cheery voice sang out.

Sandy asked for Iris Miller, then waited while she was paged.

"Yes, this is Iris Miller."

"This is Sandy Pressman, Mrs. Miller . . . from New Jersey . . . Jennifer's mother . . ."

"Yes, Mrs. Pressman. I saw Jennifer at breakfast. She's doing beautifully."

"But, Mrs. Miller, I just received a very disturbing postcard from Jen saying that she's starving."

"Really Mrs. Pressman," Iris said, laughing, "I promise you, she's not starving."

"Something about no steak and no roast beef."

"She's been here less than a week . . . she's a first-year camper . . . there's always a period of adjustment . . . and as it happens we had steak on our first night. But we refer to it as beef here. We certainly give our campers the very best, believe me."

"Well, I hope so, but you can understand how up-set I was when I got Jen's card."

"Of course. But don't worry. She'd have written a letter if she was really unhappy. The postcard is a sign that everything's fine."

"I'd like to talk to Jen."

"You know that's against the rules, Mrs. Pressman. No phone calls before visiting day. Write her cheer-ful letters. Believe me, she's well cared for here."

"I guess it's just that . . ."

"See you on visiting day and don't hesitate to call whenever you're concerned."

"Yes . . . well . . ." Sandy began, but Iris had al-ready hung up.

She'd have to write to Jen tonight, explaining about the beef, suggesting that if she was hungry to demand peanut butter and to promise that on visiting day she would bring her all sorts of goodies. Pepperidge Farm cookies, fruits, potato chips, candy. No, that was wrong. Jen had to learn to get along without her. That was what camp was all about, wasn't it? That's what Norman said. Sandy didn't know. She'd never gone herself. Mona didn't trust camps. "You want polio, that's a good way to get it," Mona had argued when Myra begged to go to sleep-away camp. "But it's hot and I want to go swimming," Myra whined. "You're hot, go sit in the bathtub," Mona answered.

Sandy barely made the nine-thirty-two and found a seat in no-smoking. She'd been looking forward to this visit with Lisbeth. They hadn't seen each other in months, not since January, when Sandy had returned from Jamaica. And on that day Sandy was sporting a full-blown herpes virus on her lower lip.

"You still get those things?" Lisbeth had asked.

"From the sun."

"So why don't you wear something to protect your lips, like zinc oxide?"

"Zinc's so ugly, all that white goo."

"No offense, San, but it's not as ugly as a fever sore."

"I know, and from now on I'm going to cover my lips before I go out in the sun. I've made up my mind, it's crazy to suffer this way."

"Didn't you have one when you and Norman were married?"

"Yes, a very small one."

"And when your father died?"

"Yes, at his funeral. I had the tail end of one at my Sweet Sixteen Party too."

"Do you think they come from emotional upheavals?"

"No, from the sun."

"But your father died in November, didn't he? The same time as JFK?"

"You know something, you're right. I never thought about that."

"You see, there's more to it than the sun."

"Maybe . . ."

Lisbeth Moseley. Born Zelda Rabinowitz. Changed her first name on her fifteenth birthday, refusing to speak to anyone who didn't address her as Lisbeth from that day on. It was she who encouraged Sandy to change the spelling of her name from Sandra to Sondra, not that it mattered. Everyone continued to call her Sandy. Lisbeth. Editor in chief of the Hillside High *News*. Girl Most Likely To . . . with straightened black hair and an inexpensive but successful nose job. The only one of the old crowd to go to Barnard. Lisbeth, who married a goy, when Sandy wasn't even brave enough to date one. A genuine goy who also happened to be her professor. An elective poetry course for those students exempt from freshman English. Blond and tall and slim, he smoked a pipe and wore tweed jackets with elbows patched in leather. The stereotypical professor. Vincent X. Moseley, from Connecticut. With background. Never mind that he also had a chunky, snub-nosed wife and two little boys in a crowded apartment on West 116th Street.

He *did it* with Lisbeth anyway.

"Really, all the way?" Sandy asked.

"Yes, and it was wonderful . . . wonderful . . . much better than we ever thought when we used to play our silly games."

"It didn't hurt?"

"No."

"Did he use a rubber?"

"No."

"But Lisbeth, suppose you get pregnant?"

"I'm going to marry him, anyway."

"But he's already married."

"She doesn't understand him. He's a poet. He's very sensitive. All she understands are diapers and bottles. He's asking for a divorce."

Their child, Miranda, was two years older than Bucky. Lisbeth's mother looked after her until Lisbeth got her degree, and then, when she had a job, a job with a real future, as a textbook editor at Harper's, Miranda went to live with her parents in New York. "She's brilliant, beautiful, and sophisticated, just as you'd expect," Lisbeth said, matter-of-factly, to anyone who asked about Miranda.

They lived in a co-op on Riverside Drive now, and had a cabin off the coast of Maine with no indoor plumbing. Lisbeth had shown pictures of the three of them, frolicking in the outdoor tub, naked.

Lisbeth, whose mother kept kosher when the rest of the crowd ate bread over Passover, whose mother never tired of singing "How Much Is That Doggie in the Window?" to her daughter's embarrassment.

Lisbeth, Sandy's best friend. Sandy's first lover.

They were twelve, going on thirteen. It was New Year's Eve. The bedroom door was closed but not locked. There were no locks on the doors in Sandy's house. A child might get locked in that way. And God forbid, in case of fire . . .

Mona and Ivan were in the basement recreation room entertaining their friends. Myra was out on a date. Sandy and Lisbeth were in Sandy's bed, under the quilt. Sandy was on top, being the boy. She moved around and around, squiggling, rubbing against Lisbeth until she got that good feeling. Then it was Lisbeth's turn to do the same. Sometimes they played *Rape* and other times it was *Just Plain Love*. They touched each other's breasts, but never *down there*.

The door opened. It was Mona. "Happy New Year!" she sang, slightly tipsy, a glass of champagne in one hand. "What are you doing in the same bed?"

"Keeping warm," Zelda/Lisbeth answered.

"You're cold?"

"Yes," Sandy said.

"I'll turn up the heat, but first, come downstairs and say Happy New Year to our friends."

"Do we have to?"

"Yes, everybody wants to see you."

"Like this?"

"Put on your robes and slippers."

Mona didn't know that under the quilt the girls were naked.

"We'll be right down," Sandy said. "Could you close the door so nobody can see us in our pajamas."

"There's nobody here but me," Mona said.

"Please, Mom, Zelda doesn't want you to see her in just pajamas."

"Since when?"

"Since I've gotten modest, Mrs. Schaedel. It just happened a few weeks ago."

"I see," Mona said. "All right, but hurry down because then you have to go to sleep even if it is New Year's Eve."

"Whew . . ." Zelda/Lisbeth said, when Mona was gone.

They got into their pajamas and robes and went downstairs, where they were hugged and kissed by Mona and Ivan's friends. Friends from the Sunday Night Club, where the women played Mah-Jongg and the men played poker, friends from the Tuesday night group, where the women played canasta and the men played poker, and friends from the Friday Night Dance class, where Mr. Zaporro came to the house and taught them the cha-cha-cha.

Sandy had to call the friends *Uncle* or *Aunt,* and let them pinch her cheeks. When she and Zelda/Lisbeth went downstairs, Aunt Totsie spilled champagne on Sandy's robe and Uncle Jerry was too busy to kiss her because he had his hand up Aunt Ruthie's dress. Aunt Ruthie wore black stockings and the girls could see clear up to her garters, even caught a glimpse of her black girdle. That was really funny because Aunt Ruthie was married to Uncle Ned and Uncle Jerry was married to Aunt Edie.

73

"Do you think they're going to do it?" Zelda/ Lisbeth whispered to Sandy.

"No, they're just good friends."

"She has her hand on his fly."

"I know, but they're just good friends, believe me. Sometimes good friends act that way."

"I never knew that."

"Yes. When it's New Year's Eve anything goes."

"Oh."

Lisbeth had such dreams! Getting married and having babies was enough for the rest of the crowd but not for Lisbeth. She dreamed of being president of Lord and Taylor's. After all, she read the New York *Times* and longed for a zebra-covered sofa and a Manhattan apartment when the rest of them were concerned with Saturday night dates and being felt up.

And later this same Lisbeth marched on Washington and no longer dreamed of zebra-covered sofas because her consciousness had been raised to such a degree that she insisted that her mother get rid of her cherished Persian lamb coat and hat. Mrs. Rabinowitz, who had a friend, who had a cousin, who knew a man who manufactured Borgana coats and the summer before they went off to college had schlepped both girls into New York, to the wholesale house, where each bought a Borgana coat for freshman year. Lisbeth had whispered to Sandy, "It feels so good against my skin I'd like to turn it inside out and wear it naked." And later, after she'd met Vincent, called Sandy to say, "You know that coat . . . the Borgana one . . . well, Vincent and I make love on it . . . in his office . . . on the floor . . . you ought to try using yours for that, San . . . it's terrific!"

"Sandy! It's been so long . . ." Lisbeth sang, hugging her, outside the Plaza. "Are you all right?"

"Yes, I'm fine, why?"

"I don't know. You looked tired."

"I've had a busy morning."

"Well, let's get a table. I've got so much to tell you."

Lisbeth was in French pants and a shirt unbuttoned halfway to her navel. Sandy felt very suburban in her linen suit.

"We're leaving for Maine on the first, taking the whole month off. Vincent is thinking about doing a book."

Vincent was always thinking about doing a book.

"I'm just going to relax, unwind, be free."

"Sounds wonderful. How's Miranda . . . is she going with you?"

"Of course. She has friends there. You should see her, San . . . I should have brought pictures . . . she's got tiny breasts and just had her first period. I taught her to use Tampax right off. Remember how we had to put up with those disgusting pads?"

Sandy nodded.

"Let's order. Then I want to hear all about you."

Sandy scanned the menu. "Did you ever have the chicken salad here?"

"Yes, you have to toss it yourself."

"You mean it's dry?"

"Yes, chunks of chicken."

"Good . . . that's what I like."

"And there's shredded lettuce on the side and mayonnaise or Russian dressing, I forget which."

The waiter came to take their order.

"Is the chicken salad all white meat?" Sandy asked him.

"If you request it," he answered.

"Yes, please, with mayonnaise on the side and shredded lettuce."

"We're not serving it shredded any more. It's leaf style now."

"Oh . . . well, that's all right."

"So . . . what's happening in suburbia these days?" Lisbeth asked.

"Oh, the usual. Plus we joined The Country Club this year."

"You didn't!"

"Norman's playing a lot of golf and tennis. It made sense."

"But what about you?"

"Oh, I'm taking lessons. Norm's head of the Grievance Committee."

"Terrific!"

Sandy laughed. "He loves it."

"I'll bet."

"His first complaint had to do with a woman who ran from the golf locker room to the parking lot in her bathing suit."

Lisbeth shook her head. "How's the new house coming?"

"We hope it'll be finished by Labor Day."

"Did you sell the Plainfield house yet?"

"No, we've had a few offers but Norm says they're not enough."

"Are you going to sell it to blacks?"

"Norm says, no, even though three out of four lookers are black."

"That's illegal, you know."

"I know, I know, I've tried to tell that to Norm, but Enid would never forgive him. You know how she feels about them."

The waiter brought their lunch. "Mayonnaise on

76

the side," he said, plunking Sandy's plate down in front of her.

They ate quietly for a moment. Then Sandy asked, "How's your mother?"

"Not too well. She's been undergoing all sorts of tests. Lost the feeling in her left arm."

"I'm so sorry. Is she in the hospital?"

"She was. She's out now. How's yours?"

"She's okay."

"And how are things with you and Norman?" Lisbeth asked, looking up from her shrimp salad.

"What do you mean?"

"In general . . . I just finished a course called Marriage in a Changing Society and I'm interested."

"We're the same as always." Sandy tossed some more of the chicken in mayonnaise. "Did I mention that Jen hates camp, that she wants to come home? And that I have this fungus or something that I can't get rid of. It's driving me crazy."

"No, you didn't mention that."

"And that sometimes I . . ."

"What?"

"Oh, I don't know."

"Are you sure you're all right?"

"I don't know that either." Sandy choked up and took a long swallow of iced tea.

Lisbeth reached across the table and patted Sandy's hand. She spoke softly. "Tell me," she said. "You'll feel better."

Sandy shook her head. "It's nothing. I'm just tired. I tire easily."

Lisbeth put down her fork and leaned close. "I'm going to tell you something, San, because I think it might help. A few months ago Vincent and I were having our problems . . . boredom with the relationship, snapping at each other . . . the usual . . . but now we've got it back together . . . better than ever . . . and it's all due to a fantastic new arrangement . . . Thursday nights off . . ."

"I don't get it."

"Thursday nights off from each other, from the marriage."

Sandy still wasn't sure what Lisbeth was trying to tell her.

"Every Thursday night I go out with another man and he goes out with another woman and then we come home and tell each other everything."

"Sleep with, you mean?"

"Yes, of course. Isn't it incredible that something so easy should bring us back together?"

"Who do you go with?"

"Right now it's this art director. He's young, his wife and kids are out at the beach for the summer, so we go to his place and just fuck, fuck, fuck."

"And Vincent?"

"He's got some graduate student doing her thesis on eighteenth-century poets."

"And do *they* know about your arrangement, the graduate student and the art director?"

"Of course. Everything *must* be out in the open . . . that's the only rule . . . no secrets . . . you see, San, it's secrets that cause problems . . . this class I took last semester in Contemporary Relationships was fabulous . . . showed us how secrets cause strains. This openness has been such a boon to our marriage . . ."

"Well, I don't know what to say."

"Don't say anything. I'm only telling you because I think it could do a lot for you and Norman."

"Norman is very conservative."

"I know, you'd have to approach the subject carefully, but I'm still convinced it could work for you."

"Maybe. I'm not sure."

"Oh, I almost forgot . . . I've got something for you." She opened her purse and pulled out a paperback book. "You haven't read it yet, have you?"

"No," Sandy said as Lisbeth handed it to her. The title was *Diary of a Mad Housewife.*

"I think you'll really enjoy it. It's funny and true. It has a lot to say."

Did Lisbeth think she was a mad housewife too? Was that why she'd given her the book? "Thanks, I'll start it on the train going home."

But on the train going home, she saw Shep. God, she hadn't seen him in what . . . almost eight years. Since she was pregnant with Jen and they'd bumped into each other at the Towers Steak House on Route 22. She'd been sitting at the bar, with Norman and another couple, and he'd walked in with a group of friends. She'd introduced him to Norman and then he'd introduced her to his wife, Rhoda. "One of my old friends," he'd called Sandy. She'd tried hard to stay calm, cool, but she'd farted when she first saw him, silently, thank God, and after he'd been shown to his table she'd squeezed her whiskey sour glass so hard it had broken in her hand, cutting her palm. The bartender had had to give her a wet towel to sop up the blood.

Shep.

"He'll never amount to anything," Mona had warned. *"Handsome* doesn't put food on the table. You can't eat love." Some people might disagree with you on that one, mother.

He'd fooled Mona all right. Fooled all of them. He'd made it big, in shopping centers. *Handsome* puts food on the table after all. And were they eating love, he and Rhoda? Probably.

They'd met at Myra's wedding. He was the date of one of Myra's bridesmaids, Margie Kott. Mona had advised Myra to choose her plainest friends as bridesmaids so that she'd really stand out. And she did. She looked as if she'd stepped right out of *Bride's* magazine. Sandy was maid of honor, in pink organza. Everything was pink and white at Myra's wedding, including the cageful of doves that were released as the happy couple said *I do*. Before they completed their circle around the room, one of them let out his stuff on Shep's head. Sandy saw it happen and couldn't help laughing.

"Jesus!" he'd said as she handed him a pink napkin with *Myra and Gordon* printed across it. "Thanks, kid. Did I get it all?"

He bent over and Sandy inspected his hair. It was thick and dark. "Yes."

"Does it stink?"

She sniffed his head. "No, you're okay."

He smiled at her. "You know something, kid? So are you."

Oh, that smile. Slightly crooked. Dazzling. Making Sandy's tummy turn over. "I'm not a kid. I'm a senior in high school. I'm seventeen. I have a driver's license."

"No, really?"

"Yes, how old are you?"

"Twenty-three."

"Myra's twenty."

"Myra?"

"My sister, the bride."

"Oh, that's your sister? Great-looking girl, Myra."

"Everybody says so."

"But I prefer you." Again, the smile.

"Who are you, anyway?" Sandy asked. "I mean, what's your name?"

"Shep. Shep Resnick, think you can remember that?"

"I'll try. I'm Sandy Schaedel."

After dinner he came over to her table and said, "Let's dance, Sandy Schaedel."

He held her close and they danced to "Blue Velvet." "You shouldn't wear a padded bra, kid."

"You can tell?" Sandy looked up at him, feeling her face turn red.

"I can always tell. And you sure as hell don't need that girdle," he told her, patting her ass.

"Shep, please!" she giggled nervously. "Everybody wears . . ."

"Never mind everybody. Next time we dance I want to feel *you* next to me, not padding and rubber." He pulled her closer and hummed into her ear.

He called the following Wednesday. Was she free on Saturday night? Was she!

He picked her up at eight and they rode around town in his 1950 Nash. "I've got no money, kid, sorry, but I blew it all renting that monkey suit for your sister's wedding."

"That's okay."

"I guess most of your dates take you to the movies."

"Yes, that's what we usually do."

"And then for a hamburger."

"Most times."

"And then what?"

"Oh, well, that all depends."

"On what?"

"You know, how much I like him."

"And if you like him what?"

81

"Well, then maybe we'll go back to my house and sit in the rec room and listen to records and . . . you know."

"I'm a lot older than you, Sandy. I'm not sure what kids do nowadays."

"Make out."

"What exactly does make out mean?"

"Shep, are you teasing me?"

He reached for her hand. "Would I tease a nice kid like you?"

So they'd gone back to her house after she was sure her parents were asleep and he made coffee because she didn't know how and she served them each a slice of Mona's homemade chocolate layer cake and sat with him at the kitchen table drinking a glass of milk and he told her she looked like a commercial for the dairy industry. She was almost sure that was a compliment. And then they'd gone downstairs to the rec room and she'd played her favorite making-out records, starting with "Blue Velvet," followed by "The Morningside of the Mountain" and "She Was Five and He Was Ten."

They danced. "Much better," he said, patting her ass, "much, much better." And then he kissed her. She'd kissed a lot of boys but never anyone like Shep. Never anyone with *experience*. His mouth was hot. He licked the corners of her lips then pushed his tongue into her mouth, running it over her teeth, then above them. He moved his lips across her cheek, to her ear, and he breathed into it licking the outside, then the inside, nibbling on her lobe. Sandy knew suddenly that she was in great danger and she pushed him away.

"What's wrong?" Shep asked.

"It feels too good when you kiss me like that."

He laughed and hugged her.

"I'm scared of you," she said.

"You don't have to be. I won't hurt you, I promise. And I won't do anything you don't want me to do either, not ever, understand?"

She took a big breath and nodded. "Okay."

He had a job in New York that summer, in the garment industry, and she was at the Jersey shore, working as a mother's helper. He drove down to see her one weekend. He had money this time. He took her to the movies and then for a hamburger and then for a ride in the Nash, parking it along the beach, showing her how the front seat folded down to make a bed. And he kissed her again and again, his body stretched out next to hers, his hands reaching under her sweater. Sandy tensed. She had to be ready to spring up if the situation demanded it. How could she allow herself to relax and enjoy it when her entire future was in jeopardy?

He unhooked her bra, his fingers on her bare breasts. Okay. She had decided it was all right to go this far, but no farther. He never stopped kissing her. Touching her. And then his hand was on her belly, his fingers creeping lower and lower . . .

She sat up. "No, Shep, you promised!"

"But, Sandy, what am I doing wrong?"

"I don't know. I just have this feeling."

"You like me to touch you?"

"Yes, you know I do."

He took her hand and pressed it to his pants. "How far do you go with your other boyfriends, Sandy?"

"I've gone this far but it wasn't the same. Besides, I don't have any other boyfriends right now . . ."

"I'm glad to hear that. You understand that I go out with other girls . . . with other women . . . because

I have to . . . but you're my favorite, kid. I really mean it, I like you the best."

"Thank you."

"The others, well, they're just for sex because I'm a pretty hot guy, Sandy, and I really need it."

"Yes, I understand."

He started to laugh. "Hey, do you believe everything I tell you?"

"Yes."

He put his arms around her. "Sandy, Sandy, I want to be your first lover. Will you remember that? Some day when you're ready I want it to be me."

"Not until I'm twenty-five or married, whichever comes first."

"Twenty-five?"

"Yes. My mother thinks I should wait until I'm thirty if I'm still single but I've decided that twenty-five makes more sense."

He laughed again, then reached inside her sweater but this time he rubbed her back. "How many cashmeres do you have?"

"Twenty-seven, why?"

"Just wondering."

"That's a pretty funny question."

"But you had the answer, didn't you?"

"Everybody counts their cashmeres."

"You see. Is your father rich, Sandy?"

"Not rich, but we're well off. He's got a tire business."

"I'm poor, but I'm going to make it someday."

"I hope you do, Shep, if you want to so badly."

"And I'm going to be able to buy my kids twenty-seven cashmeres at once."

"I didn't get them all at once. I collect them."

"I know, I'm just telling you how it's going to be for me."

He seemed so different when he talked that way. More like a little boy. Certainly he wasn't a threat when he was sharing his dreams with her. Sandy found this side of Shep very appealing. She could handle the little boy in him. It was the man that terrified her.

Sandy went off to Boston U. that fall and didn't see Shep until Thanksgiving. He was sharing an apartment with three other guys in the Hotel Albert on University Place, working for Pilgrim Knitwear, as a salesman, and taking courses in business administration at NYU, nights.

Sandy wore her beige wool dress, three-inch heels, seamless stockings, gold bangle bracelets, green eye shadow, and her Borgana coat. The picture of sophistication. She thought.

He took her out for a drink, then up to his place.

"Sandy, Sandy," he said, looking her over. "What's happened to my little girl?"

"I've grown up, Shep."

"Not too much, I hope."

"Enough." She smiled knowingly, trying to keep her voice husky, her legs from trembling. She'd rehearsed this moment for two months.

"Seeing a lot of guys?"

"I go out."

"That's not what I'm talking about."

"Well, what are you talking about?"

"You know damn well!"

"I told you once, twenty-five or marriage, whichever comes first."

He took her in his arms. "I thought you said you've grown up."

"I was just pretending."

"I'm glad."

It felt so good to have him hold her again. She wanted it to stay this way forever. He unzipped her dress and she tensed. "It's all right," he whispered, easing it over her shoulders and down, until she stepped out of it. "It's all right." He held her close. She was in her lacy beige nylon slip, her beige garter belt, her beige lace bra and matching panties. She'd bought it all in September, at Filene's, with some of her living allowance, and every day she took the set out of her dresser drawer, fondling it, thinking about how it would be when she wore it with Shep. And every day she came, picturing them together.

But she'd never tried it on. No, that would have spoiled it. She hadn't even worn it to the Tufts Homecoming Ball and her date, Norman Pressman, was a senior, vice-president of the graduating class, a BMOC. She'd let him kiss her goodnight, twice, but that was it.

"I bought it just for you," Sandy told Shep. "Do you like it?"

His answer was a sliding kiss, from her mouth to her neck to her shoulder. He picked her up and carried her to his bed. Scarlett O'Hara and Rhett Butler. He lay next to her, kissing, kissing, until she thought she would die. He lifted her slip and took it off, over her head. He unhooked her beige lace bra and tossed it to the floor. He looked down at her and kissed her bare breasts. One, then the other, making her nipples stand up, sucking on them. "Oh, Shep . . . God . . . please . . . no . . . I can't . . . I . . ."

And he rested his hand on the soft flesh on the inside of her thighs, between the tops of her stockings and her beige lace panties, and then, he let his hand rest on the panties themselves.

"So wet," he whispered, "your pussy is so wet." His

hand was suddenly inside her panties, his fingers touching her, *There*. The first person she'd ever let get inside. "No, Shep, I . . ."

"Shush . . ." He kissed her again and kept playing with her, one finger moving around inside her, the others squeezing her lips.

"I love you, I love you," she called as she came.

"I know," he answered. "I've always known."

She kissed him.

"Was that nice?" he asked.

"You know it was. I never came that way before. I never let anyone touch me *there*."

"So how did you come?"

"Oh, by myself, mostly . . . rubbing . . ."

"Like this?" And he rolled over on top of her. When had he taken off his slacks? He was just in his jockey shorts now and she could feel him against her, feel how long and hard he was. They moved together and she could imagine what it would be like to have him inside her. Yes, she could imagine it. She could want it. "No . . . stop, Shep . . ." She pushed him away.

"Sandy . . . Sandy . . . it hurts . . . please . . ." He reached inside his shorts and pulled out his penis.

She looked away.

"Don't be afraid, Sandy, come on."

"I can't, Shep."

He took it in his hand, his fingers wrapped around it, pulling, rubbing. "See, that's all you have to do."

He took her hand and put it around him. "There . . . there . . . see how easy that is?" He kept his hand over hers and together they made him come, into his handkerchief.

At Christmas he was begging her to kiss it and wanting to eat her. But she couldn't, couldn't do that. It was unhealthy, abnormal. Shep was pushing her too far.

Mona warned her. "I won't forbid you to see him, Sandy, but I want you to know how unhappy Daddy and I are about this. He's not the right kind of boy for you. He has no background. His mother scrubs floors. Did you know that?"

"No."

"A Jewish scrubwoman. They're not our kind of people, Sandy. And God forbid, he could make you pregnant."

"Mother! I'm not doing anything like that."

"I hear he's already made twenty girls pregnant."

"Who told you that?"

"Margie Kott's mother. Margie had to stop seeing him because she couldn't trust him."

"I don't believe that."

"You better believe it before it's too late . . . did you know a girl can get pregnant without doing . . . *you know what . . .*"

"No!"

"It's true. So don't go losing your head over him. He could ruin the rest of your life . . . remember that . . . look at Myra . . . look how happy she is . . . you find yourself a nice boy, like Gordon . . . somebody with a future . . . with a profession or a good business and you go after him . . . and give him enough to keep him interested but don't give him everything . . . because once he's got everything from you he'll never marry you . . . believe me, I know what I'm talking about. I gave Myra the same advice . . . and look what she got. What about that nice boy who took you to the Ball?"

"Norman?"

"Why don't you see him over vacation?"

"I might."

"He calls every day . . . a nice boy from Plainfield . . . the same background . . . that's what counts, Sandy. Remember, you can't eat love . . ."

"Please stop saying that."

So Sandy went out with Norman Pressman. He took her to the Chaim Chateau for dinner and dancing, and although he couldn't dance at all, it turned out to be a very nice evening. No pressure. Two good-night kisses. And the next day he asked her to dinner at his house and his mother served a roast and his father carved it at the table. Three days later Norman drove her back to school in his new Oldsmobile.

Still, she dreamed of Shep. She dreamed of kissing him *there* and over midwinter vacation had a sudden urge to take him in her mouth. What was she going to do about these disgusting thoughts? Decent people, normal people, didn't do those things . . . didn't even think about them. Shep was perverted. But she let him do that to her. Just once. And oh, it was so good. Like nothing she had ever experienced. She came over and over, as he licked and kissed and buried his face in her. Until she cried, "Stop . . . please stop . . . I can't take any more . . ."

And then he kissed her face and she tasted herself on him. And she liked it.

If her mother knew, she would grow faint and say: Sandy, a nice girl like you! I can't believe it. How could you? That's against our religion. All those years of Sunday school . . . didn't you learn anything?

And her sister would add: Sandy, I'm shocked! Gordy and I are married and we *never* do anything so disgusting. Didn't you take Health in school? Don't you remember what Miss O'Shea taught us? That if you engage in abnormal sexual practices you'll give birth to abnormal babies. Don't you want healthy babies, Sandy?

But it feels good, Sandy would argue.

So do a lot of things, Mona would tell her. But we don't do them.

Like what? Sandy would ask.

And then Mona and Myra would look at each other and shake their heads.

Sandy knew she had to be strong. Strong enough to stop seeing Shep before he ruined her life.

Fortunately, he was drafted before Easter and after six weeks at Fort Dix was scheduled to go overseas, to Germany.

Mona relaxed.

Shep called to say good-bye. "Will you wait for me, Sandy?"

"Are you asking me to?"

"I can't, Sandy. I'm going to be gone a long time, but someday I'll be all yours. I promise."

"I don't know, Shep. I've got to think about it."

She thought about it while she went out with Norman Pressman. To dinners at expensive restaurants. To fraternity parties. To dances and movies and plays.

By the end of the summer they were pinned.

By November engaged.

She understood Norman. Felt comfortable with him. Safe. With Norman she was in control of the situation. She didn't have to be afraid. He knew the rules.

DEAR SHEP,

I haven't heard from you in ages, but I just thought I should tell you that I am engaged to marry Norman Pressman. He went to Tufts but graduated last June and is now in his family's dry-cleaning business in Plainfield. We plan to be mar-

ried in August. I will probably transfer to Doug-
lass next fall.

Please Shep . . . call and tell me not to do it and
I'll listen. Come home and kiss me, Shep . . . hold
me . . . and I'll call it all off. My knees don't shake
with Norman, Shep. My stomach doesn't roll over . . .
but you can't eat love, can you? I mean, really? I know
what kind of life I'll have with Norman. I don't know
about you, Shep. With Norman there won't be any
surprises and that's good, isn't it? My mother says so
. . . my mother says surprises can only mean trouble . . .
Norman fits in, Shep. You don't. You'd never be
satisfied with just me . . . would you? And I couldn't
stand it, Shep, if we got married and then you went
with other women . . . I'd die . . . I have an engagement ring. A two-carat, emerald-cut, blue-white diamond. And we're going to Puerto Rico on our honeymoon. And we're renting a new garden apartment in
Plainfield. Five and a half rooms. And I'm choosing
my china and crystal and silver and linens . . . oh, I'm
so busy choosing everything . . . and my picture is
being done by Bradford Bachrach next week, Shep
. . . and please, if you care . . . if you want me the
way I want you . . . please, hurry and send a tele-
gram before my picture is in the paper and everybody
knows I'm going to marry Norman Pressman . . . before it's too late, Shep . . .

She moved into the seat behind Shep on the train,
willing him to turn around. But he didn't. He had
longer hair now, brushing his shirt collar. She thought
about touching the back of his neck. Remembered
how he'd shivered when she'd kissed him there.
Funny, she'd never kissed the back of Norman's neck.

Ten minutes later they pulled into Newark. Sandy had to change trains. She walked out past him. He was reading his paper and never looked up. She was clutching the book Lisbeth had given to her.

Sandy and Norman went out to dinner that night. Not to The Club. The Club was closed on Mondays. To the new Chinese restaurant in Scotch Plains. Everyone was raving about it. And the owner, Lee Ann Fong, had recently joined The Club herself. Sandy told Norm about Lisbeth and Vincent and their arrangement. Their Thursday nights off.

"I could never tolerate anything like that," Norman said. "Marriage is a contract."

"But Lisbeth says it's helping their marriage."

"Lisbeth is full of shit . . . always has been." Norman stirred his Scotch with his index finger as he spoke.

"Did you know McCarthy did that?"

"Did what?"

"Stirred his drinks with his finger."

"You think I'm like Joe McCarthy? Is that what you're saying?"

"No, Norm, one thing has nothing to do with the other. It's just a peculiar habit."

"You shovel corn niblets with your fingers."

"It's hard to get corn niblets onto the fork."

"It's uncouth to shovel with a finger. That habit of yours has bothered me for years."

She pushed her salad around on her plate. "I told Lisbeth you wouldn't go for the idea."

"Go for? You're not suggesting . . . Jesus . . ."

"No, of course not!"

"I wish you'd stay away from her. She's nothing but trouble. I wish you'd concentrate on making new friends, at The Club."

"I got a dress for Fourth of July."

"Good, I thought you were going to have your hair cut, too."

"I was, but I didn't have time."

"Make an appointment before the holiday weekend."

"I will, I will. It's just that I'm so busy. I've got so many lessons . . ."

"Make an afternoon appointment. I cut out a picture for you."

"A picture of what?"

"The way you should have your hair cut. Remind me to give it to you when we get home."

But when they got home Norman was ready for a little something. And when she came, when she got her dessert, she called out.

"What'd you say?" Norman asked.

"Nothing."

"I thought you said *schlep*."

"No, why would I say that?"

"I don't know, that's what I'm asking."

"No, I didn't say anything."

But she must have. She must have called *Shep*. She'd been thinking about him as she came.

9

WHAT NORMAN LIKED best about The Club was that
it wasn't one hundred percent Jewish. Besides Lee
Ann Fong, there were nine Japanese members, all
from Manhattan, three Italian families, all in the dis-
posal business, two ordinary Christians, and a black
assistant pro named Roger. Norman felt it was good
for the children to meet all kinds of people. Not that
they'd actually met any of the Japanese members
because they kept pretty much to themselves but they
had, at least, seen them eating dinner in the Grill Room
along with everybody else.

Sandy took golf lessons from Roger. Three mornings a week, at nine-thirty, she reported to the driving range dressed for battle. Three mornings a week
Roger steadied her head with one hand as she swung
at the ball. Roger smelled of Sen-Sen and old English
Leather after-shave. He was determined to get her off
the practice range and onto the front nine by mid-
July.

"Eye on the ball, Mrs. Pressman," Roger said.
"Watch your club strike the ball . . . left arm straight
. . . no, no, look at that elbow . . . is that a straight

arm? Get comfortable . . . move those feet around . . .
look at that club waggling . . . we can't have that . . .
now, take it back again, nice and slow . . . no need to
hurry . . . nice and easy . . . don't try to kill the ball,
Mrs. Pressman . . . are you comfortable . . . you don't
look comfortable . . ."

I'm not, dammit! Sandy wanted to scream. *How
can I be comfortable with you holding my head?* But
she said, "I'm comfortable . . ." and she swung at the
ball. And missed.

"You've got to *watch* the ball, Mrs. Pressman . . .
I can't put it any plainer than that . . . if you don't
watch the ball, you're never going to hit it."

"I'm trying," Sandy said, "but I'm not especially co-
ordinated."

Roger sighed.

Sometimes Roger would stand behind her and put
his arms around her and actually hold the club with
her and some of those times Sandy felt what it would
be like to really hit the ball well. And some of those
times Sandy could imagine what it would feel like to
have Roger put his hands on her breasts, as he stood
behind her with his cock hard, pressing against her
ass.

After each lesson Sandy was expected to stay at the
practice range, hitting two buckets of balls. Then she
was permitted a break.

Two afternoons a week she was scheduled for tennis lessons with Evan. Evan was not as determined as
Roger. Evan favored his more promising students. He
stood across the net from Sandy, tossing balls to her
and delivering instructions in a bored monotone.

"Racquet back . . . step to the side . . . bend your
knees . . . watch the ball . . . control, Mrs. Pressman

. . . we're after control . . . where's that follow-through . . . don't try to kill it . . . easy, swing easy!"

And after Evan had used up his bucket of balls, it was Sandy's job to retrieve them. Then they'd begin again, with Sandy panting and Evan cool and smug.

"Can I ask you a serious question, Mrs. Pressman?" Evan said after Sandy's fourth lesson.

"Yes."

"Do you like this game?"

"Not really."

"Then why?"

"Because my husband wants me to learn for our retirement."

Evan shook his head and smashed a few balls across the net.

"Very nice," Sandy said, walking off the court.

She began to pray for rain.

The phone rang as Sandy was dressing for her Wednesday golf lesson. She was trying to match a pair of peds but all she could find was one with pink trim and one with yellow.

"Hello . . ."

"This is Hubanski."

"Oh, yes, sergeant."

"Can you be down to headquarters in half an hour?"

"Well, I've got a nine-thirty appointment."

"This is very important. Can you cancel, because we've traced the laundry markings on the sheet and we've picked up the guy it belongs to."

"Who is he?"

"Can't go into that now, but we're holding him. What we want to do is put him in a lineup and see if you can identify him."

"A lineup?"

"Yeah."

"Like on TV?"

"Yeah, like that."

"Okay, I'll be there."

Sandy called The Club and canceled her lesson, assuring them that it was an emergency and that she would return tomorrow morning, as usual.

She drove downtown, to police headquarters.

Would she be able to identify the man on the motorcycle? Did she even want to?

"Now, look, Mrs. Pressman," Hubanski said, directing her to a small auditorium, "all you got to do is look them over. They can't see you, so don't worry."

"Are they all criminals?"

"We can't discuss that now. The important thing's for you to identify the guy. You got that, Mrs. P?"

"Yes." So now she was Mrs. P. How cozy.

"Here we go," Hubanski called, "Okay, Jess, send them out."

Sandy slouched down in her seat in the darkened room.

Number One wore a business suit. He had graying hair and was far too pudgy to be her man. Number Two wore jeans and a T-shirt. She mustn't be fooled by dress, though. He had a lot of red hair. Attractive. Young. The right build. But red hair? No, then he'd have red pubic hair too, wouldn't he? And freckles? Her man had dark pubic hair and no freckles, at least none as far as she knew.

She leaned over to Hubanski and whispered, "You know, I didn't see his face."

"Try to identify him by body."

"If I could just see them naked."

"Mrs. Pressman!"

98

Number Three was young, pimply, and skinny. Too skinny. Number Four wore slacks and a sport shirt. Nice build. Could be . . . could be . . . clean-cut face . . . brown hair . . . she had no trouble imagining him naked . . . nice . . . very nice. Number Five was big, with a craggy face, about fifty, looked like a caddy at The Club. God, he *was* a caddy at The Club.

"I know that man," Sandy whispered to Hubanski. "Number Five. He caddies at The Club."

"Is he the one?"

"No, he's too old."

"You're sure?"

"Yes, positive."

"Well, do you see anyone else?"

"I can't be sure, but Number Four might be the one."

"Number Four is my assistant, Mrs. Pressman. And I can assure you that on the day of the incident in question my assistant was right here, working with me."

"I'm sorry. How was I to know? The only other possibility is Number Two but his coloring is wrong. I don't think the man we're after has red hair." She wanted to say, *if only I could see them in the act I'm sure I'd recognize him . . . my man has a certain style . . .*

But then Hubanski would say, *let's not get carried away, Mrs. P. There's no way I can give you a lineup of guys jacking off.*

I don't see why, she would argue.

Hubanski stood up. "Well, this is very disappointing, Mrs. P. Very depressing, you know? I was hoping the guy with the sheet."

"Which one owned the sheet, anyway?"

99

"I can't go into that now. Let's just say you didn't mention him at all."

"Are they all left-handed?"

"No . . . but I'm not convinced the man we're looking for is either. He could have used his left hand to throw us off the track . . ."

"Do they all ride motorcycles?"

"I can't divulge that information either."

"Well, I'm sorry, sergeant, but you certainly don't want me to lie."

"Certainly not, except that now we're back to nowhere."

When she got home the phone was ringing. Florenzia never answered the telephone and made no calls herself. She'd made it clear from her first day on the job that she would have nothing to do with that machine.

Sandy threw down her purse and car keys and ran to the kitchen wall phone. "Hello," she answered, breathlessly.

"Mrs. Pressman?"

"Yes."

"May I fuck you today?"

"Excuse me?"

"I said, may I fuck you today?"

Sandy hung up. *Jesus!*

It rang again.

She picked it up. "Yes?"

"Or would you rather have me suck you?"

She slammed down the receiver. If it rang again, she wouldn't answer. Maybe Florenzia had the right idea after all.

"You got mail," Florenzia said. She was wiping

out the cabinet under the kitchen sink. "I put on your bed."

"What? Oh, thanks."

"The phone be ringing all morning. I no answer."

"Yes, okay." Sandy went upstairs to look over the mail.

DEAR MOMMY

Grandma is writing me letters addressed to *Sarah*. Will you tell her to quit calling me that. Everybody in my bunk is calling me Sarah now, all because of Grandma. I still hate camp and want to come home. My counsellor got fired for doing it in the woods. That's what the seniors told us. They are big kids who know everything. We have a new counsellor now. Her name is Fish. Isn't that a dumb name? She's dumb too. She bounces a quarter on my bed every day to make sure the covers are tight enough. I miss Banushka. Send me some of her fur. Also, I hate Bucky. He was mean on brother-sister day, just because I cried.

Love,
JENNIFER P.

This letter was dictated by Jennifer P. to Deborah Z. of Bunk 16.

And a postcard from Bucky.

DEAR MOM AND DAD,

Jen is a jerk. She cried at brother-sister day. I'm not going to any more of them. I had twenty-six splinters on the bottom of my foot. The nurse counted them when she took them out. That's the most any kid at camp has ever had at one time.

101

She put them in an envelope so you can see them on visiting day. I have thirty-one mosquito bites. You might get to see them too. Camp is great. I'm fine. See you soon.

Your son,
BUCKY PRESSMAN

The phone again. If it was *him* she'd tell him to fuck off. To get it up with someone else. She was too busy for crazies.

"Yes?" she said, picking it up on the fourth ring, sounding annoyed.

"Sandy?"

"Yes."

"This is Vincent."

"Who?"

"Vincent, Vincent Moseley."

"Oh, Vincent . . . hi . . . sorry . . . I didn't recognize your voice."

"How are you, Sandy?"

"Oh, just fine, how about you?" Why would he be calling her unless he had bad news. "And the family, how's the family?"

"They're fine, as well."

"Oh, good, for a minute there I was worried."

"No, everything's okay. Lisbeth told me she had a nice visit with you the other day."

"Yes, we don't see each other often enough."

"Look, Sandy, I was wondering if you could meet me for dinner next Thursday?"

"The four of us, you mean?"

"No, Lisbeth's busy on Thursday nights. Just the two of us . . . informally . . . a chance to talk . . ."

"Thursday, you said?"

"Right."

102

"That's Thursday, the seventh?"

"Let me check. Yes, Thursday, the seventh. Let's say Gino and Augusta's at six-thirty . . . that's on West Sixty-fourth, near the park. Is that okay, Sandy?"

"I'm writing that down. Sixty-fourth, near the park?"

"Right, you'll be there, then?"

"Well, I guess so."

"Good . . . see you then . . . really looking forward . . ."

"Yes. Bye, Vincent."

Vincent X. Moseley? On Thursday night? What was this all about? Unless . . . oh, it *couldn't* be that! Not Vincent. Then why? Strange. Vincent calling out of the blue that way. She'd just have to wait and see.

"What did you do?" Sandy asked.

"What could we do?" Gordon answered. "I gave

⚔ 10 ⚔

THEY'D PUT THE house on the market in March, right
after Myra and Gordon had returned from their midwinter vacation in Jamaica. The four of them had met
in New York for dinner at Le Périgord Park. "We were
robbed," Myra said, over paté. "We didn't want to tell
you on the phone, we knew you'd worry."

"Robbed, my God!" Sandy said.

"Robbed," Myra repeated. "They held a machete to
my throat. I was this close to death." And she held her
thumb and index finger together so that Sandy and
Norman could see exactly how close to death she had
been. "I'm telling you, this close," she said again.

"A machete, Jesus!" Norman said.

"Those fucking schvartzas . . . look at these marks."
Myra pulled her Lanvin scarf away from her neck.
"That's where he had his hand . . . one hand on my
throat . . . the other holding the machete over me . . .
they broke in through the shutters, right into our bedroom . . . in the middle of the night . . ."

"What did you do?" Sandy asked.

"What could we do?" Gordon answered. "I gave

them everything. My money, Myra's jewelry, everything. They would have killed her if I hadn't."

"You did the right thing," Sandy said. "You had no choice."

"The girls slept through it all," Gordon said.

"And Mona is never to know," Myra told them. Sandy and Norman nodded in agreement.

"We put La Carousella up for sale the next day . . . we told the agent to sell it fast . . . just to get rid of it . . . never mind if we have to take a loss . . . I never want to see the place again . . ." Myra went back to her paté. "Besides we were getting tired of Jamaica." She swallowed, sipped some wine, and continued. "We want to learn to ski next winter . . . maybe get a place in Aspen or Vail . . . more invigorating than the heat of the islands . . . better atmosphere for the twins . . . and have you seen the latest ski clothes? They're fantastic!"

Later, when Sandy and Myra went to the Ladies Room Myra said, "Gordy is ashamed of himself, can you tell?"

"No, why?"

"Because he begged and pleaded with them. He even cried."

"But that's only natural. They were threatening your life."

"And his. They said they'd kill us both, first me, then him."

"Oh, Myra, I'm so sorry," Sandy said, hugging her sister. "It must have been awful."

"And after they were gone he vomited . . . got diarrhea . . . had a nosebleed . . ."

"It was a terrible experience for him," Sandy said.

"I'm the one who almost died."

"I know, but . . ."

"And I didn't vomit, for chrissakes!"

"How did you react?"

"I don't remember. Gordy says I was angry at him for giving them my jewelry, but I honestly don't remember."

"You were probably in shock."

"Probably. I just can't wait to start skiing."

They went back to their table and ordered Courvoisiers. "I'll tell you this," Gordon said, mainly to Norm, "the natives are restless everywhere. It's only a matter of time before it really hits here. Remember the riots in Newark in '67? Plainfield is next. You better get out before it's too late."

When they got home, after Norman had paid the baby-sitter and seen her out to her car, he said, "There's something I think you should know, San."

"What's that?"

"I've got a gun."

"You've got a gun?"

"Shush, you'll wake the kids."

"Since when . . . where . . . ."

"I got it during the riots in Newark. I never wanted you to know, but now, well, Gordon is right. It's only a matter of time so I'm going to show you how to use it just in case."

"No, Norm, I don't like guns. They terrify me. I don't want to know."

He grabbed her hand and led her into his study. "Look," he said, "I keep the gun locked in this cabinet." He tapped one of the wall units. "And the key to the cabinet is here, in the bookcase, behind *Bartlett's Quotations*. Now, the ammunition is locked in a steel box in the bottom cabinet." He tapped again. "And the key for *it* is in the third drawer of my desk, under the business envelopes, so you don't have to worry about the kids getting into it."

"But Norm, if somebody breaks into the house, by the time you unlock the cabinets and the ammunition box and load the gun we'll all be dead anyway, won't we?"

"You don't understand, Sandy, but then, I didn't really expect you to."

"First, we'll try selling the house ourselves," Norman said. "No point in paying a commission if we don't have to."

So, on Monday morning, Sandy placed ads in the *Courier News,* the Newark *News* and the New York *Times,* and made appointments with three realtors to look at houses in Watchung. In May she found the right house. With a view. At night you could look down and see the traffic on Route 22. You could see the lights of the houses in Plainfield, twinkling. A fireplace in the family room. Three bathrooms. Lots of stone. Lots of glass. Lots of class. And all for just ninety-nine thousand five hundred dollars. Not only that, but the builder, Joe Fiori, who was putting the house up for speculation, would let them choose their own bathroom fixtures, their kitchen cabinets, their wall colors.

Now all they had to do was sell the Plainfield house. In any other suburb it would be worth eighty-five thousand dollars, at least. Here, they'd be lucky to get forty thousand dollars for it. Plus, they had to contend with Enid, had to promise they wouldn't sell to blacks, not even to a black doctor or lawyer. A foolish promise, since there were very few white buyers in Plainfield. But Enid refused to have *ductlas* living in the house she and Samuel D. had built.

Ductlas. Enid claimed she had invented the word because *they* had figured out what *schvartza* meant. This way she could say, *Do you have a decent ductla? How does she iron? My ductla eats me out of house and home. I have to hide everything.* And they would never guess what she was talking about.

All of the Pressman stores were staffed with blacks. A smart business move, initiated by Norman, when he took over. And the best way to keep them from stealing you blind was to hire a black manager for each store, give him a share of the profits, and let him contend with the rest of the employees. That way Norman never had to play the bad guy. And he would never drop dead while firing a cashier for stealing the way his father had. Sometimes, Sandy wished Norman would drop dead. Because then she'd be free. Oh, she knew that was a terrible thought, a wicked thought and she certainly didn't wish him a long, horrible, cancerous death. Maybe an accident with the car or a blood clot to the brain, something clean and quick. *Free, free, free.* She'd never been free, could only imagine what it might be like. She'd never been on her own. She'd gone from Mona and Ivan straight to Norman. Little girl to little wife.

Sandy and Norman took Enid to The Club for dinner. Enid was dressed to a tee, as she liked to put it. And tonight she wore her thick, ash-blonde wig, turquoise eye shadow to match her Trevira knit dress, and the most curious pair of spectator pumps. Enid never got rid of old shoes, believing that if you held onto them long enough they'd come back into style. "Today's are all made of plastic," she'd once told Sandy, slipping off her shoe and holding it out. "Smell this, genuine leather top and bottom, 1947."

As soon as they were seated and studying the menu, Roger came over to their table. "I missed you today," he told Sandy.

"Oh, sorry, something came up, but I'll be back tomorrow."

"I like your haircut."

Sandy's hand went to her head. "Thanks."

Giulio had invented a cut just for her, at least that's what he told her. It looked neat and would require very little care. Norman didn't like it, she could tell, even though he said it was cute, that she looked like an elf. "And anyway," he'd told her earlier, "it'll grow out by September and then you can have it restyled."

"But I like it this way," Sandy said.

"Don't get me wrong, for the summer it's okay," Norman had answered.

"Well," Roger said to all of them, "enjoy your dinner." And then, just to Sandy, "See you tomorrow."

"They allow *ductlas* in here?" Enid asked, as soon as Roger was out of earshot.

"He's the assistant golf pro," Norman explained. "Sandy is taking lessons from him."

"They couldn't find a white one?"

"Roger is very good," Norman said.

"Well, if you don't mind, why should I mind?" But suddenly Enid wasn't that hungry. "A salad is all I feel up to, that and some soup." And she sighed.

"Jen wrote asking me to tell you she's very unhappy about the way you've been addressing her letters to camp," Sandy told Enid. "Her name isn't Sarah, you know. You're embarrassing her in front of her bunkmates. Do you think that's fair?"

"A name like Sarah, a beautiful, biblical name like Sarah should embarrass a child?"

"No, that's not the point. It's not the name that embarrasses her, it's the idea. Everyone at camp knows her as Jennifer. That is, after all, her name."

"Not her *real* name," Enid protested.

"Oh, yes, her *real* name."

"Look, Mom," Norman said, "it would be better if you wrote to *Jennifer*. She's at that age now."

Enid sighed again and picked something out of her salad. "Look at this. You'd think such a high-class club could wash their salad more carefully."

And that wasn't the only thing wrong with dinner. Enid's soup was served lukewarm. "There's nothing less appetizing than cool soup," Enid said, calling the waiter. "Please take this back. Soup should be served steaming hot." She turned to Norman. "You'd think a place like this would know."

And the coffee was weak.

And the cream for it might or might not have been sour, but from the looks of it Enid wasn't taking any chances and ordered tea instead. But the tea wasn't brewed, it was served with a bag on the side.

"Did you shop around before you joined this place?" Enid asked. "I'm sure there are plenty of other country clubs."

"My sister belongs here," Sandy said. "It's supposed to be the best."

"Maybe tonight's an off night," Enid said.

"Yes, maybe."

"She's getting difficult," Norman said later.

Getting? Sandy thought. But she said, "Yes."

"She's driving everybody in the store up the wall."

"What are you going to do?"

"I don't know, but I've got to get her out of there."

"What about Florida?"

"I only wish."

"Your Aunt Pearl is there."

"You know they don't get along."

"That was years ago. It might be different now that they're both widows."

"And this business about not selling the house to blacks. We haven't had a decent offer yet. If we're going to be in the new house in time for school we've got to sell now."

"Maybe you could talk to her about it, explain how we need the money from this one in order to close on the new one."

"She won't listen. Nobody can make her listen, you know that. But I have another idea."

"What?"

"We can sell to a realtor, then the realtor can sell to a black family. A lot of people who don't want to sell directly to blacks are doing that."

"Oh, Norm, I don't know. I'd rather we sell it ourselves or just list it with a realtor."

"I'd rather sell it myself too because I doubt that we can get forty to forty-five selling it to a realtor, but if we haven't sold it ourselves by August first, I think that's what we should do."

"That doesn't give us much time."

"If worst comes to worst you can drive the kids up to Watchung for the first month or two of school."

"But that would eat up my whole day."

"You don't have anything better to do."

"Until you said that I thought we were having a real conversation. We were actually exchanging ideas, but you had to go and ruin it with that stupid statement!"

"What statement, what are you talking about?"

"That business about me not having anything better to do!"

"There you go again. No wonder we can't ever have a conversation—you're too goddamned touchy!"

And later, when they were in bed, ass to ass, Sandy asked quietly, "Norman, do you love me?"

"You know what I think of that question."

"Do you?"

"I'm here, aren't I?"

11

THE UNWRITTEN LAW. She had broken the unwritten law with that question. He'd told her once, when he'd asked her to marry him. "I love you, Sandy. I love you and I want to marry you. I don't think it's necessary to tell you that again."

And he hadn't.

And Sandy was ashamed for wanting him to, for wanting him to confirm and reconfirm his feelings for her. But that was her problem. And she would have to deal with it herself.

They'd been married at The Short Hills Caterers, a newer wedding palace than Clinton Manor, where Myra had married Gordon. And instead of the two hundred and fifty guests of Myra's wedding, Sandy and Norman had had only ninety. "We don't owe so many obligations this time," Mona told her. It was a more intimate wedding, more elegant, Sandy thought, without doves, without a ceremonial parade, without the bride feeding the groom. A no-nonsense wedding, with Norman breaking the glass on his first try and with a band who played the horah, just once, which disappointed both families. "That's the way the happy couple wants it," Mona explained, shrugging.

Sandy had worn Myra's wedding dress, taken in, and Myra and Lisbeth were co-matrons of honor in vivid blue, the tiny twins were flower girls, in pale blue organdy, toddling down the aisle, stealing the show.

Cousin Tish caught Sandy's bouquet and one month later ran off to Europe with Norman's Uncle Bennett, whom she'd been seated next to at the wedding dinner. He left his wife and three children, he quit his job with IBM, to live with the love of his life, who was twenty years younger and who still slept with a retainer in her mouth, although her braces had been off for years. And to think that he'd met her in New Jersey, of all places. That they'd fucked in the bride's changing room at The Short Hills Caterers, between the prime ribs au jus and the baked Alaska. Rumor had it that they were still together, running a small inn somewhere in the south of France, that they were deliriously happy, and that her teeth hadn't shifted.

Sandy and Norman spent their wedding night at the International Hotel at Kennedy Airport, found a bottle of Taylor's Brut on ice awaiting them in their room with a card reading *Thank you, thank you, thank you! We wish you a long happy life together.* Signed, *Uncle Bennett and Cousin Tish,* which neither of them understood at the time.

Norm had opened it and they'd toasted each other, then Sandy poured the rest of the bottle into her bathwater, having read somewhere that champagne baths were sexy. She emerged from the bathroom powdered and perfumed and dressed in her Odette Barsa bridal peignoir set, to find Norman already under the covers, on his back, one hand draped across his eyes.

116

"I drank too much," he said.

"Oh, I'm sorry, are you feeling sick?"

"Just the beginning of a headache."

"Can I get you anything?"

"No, I'll be all right. Just turn out the lights, okay?"

"Okay." Wasn't he going to open his eyes? Wasn't he going to admire his bride in her Odette Barsa peignoir set? Obviously not. Oh well, there was always tomorrow night. She untied her peignoir, laid it carefully over the chair, and climbed into bed beside him.

How strange to be in bed together. She'd never been in bed with a man. On a bed, yes, with Shep, but never *in* it, never under the covers.

He turned to her. "Hello, wifey, how's my little wifey?"

Sandy felt the champagne, the baked Alaska, the au jus, working their way up to her throat, thought she might be sick in her wedding bed, on her new husband. Oh, God, her husband! What a terrifying thought. Why had she done this stupid thing? Why, oh why, had she gotten married . . . and to Norman Pressman, of all people!

Norman rolled over on top of her, pushing her night gown up above her belly.

"Look," Sandy said, "we don't have to . . . if you don't feel like it . . . there's always tomorrow . . . I mean, we're going to be married for a long . . ."

"No, I'm okay and I want to, unless you . . ."

"No, it's not that."

In the rec room, in Sandy's parents' house, she and Norm had shared the couch, week after week, listening to music, kissing for hours, feeling each other, dry-humping until they both came, with Norman having to change his underwear. Even then he came quickly.

117

Rub-a-dub-dub and it was all over. He'd always carried an extra pair of boxer shorts in a Safeway bag.

Sandy needed that kissing and hugging, that petting, but maybe Norman didn't know, didn't understand, because now he was pushing his penis against her, trying to get inside. "Norm, I'm not ready yet . . . please . . ."

"Relax, San, I know you're scared. It's okay."

"No, it's just that . . ."

"It'll be over soon. Just close your eyes and try to think of something else. I put Vaseline on the rubber so it'll go in easier."

"No, Norm, wait. Please."

But he wasn't listening. He was pushing, pushing inside her. She was dry, dammit.

Sandy closed her eyes and prayed that it would be over quickly. *Some wedding night! Shep . . . oh, Shep . . . I want it to be with you . . .* "Norm, it can be good if you wait for me. Norm . . ."

Push. Shove. In. Out.

"Norm . . . ow . . . please . . ."

"Shush . . . can't wait . . . sorry, San . . ."
In and In and In and then it was over. Norm shuddered once, kissed her cheek, said "Now you're really my little wifey," then rolled over and fell asleep.

Sandy was sore and bleeding. She bled so heavily they'd had to call Gordon the next morning.

"Relax," Gordon told her. "It'll stop in a day or two. Wear a Tampax and enjoy yourself! See me as soon as you get back. I'll cauterize you and fit you with a diaphragm."

She'd left a trail of blood all over Puerto Rico, but by week's end she was beginning to enjoy the feeling of Norm's penis inside her. She was still sore but she liked the way it felt moving in and out. And she was coming, coming the way she had in the rec room, coming once or even twice every time. She wanted it more and more. She wanted it morning, noon, and night. And Norman was impressed with her responsiveness. He'd had other girls, he told her, but none like her. None who could come so fast, so hard. None who wanted it so often. It looked like it was going to work after all.

So where did things go wrong, Norm? So what happened? It seemed all right then. Comfortable. Safe. We had our babies. We made a life together. But now I'm sick. You can't see it this time. There isn't any rash, no fever, but I'm sick inside. I sleepwalk through life. And I'm so fucking scared! Because every time I think about life without you I shake. I wish somebody would tell me what to do. Make the hurt go away. I wish a big bird would fly up to me, take me in its mouth and carry me off, dropping me far away . . . anywhere . . . but far from you. I want my life back! Before it's too late. Or is it already too late? Is this it, then? Is this what my life is all about? Driving the kids to and from school and decorating our final house? Oh, mother, dammit! Why did you bring me up to think *this* was what I wanted? And now that I know it's not, what am I supposed to do about it?

and her secret made her feel sexy. But she wasn't to tell Norman. Let him discover it on his own.

12

SLINKY JERSEY WAS out. Flowing chiffon was in. Sandy had guessed wrong again. Norman would be disappointed.

This was Sandy's first Club Formal. They'd missed the Memorial Day Dance because Bucky had been sick. Norman looked handsome in his new tuxedo with his blue ruffled shirt. She'd told him so before they'd left for The Club. And he had admired her too, saying, "That's a very unusual color for a summer dress."

"Yes. The saleswoman called it *wine*. I think you can wear it all year round, don't you?"

"Yes, I suppose so."

Sandy had a secret. Like the man on the motorcycle, she wore no underwear tonight. She hadn't planned it that way, but she found that her panties showed through her slinky dress, spoiling the line, and it was too warm to wear panty hose. So she wore just a Tampax under her new dress, insurance against leakage. The jersey felt good against her naked bottom and her secret made her feel sexy. But she wasn't going to tell Norman. Let him discover it on his own.

Norm brought Sandy a whiskey sour. "Drink it slowly," he said, "so you don't get dizzy."

Sandy nodded.

Sherm Hyatt, who was Norman's partner in the holiday tournament, walked toward them with his guests. "I'd like you to meet Rhoda and Shep Resnick," he said. "Rho . . . Shep . . . say hello to two of our new Club members, Norm and Sandy Pressman."

Sandy squeezed her whiskey sour glass.

He spoke first. "Sandy Schaedel!"

"Yes."

"What a surprise!"

"Yes." She would not break her glass this time. She would not sweat or stutter or fart. She would remain calm, cool, and sophisticated.

"Well, it's certainly been a long time."

"Eight years."

"Eight years . . . imagine . . . Rhoda," he said, turning to his wife, "this is Sandy Schaedel, a friend from the old days."

"Oh, yes," Rhoda said, extending her hand, "we met once at some restaurant."

"The Towers," Sandy reminded her.

"That's right . . . of course . . ."

Shep kept smiling at Sandy while Norman and Sherm heatedly discussed the latest Club Incident. Ed Braidlow had peed on the floor of the steam room and three other Club members had lodged a complaint against him.

"Norm is chairman of the Grievance Committee," Sandy explained.

"Must be interesting," Shep said.

"This is his first important grievance . . ."

"I see."

"Do you live around here?" Rhoda asked.

122

"In Plainfield but we're moving to Watchung soon. We're building a house there."

"We're in Princeton."

"Oh. It's supposed to be nice there."

"It is, especially for the children."

"How many do you have?" Sandy asked.

"Four but we're expecting our fifth any day."

"Oh, really? You can't tell."

Shep and Rhoda laughed together, making Sandy feel foolish.

"Rhoda's not pregnant," Shep told her. "We've adopted our last two kids and our latest is coming from Vietnam."

"She's three and a half," Rhoda added, "and adorable. I can show you her picture." She opened her purse and pulled out a mini photo album. "There she is, isn't she a darling?"

"Oh, yes, lovely."

"And these are our others." She flipped the pages so that Sandy could admire all five children. "We've got two boys of our own and two girls from Korea."

"I think that's terrific," Sandy said. "Really, just so nice."

"Rho," Lexa Hyatt called, "over here . . ."

"Excuse me," Rhoda said, "I think Lexa wants me to meet some of her friends."

Which left Sandy alone with Shep.

"So," he said.

"So," she answered.

"You're looking good, Sandy."

"Thank you." Pause. "Rhoda seems very nice."

"She is."

"And all those kids."

"She collects kids the way some women collect recipes."

"But you must enjoy them too."

"I've always enjoyed kids." Pause. "Norman seems nice, too."

"Oh, yes, he is. And we have two children, a boy, ten and a girl almost eight. They're away at camp." Pause. "My sister's here. You remember Myra, don't you?"

"How could I forget? I met you at her wedding."

Sandy's mouth was dried out. She licked her lips, then tried sipping her whiskey sour but found her hand was shaking. "I saw you on the train last Monday."

"Why didn't you say something?"

"I had to get off in Newark, to change trains. There wasn't much time."

"Where are you sitting for dinner?"

"Over there," Sandy pointed, "at the table in the corner with my sister and her friends. How about you?"

"Back there, that long table. Save me a dance, will you?"

"No problem. Norman doesn't dance."

The band leader announced dinner and the parade to the tables began.

Gish sat next to Sandy, whispering, "You look sensational in that . . . shows off your little body just right . . . love your little tits . . . you know the old saying . . . anything you can't fit in your mouth . . ."

"Cut it out, will you?" Sandy whispered back.

She tried to concentrate on the meal, drank more than she should have, waited until she saw Rhoda Resnick dancing cheek to cheek with Sherm Hyatt, and knew that he would come for her soon.

"Pardon me, ma'am," he said, standing behind her, "but could I have this dance, for old time's sake?"

She pretended to be surprised. "Oh, Shep, how nice." And she excused herself from the table.

Shep took her hand and led her to the dance floor.

"So," he said, looking down at her.

"So."

"Here we are again."

"Yes."

"I feel like I'm back at your sister's wedding."

"And I've just wiped the bird crap off your head."

He laughed. "I haven't been crapped on by a blue dove since then."

"Pink, wasn't it?"

"Was it?"

"I think so. Everything was pink and white."

They were quiet for a while. The electricity was still there. Her knees were weak, she felt very warm, her hands were sweating. He held her tight. "Are you happy, Sandy? Do you have what you want?"

She didn't answer. Couldn't.

"Sandy?"

"I don't know. What about you?"

"I'm reasonably happy."

"And successful, I hear."

"Yes, but bored. I made it too fast, too soon. I miss the struggle."

"What about all those kids?"

"That's Rhoda's department."

The music ended but Shep didn't let go of her hand.

"Do you play around, Sandy?"

She shook her head.

"Norman was the first and only?"

"Yes."

"And you're proud of that, aren't you?"

"Not especially."

125

The music began again. He pressed her to him, then changed his mind. "Let's go for a walk."

"I can't, they'll notice."

"No they won't. Look at Norman with that little blonde."

"That's Luscious. She admires his tennis game."

"I thought you said he doesn't dance."

"He doesn't. She's dancing, he's just standing there."

"Yeah, I guess you're right. And look at Sherm. He thinks if he dances with Rhoda all night he'll get the contract on my next shopping center."

"Will he?"

"Probably. Come on." He led her through the lobby to the double doors.

Outside it was hot and dry. Sandy smelled roses and wisteria. She had trouble breathing. What now?

Shep held her hand and they walked quickly across the eighteenth fairway and down the road to the pool. Then, off to the side of the pool, behind the cabanas.

He turned to her, took her in his arms, and kissed her. He still had that delicious way of kissing, licking the corners of her mouth, running his tongue along her teeth, sucking on her lower lip. His breath was hot on her face, in her ear, on her neck. How different from Norman's cold, toothpaste kisses. Shep tasted of wine, of salad dressing, of sex. Shep was hard. Oh yes, she could feel it against her. Very hard. He laughed.

"Feel that," he said, placing her hand on his trousers. "Just like the old days."

"Shep, Norman would never forgive me. I have to get back."

He put his hands on her ass and squeezed. "You're not wearing anything under this are you?"

"No." She felt faint, unable to swallow, to get a deep breath, scared she might pass out from the excitement of it, grateful for the Tampax, holding in her juices, keeping her dry so he wouldn't know, wouldn't guess how hot she was for him, how close to coming just from his kiss, just from his hands on her ass.

"I have to go now," she told him. "Norman . . ."

"Norman will never know." He was easing her dress up, his fingers on her naked bottom now.

"You don't understand . . ."

"Relax." He was kissing her again, one hand tightening around her breast.

"I can't, Shep, I can't take the chance."

He let go and stepped away from her.

"Life is one big chance, Sandy. If you're not willing to take it, you can't play the game."

"Then I guess I'm not ready for the game," she said slowly, hating herself.

"Call me if you change your mind," he said and walked away, leaving her alone in the dark. He never was one to force the issue, damn it!

Sandy went back to the Clubhouse, to the Ladies Room, where she splashed cold water on her face. "I know how you feel," a strange woman said to her. "I've had a wee bit too much myself."

"Oh, there you are," Norman said when she got back to their table.

"I got hot. I needed some fresh air."

"Don't have anything more to drink."

"No, I won't."

Steph Weintraub rushed up to her. "Sandy, you haven't signed my petition yet. We want all the new members to sign."

"What petition is that?"

"A refusal to accept the archaic laws of this Club

which state that women cannot tee off on Wednesdays, weekends, or holidays until one P.M. I mean, we're members too, aren't we? So why should we just go along with this shit? I play as good a game as most of our *male* members. Why should I have to wait until one P.M.?"

"You shouldn't," Sandy said, and reached for Steph's pen.

"Bullshit!" Gish said. "The difference, my dear, Stephanie Ball Breaker, is that *we* work our tails off all week, supporting you charming creatures, while *you* get to play every goddamned day of the week. So is it too much to ask that on Wednesdays, weekends, and holidays we get to tee off first? Talk about fair, talk about selfishness, Jesus H. Chreeist!"

"Maybe Gish is right," Sandy said. "I hadn't thought about . . ."

"Think for yourself, Sandy!" Steph argued.

"I never learned how." Sandy handed the pen back to Steph, without signing her petition.

13

MYRA AND GORDON threw a swim party the next night. They'd just had the pool landscaped and lit. Mona assured Sandy that Myra's pool was the talk of Short Hills, just as her house had been a few years earlier, with its staircase straight out of Tara and its eight and a half bathrooms.

Sandy and Norm arrived early for a private tour of what used to be the backyard. "Fantastic!" Norman said over and over as Myra and Gordy pointed out the newly planted sights. "Absolutely fantastic! I only hope some day we can do the same thing in Watchung."

"You've got to give him full rein," Myra said of their landscaper, who called himself the Greek. No relation to Jackie's Greek. "He's a kook, but very talented. If you try to tell him what to do he'll quit. I told him I wanted something that blooms so the next morning I look out my window and here's this bush with the most gorgeous purple flower you ever saw. So I rush outside to get a closer look and the Greek, who's watching the whole thing, gets hysterical, laughing. Because it's plastic! His idea of a joke!"

"And you've got to be willing to pay," Gordon added, "through the nose."

Tiny lanternlike lights hung from the trees, glowing softly. The shrubbery was lush, with narrow footpaths running to the house, to the side yard, to the pool itself. Railroad ties, gravel, wood chips, wild flowers, they'd created a wooded paradise out of a bare acre lot. Sandy heard the soft sound of water splashing. She turned. Of course. A miniature waterfall tucked between the rocks. She should have known. And while it was not quite Jamaica, it was certainly as close as one could hope to get in suburban New Jersey. And not only that; it was safe here. Safe, because of an intricate burglar alarm system, hooked up to a private surveillance company who monitored it twenty-four hours a day. No one was going to get close enough to hold a machete to Myra's throat here. If someone or something weighing over twenty-five pounds fell into the pool, or wandered onto the grounds once the alarm was set for the night, it would go off, first silently, warning the family, then with a blast. "We can sleep without worrying now," Myra told them. "We can leave the girls and know it's okay."

Myra shimmered in a caftan of flimsy organza, her matching bikini showing through. Gordon had on tennis shoes and socks, bathing trunks, and a Lacoste shirt. His hair was arranged carefully to cover his bald spot. Sandy and Norman changed into their swimsuits as the other guests arrived, twenty couples, many of them Gordy's colleagues. Doctors and their wives. Norman loved it, loved to surprise them with his knowledge of diseases and treatments by tossing out statements from last month's issue of the *AMA Journal*.

Soon the party was in full swing with Justine and

her forces in charge. Justine was the ultimate caterer, the finest, the classiest, the most *gourmet*. Sandy knew the menu by heart. So did all the other guests. There would be no palatable surprises. But no one would go hungry. Crab fingers, marinated mushrooms, miniature pizzas, cheese and spinach quiche, tiny shells filled with chicken a la king, giant shrimp to hold by the tail, and later, at midnight, Justine herself would emerge from the kitchen, offering whole fillets of beef, sliced before your very eyes and placed on squares of hot garlic bread, eliminating the hostess's need for renting china or silverware. And later still the buffet table would be laden with delectable French pastries and freshly brewed coffee. *Oh, delicious . . . delicious!* they would cry, even though they used Justine for all of their parties too. Myra threw three of them a year. The seasons would change, Myra's hostess gowns would change, but Justine's menu would remain the same. And next week and the week after that they would attend other parties at other homes, catered by Justine, and at midnight, would rave about the scrumptious sliced beef on garlic bread and how dependable Justine was, how you could count on her food being perfect, every time.

The women gathered in the shallow end of the pool, comfortable in the eighty-eight-degree water, drinks in hand. The men were treading water or hanging onto the sides in the deep end, less concerned about wetting their hair. Into this steamy wonderland Norman jumped with his waterproof stopwatch, impressing them all with his ability to hold his breath under water.

Steph Weintraub was still trying to convince The Club members to sign her petition. She squatted at the pool's edge, begging for signatures, while trying to keep her paper dry, the ink from smudging. From their end of the pool the men threatened to drown her and teased Warren, "If you were a *real* man, you'd keep her in line."

"Fuck you," Steph yelled at them.

The response was more laughter.

At ten, a five-piece band arrived, complete with electric guitar and bongo drums, something for everyone. Sandy drank carefully although her glass seemed to fill up automatically each time she looked away. She was sure that before long someone would pass out and fall into the pool and was relieved that the house was full of doctors, just in case. Following the steak sandwiches someone declared that the *girls* should go topless. Myra was the first to discard her top, flinging it into the pool with a great whoop, then dancing a bouncing frug with Gordon's friend, Dave Immerman. The best-breasted followed Myra's lead, while the padded and the drooping wisely kept covered.

Gish sneaked up behind Sandy and untied her top. "Take it off . . . take it off . . . take it all off . . ." he chanted.

Sandy held her suit to her and ran for the house, away from the circus. As she passed the pool she saw that Norman was still performing his breath-holding act, as a group of bare-breasted women circled around him, oohing and aahing and shrieking for him to come up.

Sandy went to Gordon's study, a quiet, dark room at one end of the house, and she lay down on the floor, closed her eyes, and thought about Shep. Regrets, regrets . . . her life seemed to be made up of nothing but a series of regrets. Why hadn't she let herself go last night? It would have made more sense than this . . . this insane party. Fear of pregnancy had kept her a virgin, now it was fear of being caught, of having to face the consequences, that kept her faithful . . . shit . . .

"Sandy."

She sat up. "Oh, Gordy."

"It's okay, don't get up."

"I needed to get away from . . ."

He nodded. "Me too."

"It's a lovely party, really."

Gordon sat down on the floor, next to her, and rubbed her back. His hands were warm, firm. He massaged her neck, relaxing her. "You know something, Sandy, I hate this fucking house, this stupid party."

"You're drunk, Gordon."

"Goddamned right I am. Stinko, but not so drunk I don't know my life is shit, that I've had it up to here."

"Come on, Gordy, you don't mean that."

"I do. I do. I want out."

"Don't talk that way. It's the booze, that's all."

"*That's all, she says.* What am I doing here, answer me that."

"You love Myra and the twins. That's what it's all about."

"Love? I don't know the meaning of that word. I used to think I did, but no more."

"Gordy, you're talking in cliches. You better go to bed."

"Good idea," he said, pulling her down with him, kissing her on the mouth.

"What the hell?" Sandy said, pushing him off her.

"I've always wanted you, Sandy . . . always loved your little ass . . . your cunt . . . everytime I examine you I want it . . . want to kiss it . . . to fill it . . ."

"Gordon! Are you crazy?"

"Yes, but I know what I want. Please, Sandy, please

let me." He was tugging at her bikini top, pushing down her pants.

"Look, I can't. I haven't got my diaphragm in."

He jumped up. "I'll get you one. What size?"

She started to laugh. "Gordon, this is insane."

"What size?"

"Eighty . . . but I can't . . . really . . ."

He opened a cabinet and pulled out a box. "Eighty, eighty, here's one." He ran to the door and locked it, ran back to her, and said, "I can make my cock dance inside you. Just wait, you're going to love it."

He kneeled in front of her and pulled down her bikini pants. "I'll put this in for you, what kind of jelly do you like?"

"I don't use jelly."

"You use foam?"

"No, nothing."

"You don't use anything with your diaphragm?"

"No."

"You have to use something. You could get pregnant without it."

"So far I haven't. Look, Gordy, we can't . . . somebody . . ."

"It's all right."

She had never been attracted to Gordon, but now he kneeled in front of her, his penis, fat and inviting, sticking straight out from his black bush. As he inserted her diaphragm he whispered, "So beautiful . . . sweetest pussy . . ." And then he put his face between her legs and sniffed her cunt, actually put his nose into it and kissed it. She found herself not just aroused, but actually wanting him very much.

He rolled her over and entered her from behind, one hand squeezing her right breast, the other holding her pussy. It felt good. Very good.

"Your fucking sister won't let me do it this way. Says it's for animals, but we are animals, aren't we, Sandy."

He pulled out and flipped her over abruptly. "And now for my cock dance," he said. "Lie still, don't move."

She lay quietly, obediently, as his cock slid into her and then she felt it moving, seemingly on its own, *dancing,* my god, he really could make it dance. Could others do that too? Or did Gordon, her short, balding brother-in-law have some special talent?

"Myra . . . Myra . . . so cold . . . hates to be dirty . . . have to come into a rubber so I don't mess her up . . ."

This can't be happening, Sandy thought. But she couldn't lie still any longer, was too excited now, had to move with him, and then she was coming, coming and moaning and wrapping her legs around him as he shot into her, calling, "Yes, my pussy, my love."

Sandy laughed. She shouldn't have, she knew, but it all seemed terribly funny. She expected Gordon to laugh with her. To say it hadn't really happened. Instead he sobbed.

"I should be shot, I should be hung or castrated or both. I'll never forgive myself. Never. I'll blow my brains out . . . throw myself out the window . . . drive the Citröen off a cliff . . . I've ruined you, Sandy, and I've humiliated my wonderful wife . . . my beautiful Myra . . . I love her so much . . . you just don't know . . ."

"Of course you do, Gordy. Take it easy. It's okay, no one will ever know, I promise."

"My children, what would they think . . . fucking my sister-in-law . . . oh, Jesus . . . they hate me anyway . . . hate us both, me and Myra . . . I loved them once . . . when they were babies . . . soft and small . . . now they're strangers, Sandy . . . hostile, moody strangers . . ."

"They're going through a stage, Gordy. It won't last forever."

He was crying hard, had trouble catching his breath. "I want them back the way they were. I want my babies back. Most of the time I want to die, Sandy. I want to be dead, done with it. It's too hard to keep going."

Sandy stroked his hair and cradled him in her arms, the way she would Bucky or Jen.

"I want to be a little boy again."

"Of course you do. You can be my little boy." She held him, kissing his forehead.

"Thank you, Sandy, that's the nicest thing anyone's said to me in a long time."

And Sandy cried with him.

14

SANDY AND GORDON sat in his Citröen in the parking lot of Sip n' Sup on the highway. Gordon had ordered two hamburgers with french fries and Cokes and now, as they unwrapped their lunches and prepared to eat them, Sandy said, "Oh, God, I've got to go again," and she leaped out of the car and raced inside to the Ladies Room. She'd had stomach pains and diarrhea since 4 A.M., following her episode with Gordon. She knew it was nerves. Nerves and tension and anxiety. The fear of being caught. Having to face the consequences. She could see it all too clearly.

Her mother would say: I raised her to be a wonderful wife and this is what I get. She does it with Gordon, my beautiful Myra's husband.

But mother, Sandy would cry, it was Gordon's idea.

You can't blame the man! All men want to do those things. It's up to the woman to say no. Didn't I teach you to carry a magazine on every date so that if you had to sit on a boy's lap you could spread the magazine out first? I'll bet you didn't have a magazine with Gordon, did you?

No, mother. I never even thought about a magazine.

There, you see? What did I tell you? God will punish you, Sandy. He'll never let you forget how you've sinned. Thou shalt not covet thy sister's husband. That's one of the Ten Amendments.

Commandments.

That's what I meant.

Except it's not.

If it's not, it should be.

Besides, I don't covet him. I fucked him but I do not covet him!

And Enid: Whore. Harlot. Just like a ductla! I knew from the start she wasn't good enough for my Norman. He only should have listened to me then. Miss High and Mighty. With her brother-in-law yet!

And the twins: Really? We had no idea Daddy could still get it up!

And Bucky and Jen: You did it with Uncle Gordon? Eeuuuww . . . *gross!*

And Myra: I'm suing Gordy for divorce. I'm taking the house, the cash, the investments, the cars, forty-five thousand dollars a year in alimony, and The Club membership. As for you, Sandy, I'll never forgive you! I understand why you did it. Oh, yes, I understand very well. Jealousy. You've always been jealous of me because I was the favorite child. But frankly, I think you're a fool for having done it with Gordon. All he's interested in is sticking it up somebody's asshole, and him a gynecologist!

No, Myra, you've got it all wrong. It feels good from behind, you should try it. And besides, he can do a fantastic cock dance.

Cock dance? Don't make me laugh! He hasn't even learned to do the Twist!

Norman: Norman would throw her out. Throw her out and forbid her to see her children. Marriage is a contract. You broke the contract. You're out. Without a penny from me. I don't want to see you again. Just pack up and leave. I can't imagine why you'd go and do it with Gordon, of all people. Jesus, he can't even play net!

Sandy returned to Gordon's car, looking pale and worn out. "How long will it take before the Lomotil starts working?" she asked.

"You should feel better in a few hours," Gordon said.

Sandy nodded.

"What I wanted to talk to you about, Sandy . . ."

"Don't tell me," Sandy said, interrupting. "Myra knows!"

"No, nobody knows, at least not as far as *I* know. What I want to say and I couldn't over the phone, is that I'm willing to marry you."

"Marry me?"

"Yes. I've thought it all over and decided that's what we should do. We'll fly down to Juarez, or wherever you go for a quickie divorce these days, and marry before we come home. That way we can get things settled up over the summer. We might have to move away. Nevada's a possibility or New Mexico. I'll have to look into the logistics, have to arrange to sell my practice here." He sipped his Coke. "And who knows, maybe Norman and Myra will get together too. They have a lot in common."

"Gordy, in spite of my diarrhea, I know that Sunday night just happened and the best thing we can do is to forget it."

"Really? You really mean that?"

"Yes. I don't want to marry you."

She could see his relief. "I'll never be able to tell you how sorry I am it happened, San, I could apologize for the next ten years and you'd still never know."

"I do know, Gordy . . . really . . . it's okay . . . it was my fault as much as yours . . . I could have stopped you . . . I wasn't that drunk . . . as long as nobody ever finds out . . . that's all I care about . . ."

"You're a wonderful woman, Sandy."

"Did you really think I'd marry you?"

"I wasn't sure. But I felt I owed it to you to ask."

"That was very nice, unnecessary, but nice." She leaned over and kissed his cheek.

He hugged her. "It was good, wasn't it?"

"Yes."

"We could go across the street and take a room for a few hours."

She laughed. "No."

"I guess you're right."

"Oh, I almost forgot," she said, opening her purse and pulling out a small packet wrapped in Kleenex. "I brought you the diaphragm."

"Keep it."

"I can't."

"Oh, go on, I have plenty. Think of it as a memento of our time together."

"Okay, if you're sure." She put it back in her purse and opened the car door. "Bye, Gordy."

"Bye, San, take care and let me know if you don't feel better soon."

"I feel better already." She walked across the parking lot to her own car and drove home.

Sandy couldn't remember the combination number for her locker at The Club. Rather than admit this and and have the handyman break into it, she carried her things back and forth in a canvas tote. She still tried her locker each time, hoping that one of these days she would hit on the right combination. 30-45-15 45-13-30 15-35-42 Nothing.

"What's the matter?" Steph asked, catching Sandy in the act.

"Oh, nothing, why?"

"It looked like you were having trouble with your locker."

"Me? No, I was just rearranging some of my things."

"Could you zip me up?" Steph asked.

"Sure and if you're still interested I've decided I'd like to sign your petition."

"Terrific!" Steph opened her locker, which was across from Sandy's, and handed her the petition and a pen. "This means we have just seventeen holdouts and every one of them is scared shit of her husband. Glad I had you figured wrong, Sandy. Are you going to play in the ABCD tournament?"

"No, I'm not ready for tournaments yet. I'm having my first playing lesson today."

"Well, I'll talk to Roger about it. He'll tell me if you're ready or not, and if you are, I'll try to get you in my foursome. I'm glad you joined The Club. We can use some new faces around here. Not to mention some new ideas."

"Thanks," Sandy said, surprised and flattered.

It was Ringer Day. Every Tuesday was Ringer Day. A large posterboard chart hung on the wall behind the row of dressing tables. Each member's name was neatly printed down one side. On Tuesdays, after they had played their rounds they posted their best score for any one hole. Their *Ringer*. Members without official handicaps, like Sandy, were automatically assigned a 36, the highest. She imagined the chart on Labor Day, all the little squares neatly filled in with fives and fours and threes. Except next to her name. Next to her name would still be a blank row. Oh, shit! Who cared?

Sandy had to hurry. Roger would be waiting. They were going off the back nine. Sandy had never been out on the course, except in a cart with the children when they had first joined The Club.

"Hey!" Roger called, clapping his hands. "Here she is ready for her big debut!"

"Roger, please don't make it worse. I'm very nervous as it is."

"Relax, Sandy. This is supposed to be fun. Steve is going to caddy for us. Steve, this is Mrs. Pressman."

Steve nodded and said her name softly.

She had seen him before, waiting around. He wasn't an A caddy, that much she knew, probably not a B either, but he had a nice smile and seemed shy. Good. She didn't need any wise-ass caddy following her around. Most likely he was the son of a member, home from college for the summer. He picked up her bag and walked behind them.

"Now, listen, Sandy," Roger said, "you're going to stand up to the ball. Forget about everything else and hit it. The practice range is for thinking about what to do. When you're out here you stop thinking and just let it happen."

"Suppose it doesn't?"

"That's not the attitude we want to start with, is it?"

"I'm just being realistic."

"Never mind. Confidence is what we want to stress

today to prove to yourself that you can do it. Get that?"

"Yes. Sure."

Two hours later Sandy was back at the locker room. She'd lost eight balls, had come close to getting smacked in the head when her tee shot on fifteen hit a tree and rebounded, had spent twenty minutes trying to get a shot over the water on seventeen, and had promised Roger she would come out every day to hit two buckets of balls, take a lesson twice a week, and play nine holes as often as she could.

"After next week you should start playing regularly," he said. "And sign up for the ABCD tournament."

"I can't play in a tournament."

"Sure you can. Plenty of women out there can't hit the ball as well as you."

"I'll see."

Roger held out his hand. "Next year you're going to say, remember when . . ."

Sandy scraped her shoes on the mat outside the Ladies Locker Room, then went inside and collapsed on the floor in front of her locker. One thing she knew for sure. She hated the game of golf. So why had she made an appointment with Steve to caddy for her at Friday morning at eight? Because she was expected to. Because she always did what she was told. Because she was such a good little girl. Such a good little wifey.

Yes, what a mess.

"Who could have done it?"

"That's what we're trying to find out."

15

NORMAN CAME HOME at five, an hour early. He took two aspirin and lay down on the sofa in the den.

"What's wrong?" Sandy asked.

"A terrible day."

"What happened?"

"Jake died."

"Jake who?"

"This is no time to be funny."

"I'm not being funny. I don't know who you're talking about."

"Jake, the doberman in the New Brunswick store."

"Oh, the dog."

"Is that all you can say?"

"I didn't know him personally."

"He was poisoned."

"Poisoned!"

"Had convulsions in front of the customers. Died before we could get him to the vet."

"Were you there when it happened?"

"Yes, what a mess."

"Who could have done it?"

"That's what we're trying to find out."

"Are you going to get another dog?"

"I've already called the kennel."

Sandy nodded. Then, to cheer him, she said, "I had my playing lesson today. I hit my tee shot over the green on eleven."

"This is no time to talk about your playing lesson."

"I thought you'd want to know."

"For God's sake, I just told you one of our dogs was poisoned, Sandy!"

"You didn't carry on this way when Kennedy was killed. Or when my father died!"

"Just what the hell is that supposed to mean?"

"Nothing, forget it."

She went into the kitchen, cut up the salad, and set the table. Then, feeling guilty, she poured a glass of lemonade and carried it to Norman. He sat up and sipped it.

"We got two letters from Jen and a card from Bucky," Sandy told him. "Bucky just signed his name but Jen sounds like she's adjusting and having fun."

"I told you she would."

Sandy nodded. "I made stuffed peppers for dinner."

"I don't think I can eat tonight."

"But stuffed peppers are your favorite."

"Save them for tomorrow."

"I won't be home tomorrow. I'm going into New York, remember?"

"No."

"Yes, I told you. The twins are being operated on tomorrow morning. I'm taking my mother in and then spending the night with Myra at the St. Moritz."

"I guess I forgot."

"Can I bring you some soup or maybe tea and toast?"

"Soup would be good."

"Okay. And Norm, I really am sorry about Jake."

"And I'm sorry I snapped at you. I'm glad the playing lesson went well."

Sandy sat down next to him. "Hold me."

He put his arms around her. She rested her face against his. "We can make it better, can't we?"

"What?"

"Us."

"What do you mean?"

"I mean if we try, really try, we can still make it work."

"I don't get you."

"Us . . . you and me . . . the marriage . . ."

"Don't start in tonight, Sandy. I'm tired and my head aches."

Sandy picked up Mona at eleven the next morning and drove into New York, leaving the car on the Port Authority parking roof. It was hot, but breezy, and Mona protected her hairdo with a pink, gauzy scarf for the short walk to the building.

"I was up all night," she told Sandy. "I'm so worried about the girls."

"They'll be fine. It's easy surgery. They don't even have to put them out. They get a local."

"In their noses?"

"I don't know how they do it."

"It must be very painful."

"I don't think so. If it was, you wouldn't hear about so many girls having it done."

"It's a shame they got the Lefferts' nose instead of ours. We all have such good noses."

"I'm sure they'll look great when it's over."

"Did you know it costs eighteen hundred dollars a nose but because they're twins and because of professional courtesy they're getting a break—two thousand dollars for both."

They entered the building and waited for the elevator to carry them down to the main floor.

"We'll take a cab?" Mona asked.

"Yes. The hospital's uptown."

"I get confused in the city."

"So do I."

Mona held Sandy's arm as they walked through the lobby of the Port Authority building. "Sandy," she began, then looked around as if to make sure no one was listening, "I have something to discuss with you."

"What is it?"

"Not here, outside."

They went through the double glass doors and caught a cab. After Sandy had given the driver the address of the hospital she turned to her mother. "Go on." Was it possible that Mona had somehow found out about her and Gordon? What a thought!

"I met a man," Mona whispered.

"That's wonderful!" Sandy told her, relieved.

"I knew him years ago before either one of us was married and now I ran into him again at Ruth Berkow's house. He's still married. But he wants to see me. I don't know what to do."

"Do you like him?"

"If he wasn't married I could be persuaded. He brought me a bottle of perfume over the weekend—Joy. And he sent me a dozen roses for the Fourth of July—yellow."

"He must have fallen for you in a big way."

"But he's married."

"Maybe they don't get along."

"They don't, but they have a truce, he says. No

love, no *you-know-what* but they still live together."

"And he wants to *you-know-what* with you?"

"Sandy, God forbid! I have my reputation to consider."

"So what does he want?"

"Companionship, he says."

"So what's wrong with that?"

"He's *married*. A *married* man, Sandy. How would it look? Divorce your wife, I told him, and I'll think about it. *She'd kill herself,* he says."

"So what are you going to do?"

"I'm going out to dinner with him Saturday night. Then I'll decide."

"That makes sense."

"But I'm nervous. If his wife finds out, I could be named coordinator, God forbid."

"Correspondent."

"That's what I said."

"And you can't be named just for having dinner with him."

"It's all so easy for your generation!"

"It's not easy at all. But you're an attractive woman, mother, a widow, you should be going out with men. I've told you so since Daddy died."

"If you remember, I tried once."

"That was a bad experience. I agree."

"You're telling me? You don't know the half of it. That one went to Charlie Chaplin's doctor in Switzerland. *My hormones are like a boy's,* he tells me. First we go for a ride in his new Cadillac, to south Jersey, to the cemetery where his late wife is buried, and after, he takes me to dinner at Howard Johnson's."

"I never knew that."

"You think I wanted anyone to know he took me to Howard Johnson's for dinner? And that's not the end of it either. When we get back to my place he asks if he could please come up for some coffee. *Of course, coffee and a piece of Sara Lee cake, maybe?* I say. *Sounds beautiful,* he says. *And Mona, so are you.* I should have known then, but no, I had to go and believe him. Miss Innocence. So he looks around my apartment, admires everything, and asks if he could please lie down on my bed. He's not feeling well all of a sudden. Right away I start worrying that he's going to have a heart attack in my bedroom and how will that look to the world? But he's not having a heart attack. Not him! He grabs me and pulls me down on top of him. Can you imagine! He wants to *you-know-what* with me on the first date! I tell him if he doesn't let go in a hurry I'm going to scream. *Good,* he says. *I like my women to scream.* A meshugunah! I tell him I'll kill him and I mean it. I'm already thinking about my sewing scissors. Then he laughs and lets me go. *I thought you were a sport,* he says, *but let's just forget it. I have plenty of women, more than I can handle, so who needs you?* And then he gets up and walks out. Such an experience! Is it any wonder I haven't gone out since?"

The cab pulled up in front of the hospital and Sandy paid the driver.

"You should have told me before," Sandy said as she and Mona walked into the lobby.

"You think I like to bother you and Myra with my personal problems?" Mona looked around. "This is a hospital? It seems more like an office building to me."

"It does, doesn't it." They walked toward the elevator. "Does Myra know about your new friend?"

"Morris . . . Morris Minster. No, she's got too much on her mind right now, the noses and everything."

The elevator door opened and they stepped inside. "What floor did Myra say?"

"Four, I think."

Sandy pressed the button.

"Sandy, I hope you're careful with Norman."

"Careful, how?"

"Careful so you don't get into trouble."

"We're not planning on any more children if that's what you're worried about."

"Not that."

"Then what?"

"Divorce," Mona whispered.

"Divorce?"

"Yes. My friend Nettie's daughter, who lives in Connecticut, in a very swanky neighborhood, is getting a divorce. It's making Nettie sick. Her blood pressure's up to God knows what. You should take good care, Sandy. Make Norman happy. Nettie's son-in-law, a lawyer, ran off with another woman from the same street!"

"That's too bad for Nettie's daughter but it has nothing to do with me and Norman."

"I'm just saying there's so much going on these days, everything is different from when your father and I were your age. You should just watch out. I told Myra the same thing."

"Don't worry about us, Mother, we're just fine."

"Thank God."

They got out on the fourth floor and Mona went up to the receptionist. "We're looking for a Mrs. Lefferts," she said, "Mrs. Myra Lefferts. Her twins were operated on this morning."

"Oh, yes, of course, Room four-sixteen. Mrs. Lefferts said her family would be here around noon."

They started down the hall but coming toward them

were two girls with huge brown rubber noses held on by white, bloodstained tape running across their cheeks and up to their foreheads.

Mona swayed and reached for the handrail. "Oh."

"Shush," Sandy told her.

"I feel sick."

"They've just had nose jobs, that's all."

"They look like the walking dead."

"Come on, Mother. Connie and Kate will have the same kinds of bandages. You better get used to it."

"It's good I saw *them* first. Otherwise I might have fainted, seeing my grandchildren that way."

The door to Room 416 was partially opened. Connie and Kate, in identical zombie masks, were asleep. Myra sat by the window, reading the latest issue of *Vogue*. She looked up, held her finger to her lips, then joined Sandy and Mona outside, in the hall.

"How are they?" Sandy asked.

"Fine, back in their room by nine-thirty. He did one right after the other. They were awake but groggy. Now they'll doze on and off all day."

"Thank God it's over," Mona said. "Could you see anything? Could you tell how they look?"

"No, it'll take three weeks before we can tell how they're going to look but Dr. Saphire stopped by a few minutes ago to say it went very well. No problems."

"Now, if they'll just lose some weight," Mona said.

"They will, Mother," Myra answered, annoyed. "They needed the incentive. Give them a few months and you won't recognize them. I've already made appointments at Sassoon for the day the bandages come off."

"You want to go to lunch?" Sandy asked.

"Yes. I could use a little break. The nurse will look in on them while I'm gone." Myra went back into the room and wiped off the blood trickling down from Connie's exposed nostril. She smoothed back Kate's hair, planted a gentle kiss on each girl's cheek, and tiptoed out of the room.

Sandy put Mona on the four o'clock bus back to Hillside, then went to Myra's room at the St. Moritz to shower and change for her dinner with Vincent. When she'd made the date with him she hadn't realized how well it would work out, had forgotten that she was to keep Myra company for a day or so while the girls were hospitalized.

She still wasn't sure exactly what Vincent had in mind. A good visit, she hoped. Maybe he wanted to talk with her about Lisbeth, about their arrangement, or maybe he wanted to ask her to help out with Mrs. Rabinowitz when he and Lisbeth went to Maine in August, or maybe he wanted to . . . No! She wouldn't think about that. They were meeting for dinner, that was all, like old friends. Nothing wrong with having dinner with an old friend, was there?

Come off it, Sandy!

Look, I'm not going to jump to conclusions.

She walked up to the restaurant. She was ten minutes early and decided to wait outside. She wore her green dress and carried her white blazer over her arm. She was always cold in air-conditioned restaurants. Thin blood, Norman told her. She watched the people walk by. Quite a selection. A dwarf, two shirtless men arm in arm, a group of little girls in Danskins, a stunning woman who looked like . . . my God, Sandy thought, taking off after her. Was it? Yes, she was almost sure. *Jackie!* The woman walked to the corner and turned left. Sandy followed. The woman had slightly bowed legs. The right hair. Sandy crossed the street and walked quickly to the corner. Jackie reached her corner and waited for the light to change. Sandy crossed at the same time, coming face to face with her. It *was* Jackie! She wore big sunglasses but there was no doubt. Sandy knew. Jackie knew she knew. They smiled at each other. Sandy wanted to hug her, to tell her how sorry she was about her troubles, but not to worry, that things would be better. In a second they had passed each other. Jackie walked down Central Park South, not hurrying, but with long confident strides.

Sandy rushed back to the restaurant. Vincent was waiting. They kissed hello. "You won't believe this," Sandy told him, breathlessly, "but I just saw Jackie Kennedy."

"Of course I believe it," Vincent said.

"Well, I almost didn't!"

"You've always had a lot of interest in her, haven't you?"

"Yes."

"Well, shall we go inside?"

"Fine."

"Have you ever seen her in person?" Sandy asked.

"Several times."

They were shown to a table in the corner. They each had two drinks, fettuccine, a green salad, a half bottle of Bolla Soave, and cappucino. They talked about their children, the pros and cons of fad dieting, the war in Vietnam, where it all would end, how his students weren't as bright or eager as they used to be, and marriage and its future in America. Sandy found it exciting to engage in a real conversation, found she had ideas she hadn't been aware of herself.

When the check was presented, Sandy asked, "How's Mrs. Rabinowitz?"

"Not well at all. She's going in for more tests. They suspect a brain tumor . . ."

"I'm sorry."

"Yes, difficult . . ." Vincent signed the Bank-Americard receipt and checked his watch. "Well, it's just seven-forty-five. How about a movie?"

She tried to hide her surprise. She hadn't considered the possibility of anything as ordinary as a movie. "I don't know."

"Oh, come on, it's still early and you're spending the night with your sister, you said."

"Yes."

"Well then there's no hurry, is there?"

"I guess not."

"Good. I know just the film. It's playing up near Columbia. We can make the eight-twenty show."

It would probably be some artsy foreign film with titles, and after it Vincent would ask her all kinds of deep questions about its real meaning and Sandy would either have to admit, *I don't know* or make something up, the way she used to when Lisbeth dragged her to films full of relevance way back when. Yet Sandy wasn't anxious to get back to the hotel, didn't want to meet up with Gordon.

"X-rated?" Sandy asked, when she saw the marquee.

"Yes, but very high class," Vincent assured her. "I've already seen it but I'd like very much to share it with you."

"I've never seen a porno film."

"This isn't porno, Sandy, it's artistic. There's quite a difference."

"If you say so." Sandy giggled, more from nervousness than anything else. So, it wasn't to be ordinary after all.

155

Vincent bought the tickets and they went inside.

The picture began. A girl was walking down the street. She entered a building, climbed up several flights of stairs, let herself into an apartment, went directly to the bedroom, undressed, and was raped by two young men who had been hiding in her closet. Or maybe she wasn't raped. Because she enjoyed it very much. Possibly the two young men were just playing games with her. But there was no time to try to figure out the plot because she was already with a third man. This time she sat on him, her hands caressing her own breasts, as she moved up and down. Was this simulated or real sex? Oh, wait a minute . . . it was real . . . his penis was inside her . . . yes, from this camera angle you could see it gliding in and out. And now she was sucking him . . . and here were the two young men again, one of them fucking her, the other one . . . very complicated . . . Sandy lost track of which body belonged to which player. After fifteen minutes more of various sexual acts Vincent leaned close and whispered, "Does watching make you wet?"

Sandy didn't answer. She'd been dripping right from the start, shifting in her seat, trying to make the heat go away, trying to forget that Vincent was sitting next to her and most likely had plans.

"Does it?" he asked again.

"Yes," she said, thinking over her options. She could walk out, take a cab back to the St. Moritz and never see Vincent again. That was what she *should* do. But she hated to make hard feelings. Vincent's hand was on her bare thigh now. Any second now he would feel how wet she really was.

"Vincent, this is crazy."

"You're right," he said, "let's go." He grabbed her hand, practically pulled her out of the theater, across the street, down another street, past a row of stores.

"Where are we going?" she asked.

"To my office, it's right around the corner."

Oh, so that was it. "But Vincent . . ."

"Look, Lisbeth told you about our Thursday nights, didn't she?"

"Yes, but . . ."

"I was sure you understood when you accepted my invitation."

"No, I thought . . ."

"But it's *Thursday.* I made that clear when I called, didn't I? I said, *Thursday,* the seventh."

"Yes, but you see . . ."

"Never mind. Here we are." They stood in front of a small, ivy-covered building on campus, across the square from the library. Vincent fumbled in his pocket for his keys, found them, unlocked the front door, escorted Sandy up a flight of wooden stairs, unlocked the door to his office, stepped inside, turned on a table lamp, took her in his arms, and kissed her with more tongue than she found comfortable. He squeezed her breasts and whispered, "My little panda, my little bear, my mountain goat, my baby burro." Was she hearing right? Was he kidding? He pushed her down to the floor, easing her dress up and her panties down.

"Vincent, no." She tried to get him off. "I can't. I haven't got my diaphragm, for one thing."

"Not to worry," he said, licking her exposed right breast. "I've had a vasectomy. Didn't Lisbeth tell you?"

"No."

"It's all right, my little sparrow, my coyote, my wolverine, my lion cub." He had her dress pushed up around her neck now, and her panties around her

157

ankles. He was working on her shoes, trying to un-
buckle the straps, instead of just slipping them off.

"Does Lisbeth know you're with me tonight?"

"It was her idea."

"Really?"

"Well, in a way. She asked me if I could think of
anyone who might be right for you . . . said you were
ready to explore . . . *someone who isn't terribly intellectual,* she said . . . *someone sexy but not overpowering, someone Sandy can trust* . . . So I thought
of myself. Of course I'm quite intellectual but not a
snob about it like some of my colleagues. And I'm
sexy, don't you think so, but not overpowering." He
kissed her ankles as he removed her panties. "My
little alligator, my sand shark, my turtle . . . and you
can trust me . . . so why look further . . ." He had
given up on her shoes and was kissing her knees.

"Oh, no . . ." Sandy said, suddenly. "I just remembered . . . I left my jacket in the movie . . . what'll I
do?"

"Fuck me and then we'll go back and try to find it,"
Vincent answered, kneeling over her, his erection long
and slim, like the rest of him. He had blond pubic
hair and was circumcised. She'd often wondered about
that. Vincent grabbed hold of his cock, letting the tip
brush against her cunt, teasing, then pulling it away.

Sandy arched her back and raised her hips off the
floor, like the girl in the movie had.

"My little kangaroo is hungry . . . hungry to
fuck . . ." He slid into her and she tightened her cunt
around him, but as she did she felt him disappear.

"Oh, dammit. Dammit to hell!" he cried.

"What's wrong?" Sandy asked. "Did I do something?"

"No, I lost it."

"But why?"

"Because I lose it every goddamned fucking Thursday night." He rolled off her and lay on his back.

"I'm sorry, Vincent."

"It's not your fault. It's psychological, guilt or anxiety or something."

"Is it this way with Lisbeth too?"

"Hell no, with Lisbeth it's great."

"Then why bother with Thursday nights?"

"Because she wants to."

"Does she know about you?"

"No, I make up stories for her. Actually, she's better at screwing around than I am. And that's what really hurts!"

"We could keep trying," Sandy suggested, feeling sorry for him now and needing to prove to herself that she could keep him aroused.

"No, I've tried and tried."

"Maybe you need someone with a lot of experience."

"I've tried professionals too."

"What will you do now?"

"Go home and make it with Lisbeth. It's always very good on Thursday nights."

Sandy leaned on one elbow. "Vincent, did it ever occur to you that maybe Lisbeth's inventing stories too? That maybe neither one of you is really doing anything?"

"She reeks of sex when she gets back. You can smell her a mile away. I love it."

"Oh." Sandy stood up and began to get dressed.

"Look, if you're still hot I could suck you," Vincent said. "I wouldn't mind. I'm quite good at it."

"No thanks. I've got to get back to the hotel. Myra will be wondering what happened to me. And Vincent,

I'd appreciate it if you didn't mention any of this to Lisbeth."

"I've no intention of mentioning it to her."

"But I thought you don't believe in secrets . . ."

"She doesn't believe in secrets."

"Oh, I see."

They went downstairs and walked out to the street. Vincent hailed a cab and told the driver to take Sandy to the St. Moritz. "Thanks for dinner," Sandy called.

"We'll have to do it again some day," Vincent answered.

Fat chance, she thought.

When she got back to the hotel she realized they'd never gone back to the theater to look for her jacket.

Myra was in bed, reading *Cosmopolitan.* "I was getting worried," she said.

"We went to a movie. How are the girls?"

"They fell asleep around nine and Gordy and I went out for a cup of coffee. Norm called an hour ago. He'd forgotten you were having dinner with Lisbeth."

Forgotten, no. She hadn't mentioned it to him in the first place. "Well, it's too late to call him now. Did he say what he wanted?"

"No."

"I'll call him in the morning," Sandy said yawning. "I'm very tired. I think I'll get ready for bed." When she had finished in the bathroom she climbed into the other bed, still rubbing in her hand lotion. "Okay if I turn out the light?" she asked.

"Sure," Myra said, closing her magazine. "I'm tired too."

"Night. I'm glad the surgery went well."

"Yes, me too."

Sandy was dozing off when Myra whimpered, "Oh, San . . ."

"What . . . what is it?"

Myra's voice caught and she began to cry. "Oh, Sandy, I don't know what to do . . ."

Sandy sat up and switched on the light. "What's the matter?"

"It's Gordy."

"What about him?"

"I think he's having an affair." She cried hard, her shoulders shaking, her face buried in her hands. Sandy could remember having seen Myra cry just once before. Myra must have been about fifteen and Mona had taken her to the beauty parlor for a haircut. Myra came home wailing that she had been ruined for life and that she would never forgive Mona or that fruitcake, Mr. Robert. Sandy got out of her bed and sat down next to Myra, handing her the box of Kleenex from the night table. "I can't believe it," she said, "not Gordy!"

"I know. I can't believe it either, but look what I found." Myra blew her nose, then reached under the covers and pulled out a plain white envelope. She handed it to Sandy. "Read this."

Sandy's fingers shook as she opened it and took out a greeting card. The front of it showed two tiny animal creatures and a huge foot. Inside it read:

It's bigger than both of us! And then, in Gordon's almost illegible doctor's script:

I miss you.
It was wonderful.
Let's do it again some day soon.
Just bring your memento and name the
    time and place.

                    G. . . . .

Jesus! He must have written it to her, unless he gave out mementos regularly. But, luckily, he'd never addressed it. "It could be some sort of joke," Sandy said, trying to sound convincing.

"Come on, San."

"Okay, I admit it's incriminating, but still, Myra, it doesn't necessarily mean he's having an affair. It could have been a one-night stand."

"He wants to see her again. He says so."

"Yes, but he never mailed it. He obviously thought it all over and decided it was a mistake."

"I don't know what to do. If I ask him about it he might bring up. . . ."

"What?"

"Oh, San, I'm so ashamed. Years ago, when the twins were babies and Gordy was at the hospital night after night . . ."

"Go on."

"I had an affair."

"Myra!"

"I know, I know. It makes me sick just to think about it."

"Who was he?"

"Frank Monzellini . . . our neighbor in the apartments . . ."

"I remember him. He and his wife used to have terrible fights and we used to listen."

"Yes. We only did it three times, not that he didn't want to keep it up but I couldn't. I was so scared and I didn't really like him, but he was very sexy."

"Does Gordon know?"

"I don't think so, but maybe I'm wrong and this is his way of punishing me. After all, he left the card in a very conspicuous place as if he wanted me to find it."

162

"Where?"

"With the household bills."

"It could have been a mistake."

"I guess."

"You didn't say anything to him tonight, did you?"

"No. Suppose I do confront him and he says he wants a divorce. What do I do then?"

"I'm sure he doesn't want a divorce," Sandy said, reassuringly. "He loves you, anyone can see that. If I were you I'd just forget the whole thing."

"That's easy for you to say, but suppose you found out Norman was playing around."

"Well, I'd be shocked."

"And?"

Sandy nibbled on her finger. "I'm not sure."

"There. You see?"

"Do you love Gordy?"

"Of course I love him. I've never considered not loving him. I never even think about it. I love him just like I love the twins and the house and The Club and my friends and you and Mona."

Sandy had trouble falling asleep after their conversation, couldn't help picturing Myra, at twenty-three, with Frank Monzellini, who wore an undershirt, Marlon Brando style, showing off his hairy armpits. Frank was a plumber. Sandy remembered him carrying in Myra's groceries, playing with the twins on the floor, and one day, to her surprise, when she'd dropped by unexpectedly, finding him there without his shirt, under or regular, and Myra in her robe, flushing. "The toilet's stopped up," Myra had said. "Frank is fixing it for me." Myra and Frank had exchanged looks, then Frank left. Sandy hadn't guessed, hadn't even suspected what was going on. How naive she'd been then.

Thinking about Myra and Frank brought back Sandy's unfinished sexual feelings. The movie. Vincent's office. Gordon, writing her that stupid note. That fool, she thought, touching herself softly, finishing what Vincent had started. *Fool, fool, fool.* Yet she was a fool too. A fool for going with Vincent, for playing with Gordon, for her why not attitude.

16

THE NEXT DAY, when she got home, Sandy phoned Gordon. "Myra found your greeting card."

"My what?"

"You know, *It's bigger than both of us!*"

"No!"

"Yes. And she thinks you're having an affair."

"I forgot all about that card. Did she mention any names?"

"No."

"That's good."

"Gordon, this is very serious. Why did you do it?"

"I don't know. I was looking for get-well cards for the girls and I came across that one and it appealed to me. It reminded me of us."

"You better think up a good explanation."

"I'll say it was for Mrs. O'Neil."

"Who's she?"

"Our bookkeeper. Myra's crazy about her. She's about sixty . . ."

"You expect Myra to believe that?"

"I don't know."

"Maybe we'll get lucky, maybe she won't ask."

Sandy paused. "Gordy, that card *was* to me, wasn't it?"

"Well, of course it was."

"I just wanted to make sure."

"Doesn't anybody trust anybody any more?"

"It keeps getting harder."

That night, in bed, Norman looked up from the July issue of the *AMA Journal* and said, "I didn't know you were going out with Lisbeth when you were in New York."

"Her mother's very ill," Sandy said. "They think it's a brain tumor."

"That's too bad."

"Yes."

"I picked up the new dog today. The employees voted on a name for him. It's Lester."

"That's a nice name."

"I would have preferred something with a little more class, but it's important for the employees to feel involved."

Sandy closed her book and said, "Norm . . ."

"What?"

"Have you ever seen a porno film?"

"What has that got to do with Lester?"

"Nothing, I'm changing the subject. Have you?"

"Not since my college days. Why?"

"I thought it might be fun to see one together sometime."

"That sounds like Lisbeth. You know, San, she's nothing but trouble. I've warned you again and again . . . begged you to make new friends at The Club."

"This has nothing to do with making friends at The Club."

"I'll bet her fag of a husband needs porno flicks to turn him on, but I don't." He switched off the bedside lamp, pulled down her blanket, and climbed in next to her. "I'm always ready," he said, dropping his boxer shorts to the floor. "I'm ready right now."

"Yes, I know."

Three minutes from start to finish. Sandy thought about Frank Monzellini. Frank and Myra. No time for a main course tonight. Tonight she got just a snack.

After, when Norman had finished washing and gargling and was tucked safely into his own bed, Sandy asked, "Norm, are you happy?"

"You ask too many questions lately."

"I need to know. Are you?"

"Yes, I'm happy."

"All the time?"

"Who's happy all the time?"

"I don't know. That's what I'm trying to find out."

"I'm happy enough. And so would you be if you had half a brain. Now go to sleep."

Half a brain. If she had half a brain she'd appreciate him. That's what he meant. But how could she when he treated her like a trained animal? Like Banushka. No, he treated Banushka better. With more care, more respect. Well, she had news for him. She had more than half a brain. It just hadn't been working lately. Hadn't been tuned up for a long time. She'd just been letting it sit there. Going bad. Rotting away. Atrophy. Atrophy of the brain. There now, that was a grown-up word, an intellectual word. *Someone not too intellectual,* Lisbeth had told Vincent. Imagine her saying that!

I'm going to read the classics this summer. But summer was getting away. Next weekend was visiting day at camp. That meant it was half over. Half over and half a brain. Half over and what had she accomplished? Painful golf and tennis lessons. And what did she have to look forward to? More of the same. And come September? The new house. The final house. Shit. Fuck.

She thought about calling Shep, about telling him that she was ready, at last. She went to the phone, lifted the receiver off the hook but couldn't go through with it.

Why not, Sandy? Why couldn't you dial?

I'm scared.

Of what?

Suppose he says *no?*

He won't.

He might. Besides, the man on the motorcycle hasn't shown up all week.

So . . . maybe he's on vacation . . .

Maybe . . . or maybe he doesn't find me very exciting any more . . . and if he doesn't . . . will Shep?

What does one have to do with the other?

Look, I had my chance at the dance and I blew it.

And now she was due at The Club. Due at eight to struggle through nine holes, with Steve dragging his ass behind her, yawning all the way.

"Know what you need, Mrs. Pressman?" Steve said, as she tried to chip over the water and onto the seventh green, missing by inches. "You need a good ball retriever, that's what."

"I'll tell my husband," Sandy answered.

She lost six balls—not that it mattered since Norman gave her his discards—and finished with a score of 72 for nine, not counting her tee shot on eight, when, after five tries, she finally picked up her ball and carried it up the hill, where she took her three wood and really blasted it, surprising herself. "Great shot!" Steve called.

She was finished and scraping her shoes on the mat at nine-forty-five. She showered and changed, the only member in the locker room. It was nice that way, quiet and peaceful. She tried six new combination numbers on her lock, without luck. Oh well. She'd go grocery shopping now, then home to sit on the porch and read. Yes, she'd stop by the library and get something she could sink her teeth into. Something that would make her think.

She got into her car, but instead of going directly to the A&P, as planned, drove straight to the Parkway, headed South, and thirty minutes later turned off at the Mattawan Exit, where she followed signs to Ye Olde New England Village, Shep's shopping center.

Sandy was impressed by its size, by the interesting layout and the attractive shops. She browsed through them, hoping to bump into Shep. She bought a bracelet to bring to Jen at camp, some rubber band glider planes for Bucky, canasta cards for Mona, a set of lemonade glasses in a chrome carrier for the new house, a dozen terry cloth dish towels, a knit shirt with a pocket for Norman, and everywhere, she watched for Shep, turning around quickly, expecting to find him there, smiling at her. And then they would stroll off together, for lunch in a quaint country inn, followed by a walk in the woods, and there, on a rug of pine needles with the sunlight filtering through the trees, they would make love and it would be beautiful, meaningful, perfect.

"Do you, by any chance, know Mr. Resnick, the owner of this shopping center?" Sandy asked the clerk in the bookstore, where she had just bought the number-one best-seller of the summer. Fourteen weeks on the New York *Times* list.

"Certainly," the clerk said. She was an older woman with a sweet face and Sandy could see how lovely she must have been.

"Is he here today?"

"I really couldn't say. He stops by maybe once or twice a week to see how we're doing. Very nice man, very friendly and interested."

"Yes, he's an old friend of mine. I thought I might say hello."

"No telling where to find him. He's got other shopping centers and an office in New York."

"Well, thank you."

"Enjoy the book."

"Yes, I'm sure I will."

Sandy stopped for lunch at one of the two restaurants within Ye Olde New England Village. The waitresses wore long cotton skirts. "Ready to order?"

"Yes," Sandy said. "I'll have half a brain with cottage cheese on the side."

"I'm sorry, did you say . . ."

Sandy looked up and slowly repeated her order. "Half a cantaloupe, cottage cheese on the side."

The waitress laughed. "For a minute I thought you said half a *brain*. Boy, my ears must really be clogged." She tapped the side of her head with one hand.

Had she really said half a *brain,* she wondered, on the drive home? Was her subconscious beginning to take over? Could that happen? No, of course not. She had complete control. She knew exactly what she was doing and saying. Didn't she?

She wasn't home five minutes when the phone rang.

"Mrs. Pressman?"

"Yes."

"This is the plumber over at the new house."

"Yes?"

"We've got a little problem here."

"What is it?"

"You ordered American Standard fixtures in Desert Sand."

"That's right."

"And we just got word from the company that Desert Sand has been discontinued. They're putting out two new colors though, one's called Beechnut and the other's Suntan. I've got the samples here. If you'd come up we could put the order in right away."

"It's almost four."

"I can wait."

"Well, it'll take me half an hour . . . I might run into traffic."

"The sooner the better but like I said, I'll wait."

"Okay."

Sandy went outside, got into the car, and drove toward the new house. . . .

He was waiting for her, as promised, standing next to his truck, guzzling Budweiser from the can. *Hello, Mrs. Pressman.* He wiped his mouth with the back of his hand. *I'm Frank Monzellini, the plumbing contractor.*

Frank Monzellini?

That's right. I work with Joe Fiori, the general contractor. I've met your husband but I don't think I've met you.

171

Are you the Frank Monzellini who used to live in Tudor Village Apartments?

Yeah, how'd you know that?

This is so funny, Sandy said. *You used to live next door to my sister, Myra Lefferts. Of course, it was a long time ago. The twins are going on fifteen.*

Sure, I remember now. Myra Lefferts, how about that?

Frank was about forty-five, graying, with a beer belly, but still attractive, although the undershirt had been replaced by a blue work shirt.

So you were Myra's little sister . . .

Yes I'm Sandy.

All grown up now, huh?

She smiled and fiddled with the belt on her skirt.

Small world, isn't it?

Yes, Sandy said, *and about those samples . . .*

Oh, sure, right here, in my truck. He reached in, took out the samples, and handed them to Sandy. *We were pretty good friends, me and Myra.*

She mentioned that just the other day.

She did?

Yes. Do you think I could look at these tiles in the bathroom, the light might be different.

Yeah, sure. He followed her inside and up the stairs. They went to the master bath first. *Now, this here's the Beechnut and this here's the Suntan,* he told her, spreading them out on the floor, his thigh brushing against hers.

I always liked the hair under your arms and all over your chest, Sandy said.

Well, I still got it. He took off his shirt. *You see.*

Very nice, Sandy said, running her hands across his chest. *Here, let me do that,* she told him, unbuckling his belt. She unzipped his work pants, reached inside, and pulled out his cock. It was soft, but as she held it, it grew hard. *Oh, you're big!*

Yeah, ten inches, stiff.

I guess I knew you would be. Myra said you were sexy although I've read that size doesn't mean a thing. It's what you do with it that counts.

Yeah, well, I'll tell you what I'm going to do with it, he said. *I'm going to bury it in you. I'm going to move it in and out real slow until you scream.*

My mother had a friend who liked his women to scream.

Never mind your mother.

Don't hurt me, Frank. Please. You're so big I'm afraid.

Don't be scared. I never hurt a woman.

Is this how you did it to Myra? Sandy asked, her legs around his back, in a semi-sitting position, the unfinished floor rough and uncomfortable beneath her.

Yeah . . . yeah . . .

Does it feel better with me?

Yeah . . . yeah . . . real good . . .

Fuck me, Frank . . . harder . . .

Yeah . . . yeah . . . scream now . . . scream . . .

He was waiting for her on the front steps. "Mrs. Pressman?"

"Yes."

"I'm Carl Halloran, the plumber."

"Thank you for waiting."

"I have the samples upstairs, in the bathroom. I figured you'd want to see them up there, the light might be different."

"Yes, of course."

He followed her up the stairs, down the hall, and to

the master bath. Sandy looked at the samples, thought for a minute, and said, "I think the Suntan is more what I had in mind."

"I figured you'd pick that one but I couldn't be sure."

"Yes, you can order it for both upstairs baths."

"Very good. I'll call first thing in the morning."

"Thank you."

⌘ 17 ⌘

ON SUNDAY AFTERNOON Sandy and Norman played in the mixed doubles tournament at The Club. It seemed foolish to Sandy to participate in a tournament when she'd played only two games of tennis in her life, plus, of course, her series of twenty-five lessons, which weren't over yet, but Norm had it all figured out. "You just keep out of the way," he said that morning. "I'll return everything. You've got to serve and receive serves, but other than that, every shot is mine. Just move fast, away from the ball, and we can take anybody, got that?"

Sandy nodded.

"Can you get your serve in yet?"

"I think so."

"I hope so."

Before their match began Norm said, "Why don't you wipe that white goo off your mouth?"

"I can't," she explained. "I need it—it's zinc—without it, in this sun, I'll have a herpes tomorrow."

"Couldn't you use lipstick instead, just for our match?"

"We're not on TV, you know!"

175

"But there's a crowd. You want to look good, don't you?"

"I thought all that matters is how I play."

"No, that's not all. It's our image as a couple too."

"Well, I'm sorry, Norm, but I can't go out there without zinc."

"Oh, all right." He grabbed both his racquets, adjusted his sweatbands and eyeglasses and they walked onto the court.

Sandy was already sweating, one of her peds crept down inside her shoes, and she had the remains of a blister on her right thumb, which hurt, even though it was covered by two Band-Aids.

They played against Millicent and Harvey Sommers. Millicent couldn't return Sandy's serves. "They're just too slow," she cried, "too soft. Are they even legal?"

"Damn right!" Norman called.

And Harvey said, "Just keep your eye on the ball, dear."

Bounce . . . thwack . . . bounce . . . thwack . . .

"Look at that!" Millicent cried again. "He's taking all her shots. Is that fair? Is it even legal?"

"She's serving and receiving our serves," Harvey said. "That's all she has to do, dear. Just keep your eye on the ball and try to concentrate."

"I think it's very unfair! We might as well be playing singles against *him!*" Millicent threw her racquet to the ground.

Norman ran up to the net. "As chairman of the Grievance Committee it is my duty to inform you that throwing your racquet on the court is a punishable offense. Look at that mark you've made."

"Try to control yourself, dear," Harvey said. "It's only a game."

"It's not *only* a game," Millicent informed him

through clenched teeth. "It's a goddamned tournament!"

Sandy and Norman won their match 6-3, 6-2. Norman was ecstatic. "What'd I tell you?" he laughed, hugging Sandy. "You're great. I always knew you could do it."

"But Norm, I didn't do anything. You did it all."

"Never mind, never mind. As a team we're great. The best. Unbeatable!"

Until their next match, when they were knocked out of the competition by Luscious and Ben, who smashed every ball directly at Sandy.

"Jesus," Norman muttered, storming off the court. "Six-two, six-one. I told you to move out of the way, didn't I? But you didn't. You just stood there like a lump of clay."

"I was moving . . ."

"In the wrong direction. You moved toward the ball every goddamned time."

"How was I to know where they were going to hit it?"

"Anticipation! Hasn't your teacher taught you anything?"

"Which teacher?"

"Your *tennis* teacher . . . what's wrong with you . . . don't you listen?"

"I tried my best," Sandy told him, feeling the beginning of tears and hating herself for letting him get to her this way. "Do you think I enjoy this . . . this humiliation? Do you think this is any fun for me?"

"Oh, Christ! Stop crying. Everyone can see."

He took her by the arm and tried to lead her away from the crowd but she shook him off shouting, "Let me go."

They didn't speak to each other until Monday night,

when she told him she'd been busy and hadn't prepared any supper. They went to Lee Ann Fong's. Lee Ann sat down at their table and said, "Tomorrow's the ABCD tournament. It's my first. Boy, I can't wait!"

Sandy called for the weather report at seven-thirty the next morning. "Hot and humid . . . chance of thundershowers . . . temperature ranging from the mid-eighties to the upper nineties, inland . . ." She hung up and thought about staying in bed. But Norman would never forgive her. No, she had to go, had to play in the tournament. She dressed and drove to The Club. The sky was already gray and threatening.

Sandy checked the board in the locker room and found that the rest of her foursome consisted of Millicent Sommers, Brown, and Lee Ann Fong.

Great, she thought.

"It's going to be a hot one," Myra said as Sandy tied her shoelaces.

She nodded. "What did you decide to do about Gordy?"

"I haven't decided anything yet. I'm still thinking about it."

"Don't do anything foolish."

"I don't intend to."

Outside, Lee Ann Fong was waiting in a golf cart, calling, "Sandy, Sandy, you ride with me."

Millicent and Brown were in another golf cart, ready to go. If a foursome took two carts, they were also required to take along a caddy, to carry their putters and spot their balls. The lowest-ranking caddies were awarded this job.

"Oh, not him!" Millicent cried, as the caddymaster

beckoned to Steve. "He's so slow. Can't we have someone else?"

"He's not that slow," Sandy said. "I take him every day."

"Oh, what do you know?" Millicent muttered.

Sandy didn't answer. She could feel the storm brewing and hoped that it wouldn't hit until they'd finished the front nine.

"Let's go . . . let's go . . . ." Millicent called, as Sandy missed several shots in a row, winding up in the heavy rough. "You could use some lessons!"

"I'm just having an off day," Sandy told her. "I'm sure you've had your share of those." She wanted to smash her with a golf club.

They stopped for hard-boiled eggs and Welch's grape juice at the Halfway House, wet paper towels and draped them around their necks, and in ten minutes were on their way again. Sandy dreaded the back nine. The holes were long and tedious. She was already tired and hot. The sky was still gray and the humidity oppressive.

Just as Millicent hit her tee shot on twelve it began to thunder. They were as far as they could get from the safety of the clubhouse. An open shelter stood nearby but that didn't ease Sandy's fear. "Listen," she said, "wasn't that thunder?"

"Probably," Brown answered.

Try to stay calm, Sandy told herself. "Don't you think we should go back?"

"No," Millicent said.

But at her first sight of lightning Sandy, trying to keep her voice from breaking, said, "Look, it's going to storm. I really think we should head back now."

"One-two-three-four-five-six," Brown counted. The thunder followed. "It's at least six miles away." She teed off and landed in the sand trap to the right of the fairway. "Oh, shit!"

At the second lightning, when the thunder came after the count of three, Sandy told them, "I'm going. This could be dangerous. Anyone else joining me?"

"This is a tournament," Millicent reminded her. "You can't walk out on a tournament."

And Lee Ann said, "I'm playing too good to quit now. This might be my best round."

Brown said nothing.

So Sandy jumped into a golf cart and took off.

"Come back here, you bitch!" Millicent yelled. "You've got our clubs!"

Oh, god, the clubs! Rule Number One: *If caught on a golf course in a thunderstorm get rid of the clubs.* Sandy stopped the cart, dumped the clubs off, then remembered Rule Number Two: *Get rid of your spiked shoes.* She kicked hers off and left them with the clubs, jumped back into the cart, and floored it.

"You're going to live to regret this!" Millicent screamed across two fairways.

Sandy didn't turn around. *Hurry, hurry . . . lightning to the left . . . don't think about the storm . . . just concentrate on getting back.*

She left the cart outside the locker room door and rushed inside, shaking. But she was safe now. It was going to be all right.

The storm hit ten minutes later and the golfers followed, in groups of four, rushing into the locker room, drenched, some laughing, others, kvetching. Sandy hid in a toilet stall. She didn't want to see any of them.

Click . . . click . . . click . . . the sound of spiked shoes on the tiled bathroom floor. Millicent: "Just wait till I get my hands on that little bitch. Where is she?"

Myra: "Who?"

Millicent: "Your sister."

Myra: "I don't know. What'd she do to get you so riled up?"

Millicent: "Took off in *my* cart with *my* clubs before it even started to rain!"

Myra: "Sandy's afraid of lightning . . . always has been . . ."

Millicent: "That's no excuse!"

Steph: "Calm down, Mill, the tournament's been called anyway."

Millicent: "You can ignore this if you want to, but we'll see what the Grievance Committee has to say about it!"

Myra: Laughing. "Sandy's husband is chairman of the Grievance Committee."

Millicent: "I know!"

What shit, Sandy thought. What was she doing here? What was she trying to prove anyway? And to whom? *You need to control your own destiny,* Lisbeth had said. *Yes,* Sandy answered to herself. *Yes, I want to control my own destiny.* All her life she had let others decide what was going to happen to her. Maybe now it was time to please herself. Call her own shots. She laughed out loud, remembering the two times she had made her own decisions; to vote for Kennedy and to name her baby Jennifer. Two times in thirty-two years that her decision was not based on someone else's feelings, someone else's choice.

As soon as the sky was light again Sandy left the empty locker room, ran across the parking lot to her car, and drove home.

She took a hot bath and wrote to the children.

At three the doorbell rang.

Florenzia answered and called, "Mrs. Pressman, you got some company."

"Who is it?" Sandy asked.

"Some boy. He be riding a motorcycle."

Was he back? Was he really here, in person, ringing her doorbell? Should she call Hubanski? No, not yet. After all, she wasn't alone. Florenzia was here. He wouldn't do anything in front of Florenzia, would he? She ran downstairs and peeked out the window next to the front door. It wasn't him. It was Steve. Relief, and then, disappointment.

She opened the door. "Hi, Steve. I didn't know you had a motorcycle."

"For two years."

"What kind is it?"

"Honda . . . XL 175 . . . do you ride, Mrs. Pressman?"

"No." She laughed at the idea. "Just curious. Well, come on in." She turned to Florenzia, who was standing right behind her. "It's all right, Florenzia."

Florenzia disappeared down the hall and Steve followed Sandy into the house. "This is nice," he said.

"Thanks. It's for sale. We're moving soon, to Watchung."

"It's nice up there too." He held out a brown grocery bag. "I brought your golf shoes."

"Oh, thanks, that was very thoughtful." She took the bag and set it on the floor, under the foyer table, thinking about Norman, and how he'd carried his damp underwear out to the car, after their dates.

"And I took your clubs to the storage room and cleaned them off."

"Thanks again."

"And I just wanted to tell you that I appreciate what

182

you said this morning when Mrs. Sommers was complaining about getting me."

"I told the truth, that's all."

"Well, thanks. It was real nice of you." He wiped his forehead with the back of his hand. "Sure is hot. Storm didn't help much."

"No."

"Could I by any chance trouble you for a drink, Mrs. Pressman."

"Sure. Lemonade?"

"Sounds great." He followed her into the kitchen and placed his helmet on the table.

"Have you seen *The Graduate?*"

"Yes, I have."

"I've seen it three times. I really dig that Mrs. Robinson."

Sandy carried the pitcher of lemonade and two glasses to the table.

"She's older but very . . . very, uh . . ." He made circles with his hand.

"I've always liked Anne Bancroft."

She filled both glasses. He gulped his down without stopping for a breath.

"I'll tell you something, Mrs. Pressman, you're the nicest woman at The Club."

"Thanks, Steve."

"Some of the others are okay but mostly, when you get right down to it, they're a bunch of bitches, you know?"

"Yes, I know." *Okay, Mrs. Robinson, get him out of here now.*

"Mind if I have another glass of lemonade?"

"No, please, help yourself." She fingered his helmet. It was bright yellow with a tomato stenciled on one side and his name on the other.

"I designed it myself. You like it?"

"Yes, very much. I have a friend who wears a stars and stripes helmet."

"Oh, yeah, they were very big last year. The moon landing and all that, real American . . ."

"Do a lot of people still wear them?"

"Oh, yeah, a real lot. So what kind of bike does your friend ride?"

"I'm not sure. I really don't know one from the other."

"There's a couple of real good buys around now. I'm thinking of selling mine and getting a Yamaha instead."

"Oh." *Come on, Sandy, say goodbye before it's too late.* "Well, thanks for coming by, Steve . . . and for bringing my shoes . . ." She offered her hand.

He looked at it for a minute, then stood up, realizing he was expected to shake it. His fingers closed around hers. His hand was warm. "Bye, Mrs. Pressman." He looked into her eyes.

She lowered hers, walked him to the front door, closed it after him, and sighed.

18

"I STILL DON'T understand how you could have made such a mistake," Norman said. "Do you have any idea how embarrassing this is for me?" They were driving on the Massachusetts Turnpike, on their way to visiting weekend at camp.

"I've already told you, it was lightning and I was scared. I just wanted to get back to the clubhouse and I jumped into the closest cart. I never stopped to think it was Millicent's, not mine." Sandy was working on the needlepoint pillow she'd started, but somehow never finished, last summer. She cut off a snip of wool and threaded the needle again.

"Just because I'm chairman of the Grievance Committee doesn't mean I can get you off . . . it has to go before the whole committee. I wish to hell you *had* stopped to think this time."

"I don't expect you to get me off. I've told you how I feel about the whole thing and I'm sorry I've caused you so much trouble." She turned her canvas upside down and started another row.

Norman stretched his arms out against the wheel, took a deep breath, let it out, and said, "Okay, I've

185

given it a lot of thought and I've decided maybe it's better all around if you don't play any more golf or tennis."

"I'm glad you finally see it my way."

"That doesn't mean I'm not disappointed."

"I know and I'm sorry about that too, but it's making me miserable and if you care about me at all . . ."

"If I care? Who paid for all those lessons?"

"Paying isn't caring, Norm."

"You know your trouble? Your trouble is you don't know how good you have it."

"Here we go."

"Never had to work a day in your life . . . everything handed to you on a silver platter . . . you've got no *real* trouble so you've got to go looking for it . . . inventing it . . ."

"That's not the way it is at all. I might even like to go to work." She accidentally stuck her thumb with the needle, watched the blood ooze out, then sucked on it.

"Oh, sure, doing what?"

"I don't know yet." She examined her thumb, wrapped a Kleenex around it, then went back to stitching the canvas.

"Your first duty is to make a home for me and the kids. After that, you want a little part-time job, it's fine with me."

"Norman, sometimes I get the feeling that you don't know me at all."

"And sometimes I get the same feeling about you."

"But I *want* to know you . . . I want to know your needs . . ."

"My needs are very simple. I come home from work tired. All I ask is time for a drink before dinner, a chance to read the paper in peace and quiet, some good food, and a pleasant, relaxing evening."

"Those are your needs?" She looked over at him. "Your emotional needs?"

"I told you they were very simple."

"Norman, listen to me . . . please . . . I'm scared . . . I really am . . . I don't like what's happening . . . I don't like myself . . ."

"It hasn't been easy to like you this summer."

"Okay. I admit it. Let's see a marriage counsellor as soon as we get back."

"There's nothing wrong with me. You're the one with the problem. You want to see a marriage counsellor, fine. I'll foot the bill, but don't expect me to waste my time that way."

"It only works if both partners go."

"It's not our marriage that's wrong, Sandy. It's you."

"How can you say that . . . if I'm unhappy . . ."

"Aha . . . there . . . *you're* unhappy . . . you just said it . . . but I'm not . . . I don't want to change anything . . . you're unhappy because you haven't got a life without the kids. I tried to help you develop new interests, healthy interests, but you blew it."

"Dammit, Norm, I tried."

"Not hard enough."

"I think part of the trouble is that I don't feel your love," she said.

"What do you mean, you don't *feel* it?"

"It's hard to explain. I just can't *feel* any love."

"What am I supposed to do, run around kissing you twenty-four hours a day?"

"No. But there's a lot inside me," Sandy said. "A lot you don't know about."

"Have you been reading that book again?"

"What book?"

"The one Lisbeth gave you."

"This has nothing to do with Lisbeth or books. It's me and it's you. It's us!"

"I'm a busy man, Sandy. I work my ass off for you and the kids . . . to give you everything. I don't need this aggravation. I don't have the time for it. Do *you* understand *that?* So when we get back you get yourself together. You get yourself together before the kids come home from camp." He turned off at the exit to Pittsfield. "Give me a peach, would you."

She handed him one from the bag. "It's not enough to work your ass off."

"Not enough?"

"Norm, be careful, you almost sideswiped that car."

"You want to drive?"

"No, just be careful, that's all."

"I'd like you to trade places with me for just one week . . . to let you see what my life is like . . . Christ, you have no idea . . . dealing with *ductlas* day in and day out . . ."

"You mean blacks."

"I mean *ductlas!*"

"Norm . . ."

"You've got it so fucking good, what more do you want from me?"

"Love. Understanding. Tenderness."

He pushed the button to lower his window and spat out the peach pit.

Sandy began to cry, quietly at first, then harder, louder, until she couldn't control the sobbing. Her tears fell on her needlepoint canvas. There was an ache in her throat, her head, her guts.

"Stop it," Norman told her. "That's enough. You wanted conversation, you got it. You wanted com-

munication, you got it. But you can't take it, can you?
No, because you're still a little girl. You have to have
everything your way. Emotionally immature."

"I am not a little girl!"

"Ha ha ha . . . look at the baby cry . . . ha ha . . ."

"Shut up, you bastard!"

"Don't shout, little girl. I'm sitting right next to you.
I can hear you just fine."

"Norman, stop the car. I think I'm going to vomit."

He pulled over quickly, the brakes screeching. "Get
out . . . don't do it in here . . ."

Sandy opened the car door and threw herself to the
ground, feeling faint and nauseated.

Norman remained in the driver's seat, his head
turned away from her. She could see him through the
open car door. Control. Control. She had to get control of herself, of the situation. Perspiration on her
forehead but the nausea was passing. She was not going to be sick this time. Being sick didn't solve anything. Yes, it was passing. She felt stronger now. In a
few minutes she climbed back into the car.

"Did you?" Norman asked.

"Yes," she lied.

"I can smell it."

"Really?"

"I'll pull in at the next gas station so you can wash.
You know that smell is enough to make me sick." He
pulled in at a Gulf station and Sandy got out to use the
Ladies Room. She splashed her face with cold water,
combed her hair, applied fresh lipstick, and pulled her
T-shirt down inside her denim skirt. There, that was
better. She fished around in her purse for a breath
mint and dropped it into her mouth, then sprayed a
little cologne on her neck, wrists, behind her knees.

All right. All right. It was true that Norman worked

hard and provided well for her and the children. So, was she wrong to want more out of life? She wasn't sure any more. A good wife wouldn't complain. If he beat her, she could complain. If he drank, she could complain. If he ran around, she could complain. But Sandy had no *real* reason to complain. Not an acceptable reason anyway. *Nobody loves a kvetch,* Mona had said. *Remember that, Sandy . . . especially not a man who's worked hard all day.*

I'm sorry, Mother.
I'm sorry, Norman.
I'm sorry, everybody.

What happy, smiling faces they put on for the children. What a wonderful family they appeared to be for the counsellors, the camp directors, the other parents. What wonderful families they all were for each other, ignoring the rules that had been so carefully spelled out in the visiting day brochure. *Please do not bring any food into camp. All food will be confiscated. Please do not bring bunk gifts. We suggest a book or a game instead. Please do not tip our staff. Our counsellors are professionals who are paid a professional salary.*

But that didn't stop Sandy and the other mommies from arriving with carloads of fresh fruit, cookies, pretzels, sugarless bubble gum, and bunk gifts. And it didn't stop Norman and the other daddies from tipping the counsellors, to make sure that *their* children received special attention.

Norman's Nikon captured visiting day at Camp Wah-Wee-Nah-Kee. Jen, diving into the lake. Imagine that! Little Jen who used to be afraid to put her face in the water. Jen, playing third base in a lower camp softball game, at dramatics, in a rowboat. Jen, running off with her bunkmates, laughing.

At rest hour Sandy trimmed Jen's toenails and handed out bunk gifts. "Oh, Mom," Jen said, her face full of disappointment, "I told you to buy something different. You're the third mother to give out jacks."

"I'm sorry, honey, I thought jacks *were* different."

That afternoon Bucky and the other brothers from across the lake were brought over to visit. And Norman caught him showing off his mosquito bites, with a mouthful of watermelon and teasing Jen's bunkmates with a fake snake.

When it was time to say good-bye the children walked them down to the field where they had parked. All the Cadillacs and Continentals and Mercedes were neatly lined up. Sandy had never seen so many low-numbered license plates in one lot. She put on her sunglasses so the children wouldn't see her tears. They're on their way to becoming independent, she thought. Soon they won't need me at all. Maybe that was why Mona had never let her girls go away to camp.

"I'm ready for a little something," Norman said that night when they got into their beds at the motel.

"Oh, Norm . . . I'm so tired . . . and tomorrow will be just as hectic at Bucky's camp."

"It'll make you feel better. It always does."

"And I didn't bring my diaphragm. I didn't think we'd need it."

"But it's Saturday night."

"I know."

"And I'm in the mood."

"You certainly don't want to take a chance, do you?"

"No."

"Then . . ."

"I'll pull out in time . . ."

"Coitus interruptus, at our age?"

"Just this once." He pulled down her covers and lay beside her, taking her hand and cupping it around his balls. "Ready, San?"

She'd never refused him. Not once in almost twelve years. *When he's in the mood, you're in the mood.* Oh, Mother, go away. Please, please, go away!

"You're sure this is safe?" she asked, as he entered her.

"Yes."

"Because I really don't want to get pregnant."

"You won't, although another baby might be just what you need. Another baby would keep you busy, San."

"No, that's not a good enough reason to have a baby."

He came on her belly and feeling him against her like that, feeling his wetness, excited her. "Rub it into me," she said.

"Here's some Kleenex."

"No . . . I want you to rub it into me . . . all over . . ."

"Come on, San . . . don't talk like that . . . you better go wash up or you'll be all sticky in the morning."

He got out of bed and went to the bathroom. She heard the water running, then Norman, gargling. Some things never change, she thought. She masturbated, remembering the way Shep had once rubbed his cum all over her.

Norman returned to his bed, pulled the covers around his head, and said, "I know you've been tense lately, San, but I think you'll be a lot happier once we move into the new house. It's going to change your whole outlook."

"It's not the house, Norm. It's us."

"You're going to have to stop talking like that. Everything's fine between us. It's just like always except you haven't had enough to do this summer. It's just a little depression at having the kids away. As soon as they're back you'll be fine."

"It's not that easy."

"It is! We have a good life together and don't you go messing it up."

19

On Monday morning Hubanski called. "How're you doing, Mrs. Pressman?"

"Just fine. Anything new with our case?"

"I'm sorry to tell you, Mrs. Pressman, we aren't making much headway . . ."

"Well, he hasn't been around here lately."

"Lately, did you say *lately?*"

"What I meant was, I haven't seen him since . . . since the first time."

"Oh, it sounded as if . . ."

"No . . . I meant that he hasn't come back here at all."

"I see." She heard him smack his tongue against his teeth. "We'll just have to keep trying, then."

"Yes."

Sandy wondered about the man on the motorcycle, even worried about him. The last time he'd paid her a visit he'd waved to her when he'd finished his act, and she'd waved back. Maybe that was what had scared him off, her aggressiveness.

Aggressiveness. Yes. Okay. It was time. On Tuesday morning she called Shep's New York office.

195

"He's at the Berkeley Heights site today. He can be reached at area code 201-KL-5-5579."

"Thank you." Sandy hung up, then dialed the New Jersey number.

"Yeah, hello." It was a man, but not Shep.

"I'd like to speak to Shep Resnick, please."

"Yeah, hang on." She heard him call, "Hey, Shep, for you . . ."

And then *his* voice. "This is Shep Resnick."

Control. Control. Keep your voice steady. He can't see you . . . has no way of knowing you're shaking. Or you could just hang up. Hang up now and forget about it. No . . . no! "Shep . . . it's Sandy . . ." There. Not bad. But he didn't respond right away so she added, "Sandy Pressman . . . Sandy Schaedel . . ."

"Sandy! What a surprise."

"You said to call."

"And I meant it, but I didn't expect it."

Her turn. "I'd like to see you, Shep." An uncomfortable pause. Why didn't he say something? Answer me, dammit. "Shep, are you there?"

"I'm thinking," he said. "How about lunch. Let's say Linda's Fireside at twelve-thirty, that's by the old bridge going up to Berkeley Heights. You know where that is?"

"I've passed it, I think. I'm sure I can find it."

"Good. I'm glad you called, Sandy. See you soon."

Oh, God, she'd done it. She'd actually done it. Committed herself. Would have to face the consequences this time. But wait, she could still change her mind. Just lunch. It didn't have to be more than that.

She showered and shampooed and nicked both her legs shaving. Worse than an adolescent. She inspected herself in the full-length mirror, naked, and was shocked to find hairs on the back of her thighs. She'd

196

never thought of shaving there before. She trimmed and polished her toenails, buffed her fingernails, douched with vinegar, and inserted her diaphragm, just in case. Oh, hell, who was she kidding? Of course they were going to make love. But she didn't have to. She would only do it if she really wanted to. She was through giving in to Norman because he was in the mood, through saying *why not* to Gordon or Vincent or whoever. From now on it was to be her choice. And her choice was Shep. Had always been Shep.

What to wear? She looked over everything in her closet and settled for a simple shirt and skirt. Casual, as if she were going to the A & P. But underneath she wore her best beige lace-trimmed bikini panties. Just like the old days. And no bra. Should she put rouge on her nipples? She'd read that some women did that. But suppose it rubbed off against him? No, better to just leave well enough alone.

She drove up ahead of time, in case she got lost. He was already there, waiting for her in his white Porsche. "Hi Shep . . ." How girlish she sounded. *Remember, Sondra Elaine, you're not seventeen any more. You're supposed to be a woman now.*

"Hi, Sandy, I phoned for a table," he said, getting out of his car and taking her arm.

"I've never been here but I've heard it's good."

"Linda makes a great veal piccata."

"I usually eat peanut butter for lunch."

"I'm not surprised." He laughed.

They went into the restaurant and were shown to their table. "So . . ." he said, after they were seated.

"So . . . did your little girl arrive from Vietnam yet?"

"No, the latest word is the end of September. There's a lot of red tape involved."

She pretended to read the menu. The waitress approached their table. "Have you folks decided?"

"Sandy?"

"I think I'll have the chef's salad." She looked over at Shep. "I'm not very hungry," she explained.

"Make it two," he said, "and a bottle of Pouilly Fouissé."

The waitress left and Sandy said, "I thought you were going to have the veal."

"Changed my mind. I'm not that hungry either."

They looked directly at each other for the first time. Sandy cleared her throat twice, felt her face grow hot, her stomach climbing into her chest cavity. Maybe Dr. Ackerman had been right, after all. "Shep . . ."

"Yes, Sandy . . ."

"I'm scared."

"About what?"

"You know . . . this . . . everything . . ."

He took her hand and held it between both of his. "It'll be all right."

She nodded.

After lunch they went out to his car. Sandy, feeling fuzzy from the wine, got in beside him and flipped her sunglasses up on her head. "Too bad you gave up your Nash." She touched the soft leather upholstery. "This one's not bad but the seat doesn't go back, does it?"

"I don't have much use for a car seat that turns into a bed these days. In fact, I haven't since the summer of . . ."

"Fifty-five, wasn't it?"

"You have a good memory."

"I haven't forgotten one minute of it." She faced him. "Kiss me."

He put his arms around her. "I will . . . I will . . . but first I want to just hold you close."

She placed her cheek against his, her hand on the back of his neck. Her fingers played with his soft, curling hair. She touched his face tenderly, then kissed him on his lips. A soft, gentle kiss, without the urgency, the passion of that night at The Club.

He kissed her back, harder now, stronger, his tongue in her mouth. She sucked on it, trying to keep a part of him inside her. "Can we go someplace?" she whispered.

"Not today. I want you to think it over first. I want you to be very sure of what you're doing."

"I'm sure. I'm sure right now and I want you so much."

"I want you too and if you feel the same way tomorrow, we'll go someplace, I promise."

Driving home, she considered the possibilities. He was too busy this afternoon. He had meetings that he couldn't possibly cancel at the last minute. He had another woman lined up for today.

He had to discuss it with Rhoda.

He wasn't attracted to her any more.

He'd become impotent since July Fourth.

Endless possibilities.

Or, the truth. He really wanted her to think it over, to be sure she knew what she was getting into.

Yes, she liked the truth best.

She found Myra waiting for her in the den when she got home. "Hi . . . Florenzia said you'd be back soon."

"Is everything all right?" Sandy asked. Myra wasn't in the habit of dropping in this way.

"Yes, sure, everyone at The Club is asking for you."

Sandy sank into the sofa, her legs tucked under her. "I've given up on golf and tennis . . . with Norman's permission."

"But San, that's so silly. Millicent's a bitch. Everyone knows that. Her complaint won't be taken seriously."

"It's not just that."

"Steph wanted you to play with her one day this week and a lot of the other girls were rearranging their schedules to include you in some games . . ."

"That's nice of them, but I'm not going back."

"That's crazy, San. I'd hoped . . ."

Sandy shook her head. "It's just not my thing."

Myra sighed. "I suppose you haven't heard the news."

"What news?"

"Barbara and Gish . . . they're splitting up . . . and I'm just sick about it . . . I was with her last night . . . it's awful . . . her kids will be back in a few weeks . . . they don't know yet."

"What happened?"

"Oh, who knows? She says Gish wanted out . . . ever since his brother died he's been different . . . afraid he's missing out . . . freedom . . . that whole number . . ."

"I knew he was a flirt, but . . ."

"Everyone knew that, including Barb, but she accepted it and look where it got her. He's keeping The Club membership . . . she can't afford to join another one. I don't know what she's going to do, how she's going to manage." Myra reached into her purse for a Kleenex and blew her nose.

"He'll have to support her and the kids, won't he?"

"Oh, sure, up to a point."

"I'm sorry to hear it but I can't say I'm surprised."

"Who can be surprised any more? It's happening all around us." They were quiet for a moment. "I have to admit, I've considered divorce myself . . . especially since I found out about Gordy's affair. I can't go to bed with him. I keep imagining him with *her,* whoever she is. I've decided not to go to the AMA convention, even though I adore San Francisco. I'm going to tennis camp instead. I need to get away by myself to think things over . . ."

"I know Gordy loves you, My. Don't turn his one mistake into a reason for divorce."

Tears came to Myra's eyes. "I really don't want a divorce. What would my life be like without Gordy? What am I without him? With him I'm a somebody, I'm a doctor's wife. Oh, I get lonely, but I fill my days with activities, keep as busy as possible." She blew her nose again, harder this time. "If I divorced him, I'd have to give up the house and move to an apartment in Fort Lee, with all the other divorcees, eat at Howard Johnson's instead of Périgord Park, get a job in a department store. My friends would invite me to dinner parties, trying to fix me up with some recently divorced man. It's all too terrible to even think about. Poor Barb, that's the kind of life she has to look forward to now. I think I'd kill myself first, I honestly do. The only way to a decent divorce is through another man, but where am I going to find another man who can give me all that Gordy can?"

"I've thought about divorce too," Sandy said, quietly, the first time she'd ever said it out loud.

"Sandy!"

"I can't help it. I'm not happy with Norman." There, she'd admitted it. It was on the record now. It was official.

"Sandy, I'm shocked, truly shocked."

"Don't be. Norman and I are very different. I'm emotional and he's . . ."

"Phlegmatic."

"Yes."

"Daddy was right."

"Yes. He was right about a lot of things."

"Do you ever wonder what kind of marriage he and Mona had?"

"Sometimes."

"I've been thinking a lot about them lately. I'm beginning to see things the way they really were."

"Daddy wanted a dog, did you know that?"

"No."

"He took me to a kennel once . . . it was our special secret . . . he picked out a puppy for me . . . for us . . . but we never got him . . ."

"He *let* her bring us up . . . he didn't have to withdraw . . ."

"He didn't like making waves."

"She would have appreciated him more if he had."

"Maybe."

"Well, no point in dwelling on the past, is there?"

"I guess not."

"Could I have a glass of juice?" Myra asked.

"Oh, sure." They went into the kitchen and Sandy poured two tall glasses of grapefruit juice.

"Thanks," Myra said, taking a long swallow. "I've signed up for a course in art appreciation this fall . . . art is going to be very big next year . . . everyone is getting into it . . . why don't you come with me . . . it's going to be fun . . . Wednesdays in New York . . . lunch . . . a tour of the galleries . . . I may even start collecting . . . and you'll need some things for the new house . . . they say art is a wise investment . . ."

"I don't know . . ."

"Keep busy, Sandy . . . when you're busy you don't have time to brood . . ."

"Life should be more than keeping busy."

"Maybe it should be, but for most of us, it's not." Myra stood up. "You know, San, you don't have a bad life with Norman . . ."

Sandy's eyes filled up and she chewed on her lower lip.

"I've got to run," Myra said, hugging Sandy. "I feel closer to you than I ever have. I hope we can keep it this way. Take care. Talk to you tomorrow . . ."

⚔ 20 ⚔

SHEP CALLED AT nine the next morning. "So what's the verdict, kid?"

"Guilty," she told him. "So where should I meet you?"

"You're sure?"

"I'm sure."

"Okay, twelve-thirty at the Monterey Motor Inn on Route 1, South. Park your car in the bowling alley lot next door and I'll park mine across the street in the shopping center."

"You certainly think of everything."

"I have to . . . and Sandy . . ."

"Yes?"

"I'm glad you didn't change your mind."

A few minutes later Norman called. "Four Corners made an offer."

"Who?"

"Four Corners . . . the realtors . . . they're offering thirty-seven thousand, five . . ."

"What do you think?"

"I'd like to get them up to forty."

"Did you explain about Enid?"

"I can't, how would that look?"

"I see what you mean."

"We have to do what's right for us at this point. I'll call you back when it's firm."

"I'm leaving before noon. I've got an appointment."

"What time will you be back?"

"I don't know, late this afternoon, I guess."

"Maybe we can reach an agreement before you leave."

The phone rang almost as soon as she hung up. What now? Shep, canceling?

"Mrs. Pressman."

"Yes?"

"May I fuck you today?"

"Oh, not you again!" She hung up and waited, knowing that he would call right back. He always did, at least once a week. Her friendly caller. She should have mentioned *him* to Hubanski. Maybe next time she would. Maybe there was some connection between him and the man on the motorcycle. "Go to hell!" she shouted into the phone when it rang again, before he had a chance to say anything. She slammed the receiver down. At least she'd be rid of *him* when they moved to Watchung.

She went into the bathroom, repeating yesterday's rituals, except for polishing her toenails. They still looked fine. She looked for her diaphragm but couldn't find it. It wasn't in its blue plastic case or any of the bathroom drawers. Damn! Then she remembered and laughed with relief. She'd forgotten to remove it yesterday afternoon. She washed it out and inserted it again.

Norman called back at ten-thirty. "Thirty-eight thousand seven hundred and fifty is as high as they'll go."

"What'd you say?"

"I told them I'd have to think it over."

"Enid won't like it."

"Enid won't know."

"I'll bet she finds out."

"Look, I think we should take it, San. It's the only decent offer we've had."

"Okay, whatever you decide is fine with me."

"I'll call him and get right back to you."

She sat on her bed and waited. When the phone rang she picked it up immediately. "Yes, hello?"

"It's a deal," Norman said. "We sign the papers tonight at six-thirty, our house. And after, we'll go out to celebrate."

"With Four Corners?"

"No. Just us."

There was a knock at Sandy's bedroom door. "Mrs. Pressman . . . that's me, Florenzia . . ."

"Yes, Florenzia?" Sandy opened her door.

"So many telephones today . . . everything is all right?"

"Yes, fine."

"I no like when so many telephones."

"I know and there shouldn't be any more for a while."

"Good, because my ears be ringing. It be making me very *nervoos*. I no can clean with so many telephones."

"Yes, well, I'm sorry. It should be quiet now." Florenzia was right. Sandy spent too much of her life on the phone, dealing with trivia.

She drove to the motel and parked in the bowling alley lot, as instructed. Shep was waiting for her, sitting on the steps, a wicker basket at his feet.

"I brought a picnic lunch," he said.

"You really do think of everything."

"I try."

They walked over to the motel. "We're in Room twenty-eight," Shep told her. "Mr. and Mrs. Shepherd."

They smiled at each other, Shep took the key out of his pocket, unlocked the door, and they stepped inside. "Hmm . . . let's see . . ." he said, setting the wicker basket on the bureau top. He moved a table and two chairs out of the way, making room on the floor for their picnic. He spread out the checkered tablecloth and unpacked the basket. Cold chicken, potato salad, and a chilled bottle of champagne.

"Beautiful!" Sandy said.

"You're not bad yourself, kid." He pulled a small tape recorder out of the basket. "For you." He handed it to her. "Turn it on."

She turned the switch. Nat Cole was singing "Blue Velvet." "Shep, you remember everything . . ."

He reached for the champagne. Taylor's Brut. *Uncle Bennett and Cousin Tish. Sandy and Norman's wedding night. A champagne bath. Oh, shit . . . don't think . . . don't . . . you'll spoil it . . .*

It popped when he uncorked it and dribbled down the front of him, wetting his shirt and pants. They both laughed. He poured them each a glassful and raised his in a toast. "To us!"

She clinked glasses with him. "To us!"

He offered her a chicken leg.

"I'm not sure I can swallow," she said. "I'm too . . ."

"I know. That's why we're having lunch, first, to relax you."

"I'd feel better if you kissed me," she said.

"All right, but just one."

"Just one. I promise."

He leaned across the picnic cloth and kissed her lightly. "No more now. First you have to eat."

She nodded, kicked off her sandals, and attacked her lunch.

When they'd finished, Shep wrapped everything up in the cloth and stuffed it back in the basket. "Now," he said. "Now I'm going to love you." He pushed her gently to the floor and kissed her. The tape recorder was playing *Here I go again . . . I hear the trumpets blow again . . . all aglow again . . . taking a chance on love . . .*

She held him to her, inhaling him, tasting him, her hands in his hair, her mouth open to his. He unbuttoned her shirt, slowly, watching her, then kissed her breasts, sucked on her nipples, slipped off his own shirt so that he could rub his chest against her nakedness. "Please, Shep . . . please . . ." she begged.

"Not yet . . . not yet . . ." he said, lifting her onto the bed. He unzipped her skirt and slid it off, then got out of his denim pants and jockey shorts. She looked down at him. How ready he was. How stiff and beautiful. She told him so.

He laughed and said, "I've put on some weight."

"I don't mind." She reached for his penis and held it in her hand, tracing his swollen tip with two fingers. A silky mushroom. She squeezed him and felt a drop of his liquid, exciting herself even more.

Now he moaned softly, pulled down her panties, kissed her belly, her inner thighs, licked his way back up to her breasts, to her face. He kissed her lips and she buried her tongue in his mouth.

"I love you," she told him. "I've always loved you!"

209

"You didn't come," he said, after.

"I know . . . I couldn't . . . I was too excited."

"Too excited to come?"

"Yes."

He laughed. "That's a new one."

"I'll come next time," she told him.

"I hope so," he said. "I'd hate to think I've lost my touch."

Next time was in half an hour and she came three times, which pleased him. "Soup, main course, and dessert," she said without thinking. Then she blushed. How could she play Norman's game with Shep?

"Tomorrow, Sandy?" Shep asked as they soaped each other in the shower.

"Yes."

"How about a five-course meal?"

"Maybe, but I'm not always that hungry."

"Don't eat any breakfast."

"I always have breakfast. Rice Krispies and toast."

"Always?"

"Well, sometimes I have cornflakes."

"I'm glad you haven't changed, kid."

"I'm glad you haven't either."

❧ 21 ❧

THAT NIGHT SHE and Norman signed the papers, selling their house, Enid's house, to Four Corners Realty Company, who, in turn, would almost certainly sell it to blacks.

"We hope to move by the second week in September," Norman explained to Mr. Podell, the representative from Four Corners, "and we'd appreciate it if you didn't show the house until we've gone."

"We understand your feelings on this matter," Mr. Podell said, scratching his head.

"It's not us," Norman added, hastily. "It's my mother. She and my father built this house, spent a lot of years in it . . ."

"Of course, of course." Mr. Podell examined the fingernails on the hand that had scratched his head. What did he expect to find there? "Don't worry, Mr. Pressman, we're known for our discretion at Four Corners. We'll bring our clients in after dark, on nights when you and the family are out."

Norman nodded.

"Is that legal?" Sandy asked.

Mr. Podell flushed.

"Damn right it's legal!" Norman told her.

"We'll keep an exclusive on it until you move so that we can control the prospective buyers. Then, if we still haven't sold it, we'll put it on multiple listing, but by that time you'll be comfortably settled in Watchung and I seriously doubt that we'll have to go to that. I have in mind a very successful attorney. I think this might be just what he's been looking for."

Norman and Mr. Podell shook hands, then Sandy showed Mr. Podell to the front door. "You made a wise decision," he said.

"Yes." She went back into the den, where Norman was carefully studying the ten-thousand-dollar check of deposit. The balance was due at the closing, in a few weeks.

"We're on our way to Watchung!" Norman sang, hugging her. Banushka barked, jealous of the attention Norman was showing Sandy. Norman scooped him into his arms. "You're going to like it up there, little fellow, just you wait."

"I hope he doesn't have an adjustment problem," Sandy said. "Dogs sometimes do, don't they?"

"Not our little guy. He'll be fine. How many sticks did he make today?"

"Two sticks and four wees," Sandy lied.

"That's good, I didn't see it on his chart."

"Oh, maybe I forgot to mark it."

"I wish you'd try to remember that, San. It's important for me to know how he's doing." He put Banushka down. "Well, we better get going. Lucille and Ben will be waiting."

"Lucille and Ben! I thought we were going out by ourselves."

"Ben called this afternoon, to check on our weekend game, and asked if we'd like to join him and Lucille for dinner at The Club. I accepted."

"I don't want to go there, Norm."

"You'll have to get over that, Sandy, the sooner the better. It's still *our* Club and I intend to make the most of it."

"To Watchung!" Lucille and Ben toasted. "To a happy and healthy new life there!"

"Hear . . . hear . . ." Norman raised his glass to theirs. "I'll drink to that . . ."

To us! Sandy thought. *To a new life.*

"Sandy," Ben said, "you can't be serious about quitting golf . . ."

"I'm serious."

"It doesn't take much to upset Sandy," Norman said. "She's very . . ."

"I'm emotionally immature," Sandy told them, before he'd finished. "In fact, I've only got half a brain. Right, Norm?"

Lucille and Ben looked at each other. "To each his own," Ben said, drinking.

"Isn't it terrible about Barbara and Gish?" Luscious asked.

"It's the women's lib thing," Norman said. "None of them know how good they have it . . ."

"Oh, no . . . you've got it all wrong," Sandy said, "Gish walked out . . ." But the others weren't really listening.

When they got home and into bed Norman snuggled up to her and said, "I feel like a little something."

"Well, I don't."

"What do you mean, you don't?"

"I'm tired."

"You don't have to do anything but lay there and open your legs. I'll do all the work."

"No, Norm."

"What do you mean, *no?*"

"I mean, *no!* I mean I don't *want* to."

"This is supposed to be a celebration."

"We celebrated over dinner. I drank too much. I'm feeling very gassy."

"A little something will make the gas go away."

"A little something will probably make me fart."

"Forget it," he said, rolling over.

She got a letter from Jen the next morning.

DEAR MOMMY,
Since visiting day I had a fight with Beth. She used to be my best friend. Now I hate her. She is getting everyone in my bunk to hate me. I think I should come home right away.

Your poor little unhappy daughter,
JENNIFER P.

Sandy shook her head. No point in calling camp this time. No point in writing about it either. By the time her letter arrived at camp bunk politics would have changed, possibly more than once. And camp would be over in less than two weeks. Jen and Bucky would be home. They'd be a family again. She'd have to start sorting out junk, deciding what to take to the new house and what to get rid of. They'd have to arrange for the movers and start packing. She'd have to shop. They'd need new linens, new kitchen dishes. Maybe she should work with a decorator. Myra did. Oh, shit, she wouldn't think about any of that now.

Wouldn't think about real life. She was going to spend the afternoon with Shep. And that was all that mattered.

"Hello, kid . . . how's it going?"

They met at the Holiday Inn on Route 22, where it meets the Parkway.

"Look what I have." She showed him the sexual encyclopedia she'd bought last January, when she was still full of new New Year's resolutions.

Shep laughed. "We don't need that."

"Maybe you don't but I do. I don't have any experience."

"You don't need experience to know what feels good."

She thought about that, then dropped the book to the floor and kissed him. "You're right . . . you're always right . . . and I love you, Shep . . ."

"I love you too."

"Do you know I've never been on top?"

"You've never?"

"Never."

"You've got a lot to make up for . . ."

She wasn't sure whether she liked the sex best or the closeness following. She felt so safe sleeping in his arms, their bodies curved around each other.

"Come away with me for the weekend, Sandy."

"How can I?"

"You'll think of a way if you really want to."

"I want to . . . I want to . . . it's just that . . ."

"No excuses this time."

"What about you? What will you tell Rhoda?" There. The first time she'd said *her* name to him. She didn't want to think about Rhoda, didn't want to acknowledge her existence. She hated Rhoda, hated her for having Shep all these years, for sleeping next to him and waking up with him and having babies with him and sharing life with him. She wished Rhoda were dead. Rhoda and Norman, killed in an accident together. How easy that would make it for them. How wicked she felt for her thoughts. Rhoda was a decent person, raising four, soon to be five, kids. Who was *she* to wish her dead?

"Rho and the kids are going to the beach this weekend. We have a place down on Long Beach Island."

"Don't you go with them?"

"Usually, but there are times when I have to go looking at land."

"What'll I tell Norman?"

"That's up to you."

"Where will we go?"

"I'll think of someplace. Let's get an early start. Say, nine at Newark Airport."

She nodded and wrapped her arms around him. "There's so much time to make up for. So many years."

"I know. You were such a scared little girl then. Always thinking your mother was looking over your shoulder."

"She was."

"And now?"

"Now I don't care any more."

"I'm going to make love to you all weekend until you can't take any more."

"I can take a lot."

"We'll see who gives up first."

"I love you, Shep. I don't know how to tell you how much I love you."

"I can feel it."

On the way home she remembered that she'd left the sexual encyclopedia on the floor of the motel. Oh, so what? It didn't have her name in it. Maybe the maid would appreciate it. With Shep there was no need for how-to's. She laughed out loud, feeling giddy. Giddy with sex and adventure and love.

She could imagine what they'd say when they found out she was going to divorce Norman and marry Shep. Norman wouldn't believe her at first, wouldn't take her seriously. *What are you talking about . . . a divorce . . .*

Just that, she would tell him, I'm in love with another man and we're going to be married. It's very easy to understand if you try.

You're crazy.

No.

Emotionally immature.

Not that either.

I'll get custody of the children. You'll never see them again. You're an unfit mother and I can prove it.

You can't scare me with that crap, Norman.

All right . . . go ahead . . . get a divorce! You'll come crawling back to me in a year . . . you've never known how good you have it with me . . . now you'll find out the hard way . . . and you won't get a penny . . . I can promise you that . . . not one fucking penny from me.

I don't want a penny from you. I don't want anything from you.

Enid would phone Norman: What did I tell you? Right from the start I said she's going to bring you trouble, didn't I? So now you've got it. I warned you, Normie, but that's water over the dam . . . so now you might as well say good riddance to the whore

. . . you can do better . . . I know plenty of women who would give their eyeteeth for you. She'll live to regret it, don't worry . . . she'll get her comeuppance . . . I only hope I'm still around to see it.

The children would say: What? You and Daddy are getting a divorce? That means next year at camp we can have two visiting days . . . all the kids with divorced parents get two visiting days . . . one for their mother and one for their father. Where will we live? Will we live with you or Daddy? Who wants to live with Daddy? He can't cook.

Mona: Oh my God . . . a divorce . . . how can you do this to me? What am I going to tell people? What about the new house? What about the children? Who's going to support you? I can't afford to touch my principal, you know that. What? You're going to marry Shep Resnick? Why didn't you say so in the first place? I hear he's done very well for himself . . . in shopping centers, no less . . . I don't like the idea of divorce . . . but I'm grateful that you've found another man to take care of you. A woman shouldn't be without a man to take care of her . . . believe me, I know.

Myra would give her blessings. I told you, San, the only way to do it is to go straight to another man. And you certainly didn't waste any time. I'm proud of you. Not only that but he's rich. You've got it made. I should only be so lucky.

Yes, she could almost look forward to telling them. Telling the whole world. Special to the New York *Times:* Mrs. Mona Schaedel announces the marriage of her daughter, Sondra Elaine Schaedel Pressman, to Shepherd James Resnick. Mr. Resnick is in shopping centers and Mrs. Resnick is in love. Their six children attended them. The bride wore pale beige lace bikini panties . . .

"Norm, I'm thinking about going away for the weekend."

"What?"

"I'm thinking about going away for the weekend to visit Lisbeth in Maine. She called and invited me up today."

"You know what I think of Lisbeth."

"That doesn't matter. I'm not asking you to go with me. I know you've got games all weekend."

"I don't like the idea of it, Sandy."

"Well, I do. And I've already told her I'll be there. I'm flying to Boston in the morning and taking the bus from there. I'll be back on Monday."

"Monday? What's wrong with Sunday."

"It's a long trip, Norm, it doesn't pay to travel on Friday and come back on Sunday. I'd get too tired. You know how tired I get when I travel."

"If you're so tired, you should stay home and sit at the pool at The Club."

"I didn't say I'm tired. I said I *get* tired when I travel too much all at once. I need to get away, Norm, to think."

"The less thinking you do the better off you'll be."

"That's a new one."

"Most wives wouldn't desert their husbands over a weekend."

I will not answer that statement. I will not get into a fight over this. "Myra and Gordon are taking separate trips this week. He's going to the AMA convention in San Francisco and she's going to Amherst, to tennis camp."

"What's that got to do with us?"

"Nothing, I'm just making conversation."

"What'll I eat?"

219

"Come on, Norm, you're a big boy. You can eat at The Club."

"Suppose there's an emergency?"

"Then you'll take care of it."

"Leave your phone number."

"Lisbeth doesn't have a phone in Maine, but I'll call from a booth and let you know I arrived safely, okay."

"No, it's not okay, but it looks like I have no choice."

That's right. This time the choice is mine.

"You need money?"

"No, I have enough."

"What about the airline ticket?"

"I'll write a check."

"Here . . ." he said, reaching into his pocket, "take some . . ." He counted out five twenties. "You never know . . ."

She turned the money over in her hand and felt a lump come up in her throat. "Thanks, Norm . . ."

"Just be careful."

"I will."

"Who knows . . . maybe the change will do you good."

She nodded.

"But don't plan on taking off whenever you feel like it . . . because there's only so much I can tolerate . . ."

She nodded again.

When she went downstairs the next morning she found a list taped to the refrigerator.

Sandy: Before the end of next week

1. Arrange for movers
2. Arrange for painters
3. Arrange for fixtures with electrician

4. Arrange to get Banushka to the vet for shots

5. Arrange for the kids to transfer to the schools in Watchung

6. Arrange for live-in Ductla for new house

Arrangements and more arrangements. Sandy didn't know whether to laugh or to rip the list in shreds.

The phone rang just as she was about to leave the house. "Sandy, it's Myra. I've changed my mind. I'm going to San Francisco after all."

"I'm glad. I've thought you should go all along."

"Our plane leaves at noon."

"Have a wonderful time."

"I hope so. See you next week."

"Right, bye."

Sandy drove to the airport, wishing she were going away for good, never coming back to Norman or the house. But what about the children? Oh, she'd send for them. Maybe.

Sandy! What are you saying? You'd give up your children?

I don't know.

You should be punished for even thinking that!

I'm sorry! I don't know what got into me. You're right. I should be punished.

Of course she wanted the children. They needed her, didn't they?

Are you sure? At camp they . . .

Yes, but that was only for eight weeks. They knew they were coming home afterward.

They might do just as well without you.

No! I am not giving up my children. I know what he'd do to them. Make them just like him. No! The children are mine. And that's final. Shep and I will

marry and I'll get custody. He can't prove I'm an unfit mother. I'm not! Well, I'm not, am I?

Would a fit mother be running off with another
man for the weekend, leaving a trail 'of lies behind
her?

One thing has nothing to do with the other. Look at
Myra. She was fucking Frank Monzellini when the
twins were babies.

So maybe that's what messed them up.

No, it's just a phase they're going through. It's adolescence. Ask Myra. She says they're coming out of it
now. They've already lost twenty pounds at their fat
camp in Southampton. So, you see, she is a fit mother
and so am I!

Sandy pulled into the airport. *Long-term parking,
short-term parking,* where was *weekend parking?* Why
did they have to make it so confusing? Finally, she
parked successfully, grabbed her bag, and locked the
car. She'd better write down the section and number
or she'd be looking for the car all day when she got
back. *If* she got back. Suppose they flew somewhere
and the plane crashed? Would Norman and Rhoda
put two and two together? So what if they did? She
and Shep would be dead anyway. But the children.
What would Norman tell them? That Mommy ran
away with another man? No, he'd never admit to that.
That wouldn't do his image any good. Besides, it
wasn't going to happen. Flying was safer than driving.
Everyone said so. The statistics proved it. And if the
plane was going to crash, it had to be on the way back
so they could at least have their weekend together.
Making love until she couldn't take any more. That's
what he promised. Her knees felt weak just thinking
about it.

Upstairs, in the terminal, she had pains in her stomach. Just nerves, she told herself. Relax, relax, don't give in to them and they'll go away.

She searched for Shep at the Eastern counter. He had said Eastern, hadn't he? So where was he? Suppose she saw someone she knew? *Hi, there . . . going away for the weekend? Me too . . . my old girlfriend . . . Maine . . . plane to Boston . . . how about you?*

Where are you, Shep?

He must be on his way. He should be here any minute, unless . . . unless . . . No! That was too terrible to think about. Shep, lying on the street, blood pouring out of his head. Shot . . . like Kennedy? No, an automobile accident. The slick highway. Last night's rain. Ambulance attendants bending over him, shaking their heads.

"Hello, kid."

She turned around. "Shep!"

"Who were you expecting?"

"I'm just so glad to see you. I thought . . ."

"Sorry I'm late, traffic."

"It's okay now."

"Here's what I thought we should do. Take the shuttle up to Boston, rent a car and drive out to the Cape. I've found us a little cabin on the ocean."

"Sounds wonderful. And you won't believe this but I told Norman I was flying up to Boston, then taking the bus to Maine to visit my old friend, Lisbeth."

"Now you can show him your ticket and prove it."

"Yes. It's all working out for us, isn't it?"

"Did you think it wouldn't?"

"I wasn't sure."

"Have faith, Sandy."

"I'll try."

"Let's go. There's a nine-forty-five shuttle."

As they lined up to get on board Sandy noticed Mickey. Oh, shit! Was Funky here too?

She whispered to Shep. "I know that man and I think he's seen me."

"Just play it cool."

"Hey, Sandy, I thought it was you," Mickey said, approaching her. "What are you doing here?"

"I'm on my way to Maine to visit my friend for the weekend. How about you?"

"Business in Boston. Just for the day."

"Oh."

"I heard about that episode at The Club. Phyllis tells me you've stopped playing because of it."

"No, it's not that."

"Because, hell, some guy once lodged a complaint against me. I just paid my fine and forgot about it. That's what you should do."

"It's not just the complaint . . ."

"Say, why don't we sit together on the plane?"

"Do you smoke?" She knew he did.

"Yeah."

"Sorry, but I'm in *no smoking*."

"Oh, well, have a nice weekend. If you feel like hanging around in Boston for a couple of hours, I'd be happy to take you to lunch."

"That's very nice of you, Mickey, but once we land I've got to run. My bus to Maine . . ."

"Oh, yeah, I forgot about that."

"Oh, and if you happen to see Norman over the weekend tell him we were on the same plane."

"I'll do that . . ."

"Whew," Sandy said, when he'd finally left.

"You handled that very well. I'm impressed."

"I don't like lying."

"I know."

They boarded the plane and Sandy held Shep's hand tightly as they took off.

"Don't tell me you're a white-knuckle flyer," Shep said.

"Sort of."

"I should have guessed."

The flight attendant was tall, blonde, green-eyed, and overattentive, especially to Shep. At first Sandy found it funny, but by the fourth time she paraded up the aisle, pausing at their row, Sandy began to feel uncomfortable, and then slightly nauseous at the way Shep eyed her back, at the way their hands touched as she handed him his raincoat when they landed.

"Good-looking girl," Sandy said as they deplaned.

"Who?" Shep asked.

"The flight attendant."

"Really, I hadn't noticed. I only have eyes for you," he said, patting her ass.

The cabin smelled of mildew but it didn't matter. They threw down their things, changed into bathing suits, and raced down to the ocean's edge. The water was freezing. They only wet up to their ankles, then sunbathed, took a bath in the oldfashioned tub in the cabin, and made love. Endless hours of lovemaking, as promised, with Shep climbing on top of her each time he neared his climax, pumping her full, making her come one last time when she was sure there was nothing left in her. They slept in each other's arms, Shep more soundly than Sandy. She awakened every few minutes, kissed his face, his neck, his arms, and dozed off again.

She didn't remember to call Norman until Saturday

morning at seven. "Where were you last night?" she asked. "I tried and tried . . ." She was ready with all sorts of excuses if he said he'd been home all evening, waiting for her call. *Out of order. Operator's error. Tiny village. Crossed lines.*

Norman yawned into the phone. "I was at The Club playing in the Twi-niter, then Lucille and Ben convinced me to stay for the dinner-dance." He yawned again. "I didn't get home till after one."

"No wonder I couldn't get you."

"You didn't want me to sit home all alone, did you?"

"Of course not. I'm glad you had a good time. I just wanted you to know I'm here and everything's okay."

Shep rolled over and began to kiss her breasts.

"Mickey told me he saw you on the plane."

"Yes, wasn't that a coincidence?"

"He was surprised."

"So was I."

"Well, have a good weekend."

"You too, Norm."

"See you on Monday. You'll be back before dinner, won't you?"

Shep's hand was between her legs.

"Yes, I think so."

"I hope so!"

She hung up and Shep kissed her. "I've never kissed anyone without brushing my teeth first," she told him.

"Then it's time you did," he said, sweeping the inside of her mouth with his tongue. And then Shep was on top of her but suddenly he cried out and jumped off the bed. "Jesus . . ." He paced up and down.

"What is it?" Had she done something? Hurt him in some way?

"My leg, it's my leg."

226

Polio? A blood clot?

"A cramp . . . God, it hurts . . ."

"Can I do something?"

"No . . ."

She waited quietly.

"It's letting up now." He came back to bed and lay down. He was covered with perspiration. She got up, went to the bathroom, and returned with a wet washcloth. She mopped off his face, pulled the covers up, held him in her arms, and watched him sleep.

When he awoke again it was nine-thirty and he reached for the phone to call Rhoda at the beach.

"Hi, honey . . . how are things . . . good . . . and the kids . . . good . . . send them my love . . . miss you too . . . take care . . . see you Monday . . . yes . . . kisses to all of you too . . ."

Sandy turned her back to him, hurt by the concern, the love, in his voice.

"Sorry, kid," he said, after he'd hung up.

"It's just that . . ."

"I know. Let's try to forget about it, okay?"

They went to breakfast at Josie's House, a beautiful, old Cape Cod, turned into a restaurant, where the tables were set with white lace paper doilies and baskets of fresh flowers. The waitresses were suntanned girls, their shiny hair tied back, their long, sleek legs exposed beneath miniskirts. Sandy wondered how Shep could want her, love her, when there were so many more beautiful girls in the world, every one of them ready to jump into bed with him. She could feel it. The way the redhead looked at him as she poured his coffee. The way the one with the brown eyes smiled at his smile. Sandy couldn't help feeling jealous, jealous of their beauty, their youth, their freedom. Yes, most of all, their freedom.

"Let's have the works," Shep said, "cereal, bacon, eggs, muffins. I'm famished. We forgot to have dinner last night."

"I know. We were too busy."

He smiled and took her hand, kissing her fingers.

"I love you, Shep. I want to live with you forever."

"I know."

"I want to wake up next to you every day."

"And I want to wake up with you in my arms, looking at your funny, sleepy face."

So what are we going to do about it? she felt like asking. But she couldn't. Not yet.

❧ 22 ❧

THE PHONE WAS ringing as Sandy unlocked the front door on Monday afternoon. "Yes, hello?"

"Sandy? It's Vincent."

"Vincent, what a surprise."

"We've been trying to get you since yesterday."

"I was away for the weekend. I just got back."

"Lisbeth's mother died. The funeral's tomorrow at ten. At Apter's."

"Oh, Vincent, I'm so sorry."

"It's a blessing, actually. She'd been going steadily downhill and at the end she didn't even recognize Lisbeth."

"I'll be there tomorrow," Sandy said, her voice cracking. "Send Lisbeth my love and my sympathy."

"Yes, I'll do that."

"And Vincent . . ."

"Yes?"

"You didn't by any chance reach Norman, did you?"

"No, there was no answer at all. Why?"

"No reason. See you tomorrow."

"Right."

Trying to get us on the phone all day yesterday,
Sandy thought. Suppose Norman had answered. Then
what? Then she would have had to face the consequences. Luck was with her and Shep. Somebody up
there liked them. Wasn't that what Mona used to say?
Yes, when she fell off her bicycle and came home with
only scraped knees, Mona said, *Well, it could have
been worse. Somebody up there likes you, Sandy.*
And Sandy used to wonder what the somebody looked
like. Was it God, himself? Was it one of his angels?
Was it Moses, or Esther? What a mess it would
have been if Norman had been home to take the call.
Not that Sandy wasn't prepared to leave him. She
was. But first she wanted to put everything in order.
She had to discuss it with Shep. The sooner the better.
Before something like this came up again. Before
Norman could gather evidence to use against her in a
custody battle. Wednesday. She would tell him on
Wednesday afternoon when they met at the Country
Squire Inn in Basking Ridge. She couldn't go on sleep-
ing with Norman, playing wifey, when all she could
think of was Shep and the way she loved him.

"Her mother died while you were visiting?" Norman asked that night.

"Yes."

"And they flew back but you stayed?"

"Yes, I stayed to get things in order up there."

"You stayed all alone in some godforsaken cabin
in the woods?"

"Yes."

"Did you ever stop to think of what might have happened to you with no phone, no running water.
Jesus!"

"Nothing happened. I'm home and I'm fine. The funeral's tomorrow morning."

"I hope you don't expect me to go."

"I don't."

"Because I'm really bogged down at the plant. August vacations and . . ."

"I said I don't expect you to go."

Lisbeth conducted the service for her mother. She read poetry, then told the small gathering of friends and relatives how her mother had always encouraged her, how she'd brought her up to believe that she could become anything she wanted. That it was her life, her only life, and the decisions were hers to make. "I'll always be grateful to the wonderful woman who was my mother. And I'll remember the happy times we had together. I know she'd want you to remember those times too."

Miranda, every bit as poised and lovely as Lisbeth had said, spoke next. "My grandma took care of me when I was a baby. She loved me even when I was bad. She let me sit on the kitchen counter while she baked. She gave me dough to play with and laughed when it got stuck in my hair. And as I got older, I still loved to go to stay with her. She was old-fashioned in lots of ways, but not in loving. She really knew how to love. And I'm going to miss her a lot." Miranda put a pink rose on the closed coffin. "Good-bye, Grandma. I miss you already."

Sandy's tears were confused. They were not only for Lisbeth and Miranda and Mrs. Rabinowitz, but for herself. For her life, her only life, and the decisions she had never made.

After, Sandy kissed Lisbeth's cheek. "I'm so sorry."

"I know."

"It was a beautiful service."

Lisbeth nodded. "Come to the house after the cemetery. I want to talk to you."

"Okay."

Mrs. Rabinowitz's neighbors had set up a feast. Such a delectable spread of goodies that Sandy could have sworn she was at a catered affair, maybe even at The Club. Cheeses, breads, vegetables, salads, white fish, herring, homebaked cookies and cakes. She could never understand why people felt so hungry after funerals but she knew it was true. She remembered it from her own father's funeral and from Samuel D. Pressman's. She remembered it from when she was small and wasn't permitted to go to family funerals. They always came home from the cemetery starving and Sandy wondered what they did there to get themselves that hungry. Now she knew. A celebration of life, through death.

Sandy and Lisbeth went upstairs, after lunch, to Lisbeth's old bedroom, which was exactly as she had left it sixteen years ago to go off to Barnard. They sat on the bed together the way they had when they were teens; Lisbeth propped up against the pillows, Sandy, hugging her knees to her chest.

"Vincent said you were away for the weekend."

"I was."

"Without Norman, I gather?"

"Yes."

"Well, tell me all about it."

"I went to Cape Cod, with a man, but Norman thinks I was with you, in Maine. That I was there when the call came through about your mother. I've turned into an incredible liar. I hate myself for it."

"Don't worry, I'll cover for you any time. So who is he?"

Sandy hesitated.

"Come on, San . . . this is me, Zelda, remember?"

"Zelda?"

"I've been thinking about changing it back. Did you know my mother named me for F. Scott Fitzgerald's wife?"

"No."

"I just found out myself. Supposedly I was named for my great-grandmother, but when my mother realized she was dying she told me the truth. So who is he and do you love him or is it just a fling?"

"I love him. It's not a fling."

"How long have you been seeing him?"

"Just a week, but it seems like months . . . years . . ."

Lisbeth shook her head. "It's serious, isn't it?"

"Very."

"You know something, Vincent and I have given up our Thursday nights off. We've decided it's just too risky. And to tell you the truth, it was getting boring. I love Vincent. I don't *need* anyone else and he feels the same way. It's as if we've discovered each other all over again. Ever since my mother got sick, he's been just wonderful. I've fallen in love with him, Sandy, like a schoolgirl."

"I'm glad for you." *Thank you, Vincent . . . thank you for not telling her about us . . .*

"I've often wondered why you've stayed with Norman this long."

"It takes guts to get out."

"Sandy, did you hear what I said at the funeral? You can't wait around for your next life. This *is* your life. It's very short, very precious. Don't waste it."

Sandy cried. Lisbeth put her arms around her and said, "It'll be all right."

On her way home Sandy stopped to pick up some cold cuts for supper. She and Norman ate early, then he took Banushka for a walk while she cleaned up the kitchen. The doorbell rang before she had finished. She wiped her hands on her pants and went to the front door. It was a man she had never seen before. "Yes?"

"Mrs. Pressman?"

Sandy nodded.

"I'm Mr. Martinez. Is Mr. Pressman in?"

"He'll be back any minute. He's walking the dog."

"I'll wait in my car, then."

"Is it about the house?"

"The house? No, it's a private matter."

"I see." She double-locked the door, and watched from the front window. What kind of private matter? Someone from the Anti-Defamation League? Someone who found out they'd sold to a realtor instead of a black? Now they'd really be in for it. She'd warned Norman. He should have listened. Could he be sent to jail for not selling directly to a black family? How many years? Five . . . ten? Could she divorce him if he was in prison? She saw Norman approaching with Banushka. Mr. Martinez got out of his car. Norman seemed angry. Martinez held up a portfolio and shook it at him. Both men walked up to the house. Sandy ran to the front door and unlocked it. "Hi," she said to Norman.

"Sandy, this is Mr. Martinez. Martinez, my wife, Sandy."

"Yes, we've already met," Sandy said.

Martinez followed Norman into the house. "I'll be right with you," Norman told him. He ushered Sandy into the kitchen.

"What's going on?" she asked.

234

"Myra came to me weeks ago, suspecting Gordon of having an affair. She asked me to help her. I hired Martinez. He's a private detective."

"Oh, no."

"When you told me Gordon was going to San Francisco and Myra was going to tennis camp, I put Martinez onto it."

"Oh, no."

"He's got the goods on him now. Photos and everything."

"But, Norm . . ."

"Let's go have a look."

"Caught him red-handed," Martinez said. "In the act. Wait till you see these." He tapped his portfolio.

"Go ahead," Norman told him.

"In front of the little woman?"

"It's her sister we're trying to help."

"If you say so." He untied the portfolio and spread out the evidence on the dining room table. Six 8X10 black and white glossies of Gordon and Myra. Two of them showing the happy couple fucking in the missionary position, two showing them sucking, one, making it from the rear.

"Jesus Christ!" Norman said, holding up a picture.

"I tried to tell you," Sandy said.

"Pretty good, huh?" Martinez asked. "Really professional."

"This is my sister-in-law, you idiot!" Norman said, holding the picture under Martinez's nose.

"What?"

"His wife! This is his wife!"

"This woman is his wife?" Martinez asked.

"Yes. I showed you pictures of her, didn't I?"

"Yes, but I thought . . ."

"Never mind what you thought. You're off the job.

Fired! Give me the negatives and get the hell out of here."

"But my expenses . . ."

"I'll pay your goddamned expenses but not one penny more. Now, give me the negatives."

Martinez reached into his portfolio and dropped the negatives on the table. Then he hightailed it out of the house.

"Stupid goddamned fool!" Norman muttered.

"I can't believe you hired a detective."

"Your sister came to me crying. What was I supposed to do?"

"I don't know. You could have discussed it with me."

"With you? If she had wanted you to know, she would have gone to you in the first place."

"She did. She told me all about it."

"She told you?"

"Yes, I advised her to think it over carefully. Not to do anything foolish . . ."

"Wait till I tell Hubanski about this guy."

"Hubanski! What's he got to do with it?"

"I called him, asking him to recommend someone. I'm not in the habit of hiring private detectives, you know."

"And Hubanski recommended Martinez?"

"Yes, they used to work together. Did you know your sister was going to San Francisco?"

"Yes, she called me right before I left on Friday morning. I didn't think it was that important. I didn't know you were having Gordon tailed."

Norman picked up one of the pictures. "Myra looks great, doesn't she? And who would have thought Gordon had it in him? You just never know . . ."

I know, Sandy thought.

Norman made a fire and burned the pictures and negatives.

Later, he wanted a little something. Sandy knew he would. He was excited by the pictures of Gordon and Myra. So was she. But she couldn't do it with Norman. Couldn't be unfaithful to Shep. So she said, "I'm very tired . . . the funeral . . . and now, this . . ."

"Come on, Sandy."

"No, not tonight, Norm."

"What is this shit? You've been away all weekend and now it's *no, not tonight, Norm.*" His imitation of her came out sounding like Enid.

"I just don't want to."

"It's your marital duty."

"Oh, shut up. What do you know about marital duty?"

"There's only so much I can take, Sandy. You're pushing me to my limits."

"Go to sleep."

"Bitch!"

She met Shep the next afternoon. "I've missed you," she said. "So much has happened in only two days."

"And I've missed you."

They made love, then talked. Sandy told him about Mrs. Rabinowitz, how Lisbeth and Vincent had been trying to reach her all weekend, how Norman would have found out something was wrong if he had been home to answer. She told him about Myra and Gordon and the detective, and then about refusing Norman last night, and his anger.

"I couldn't make it with Rhoda either. Told her I thought I was coming down with a bug."

"Shep, we've got to do something. I can't go on like this." *So tell me that you're leaving Rhoda tomorrow . . . that you're going to marry me . . .*

"I know, I've been giving it a lot of thought. I just didn't think it would come up this soon. I thought we'd have six months, maybe a year, before this happened."

"I love you, Shep. I'm ready to leave Norman now."

"I know you are."

Then say it . . . say it . . . "We'll be happy together."

He held her in his arms, brushing the hair away from her face.

"I want to spend the rest of my life with you," she told him, kissing his neck, then his face. *Please tell me you feel the same.*

"I wish it were possible, kid."

She looked up at him. "It is. It has to be."

"I can't leave Rhoda and the kids. Not now."

She shook her head and felt her throat tighten. "But you love me."

"Yes."

"Then?"

"I love her too."

Sandy panicked and wriggled away from him.

"Try to understand," he said.

"Understand?"

"Rho and I have shared to lot. Come a long way together."

"Now you tell me!"

"Sandy, this has been the best week of my life. I mean it."

"Stop it. Just stop it, will you."

"I don't want to let you go." He reached for her but she wouldn't let him touch her. She couldn't think.

Couldn't get beyond the tears, beyond the hurt and humiliation. She had been so sure.

"We could arrange something," Shep said. "Get a little place . . . see each other twice a week . . ."

"I hate arrangements!" she cried. "I can't live that way."

"It's a lot to ask, I know," he said, "and I don't want to push you, but a lot of people do live that way, Sandy, and it works."

"Don't tell me what works. I'm not a lot of people."

Shep sighed. "I warned you, didn't I? I warned you to think it over carefully."

"And I did. I did."

"No, you never thought about the ending."

"I didn't know there had to be one." She knew how ugly she looked when she cried. How her face contorted. But she couldn't stop. "I thought we were going to get married and live together happily ever after. What a little girl I am. What a silly, stupid little girl . . . with little girl dreams!"

"Sandy, Sandy." He stood behind her and put his arms around her. "I'm so sorry."

"Don't be," she told him, trying to control herself. "It's my fault. I should have known. What did I expect in just a week?" *Just a week . . . but it seems like months . . . years . . . my whole life . . .*

"If you don't love Norman, leave him. I'll help all I can—money, a job, a place to live."

"No! I'm not going to live a lie."

"At least let me be your friend. I can help make the transition period easier for you."

Her friend. Yes, she wanted him as her friend, but she wanted him as her lover, as her husband too. "I had it all figured out. Don't you see, I had everything figured out."

"Leave him. You'll be better off. Find yourself, kid."

"I don't know where to look."

She'd never felt such despair, such hopelessness. Nothing mattered now. Life was over because life had become Shep. Crying didn't help any more. The empty feeling inside her remained. The love of her life and her passport to freedom, all gone, down the drain together. What now, Sandy? What now? She thought about getting sick. A high fever. A raging virulent infection. Oxygen tanks. Intensive care. The critical list. Shep would rush to her bedside, blaming himself. *No!* That wouldn't solve anything. No more illnesses. No more fantasies. Divorce Norman anyway? And then what?

Myra would say: Sandy, are you crazy? You want to live on Kentucky Fried Chicken and pizza? Work in Bloomingdale's and get varicose veins? Come home exhausted to nasty children who blame you for messing up their lives? Think! The only way to a decent divorce is through another man. So get busy and find one if you're so unhappy. Never mind Shep. It's not practical for you to go on loving him.

Mona would catch her breath: Sandy! A divorce? I can't believe it. Don't do this to me. Don't do it to the children. Don't do it to yourself. You have a good life with Norman. So what if you don't love him the way a schoolgirl loves her boyfriend? Love changes as you grow older. Accept him for what he is. You're lucky. A lot of women would give their . . .

Yes, Mother, I know, their eyeteeth for a man like Norman.

Exactly.

She would tell the children: Daddy and I are getting a divorce. We're not going to have much money from now on.

Then we'll live with Daddy. He's got plenty.

But you belong with me. Don't you want to live with me?

Not in some crummy apartment, Bucky would answer. We want to live in the new house.

Why doesn't Daddy get an apartment? Jen would ask. And we'll live in the new house with you.

Because I can't afford it. And besides, I wouldn't be happy there without Daddy.

Then why are you getting a divorce? they'd say together.

Bitch, Norman would cry. Goddamned bitch!

And so, what was left? What were her choices now?

I keep the gun locked in this cabinet and the key to the cabinet is in the bookcase, behind *Bartlett's Quotations*.

Sandy went downstairs, to the den, unlocked the cabinet and looked at the gun. *A way out. The end.* She touched it. How cold it was. She lifted it and pressed it against the side of her head, feeling dizzy. She pictured her brains splattered all over Norman's desk, all over the Mark Cross desk set she'd given him on their tenth anniversary. Better do it someplace else. The bathroom? Yes, it would be easier to clean up the mess in there. Mr. Clean, Windex, Ajax—that should do the job. Would she hear the explosion as she pulled the trigger? Had Jack heard it? She remembered the blood and gore on Jackie's pink suit and looked down at her robe, her Mother's Day robe. The children

might take that personally. Maybe she should change
first. No, the undertaker would get rid of the robe. Or
did he send his customers' clothes out to be cleaned
and pressed so that he could return them to the be-
reaved family? She didn't know. She'd have to ask
Norman about that. But if she pulled the trigger now
she wouldn't be able to ask him. She would die without knowing whether or not he got business from the
local morticians. Oh, so what! Besides, you don't always die, she reminded herself. If you miss, you could
wind up a vegetable. She'd read about a man who'd
missed. He'd blown off half his face but they'd managed to save him so that he could lie in a nursing
home, a blob, a nothing, the rest of his life. Would
their insurance cover the cost of a nursing home or
would Norman leave her to rot in some public institu-
tion? No. How would that look to the family, their
friends? No, she'd have a private room somewhere,
plenty of fresh flowers, and every Sunday after tennis
Norman would drag the kids to see her. *That ugly
thing isn't Mommy,* Jen would cry, pointing. *Yes, it
is, you dummy!* Bucky would tell her. *It's Mommy
with her brains blown out.*

You know, Luscious would announce at the Labor
Day Dance, *she had only half a brain to start with.
She told me herself the last time we had dinner to-
gether.*

Sandy laughed out loud at that one. Oh, what the
hell . . . she didn't know how to load it anyway and
with her luck she'd probably blow off a foot. As she
put the gun back she noticed an envelope inside the
cabinet. Funny, she hadn't seen it before. The war-
ranty? The instruction manual? She opened it. How
strange. A canceled check, dated November 19, 1969,

made out to Brenda Partington Yvelenski for five
thousand dollars. What was this all about? Who was
Brenda Partington Yvelenski? November 19, 1969—
the week Sandy had been so sick. The week Dr. Ackerman had stood at the foot of her bed, listing possibilities. Thoracic cancer . . . leprosy . . . leukemia
. . . lupus . . .

Who was this Brenda Partington Yvelenski to
whom Norman was writing a substantial check while
she lay upstairs, desperately ill? Unless . . . unless she
was a faith healer and Norman had been so fright-
ened at the idea of her impending death he had actually contacted a mystic, called Brenda Partington
Yvelenski, who agreed to pray for her swift return to
health for the meager sum of five thousand dollars.
But Norman didn't believe in the spiritual. He didn't
even believe in Bar Mitzvahs. Still, as a last resort?
No, that's crazy! Then what else? Then why hide the
check?

Blackmail. No, for what? A homosexual, Norman?
Come on, not Norman! Okay, so the wife is always
the last to know but . . .

A hooker. A specialist in black leather boots,
chains, whips because he's too ashamed to tell her
what really turns him on. A year's supply at once,
three times a week. No. Not likely.

A landlord. He's rented a small apartment from
Brenda Partington Yvelenski. A place to rendezvous
with . . . Who? Luscious . . . Brown . . . Funky
. . . all three at once? Myra, to get even with her for
fucking Gordon? The twins . . . for kicks? Her
mother? No. Absolutely not! He didn't have the time
for anything like that. Okay, so they can always make
time, but Norm wouldn't give up his golf or tennis or

holding his breath under water just to get laid, would he?

A shrink? Yes, could be. He's finally realized he's got problems and has decided to deal with them. Dr. Brenda Partington Yvelenski, Shrink. Except that Norman didn't believe in shrinks. Besides, he would have made out the check to *Dr.* Yvelenski, in that case . . . tax deductions and so forth.

She put the check back in the envelope, the envelope back in the cabinet, relocked it and put the key in its place, behind *Bartlett's Quotations,* then went to Norman's desk. She took out the check register and thumbed through it. November . . . November . . . yes, here it was. Number 402, Nov. 19, Brenda Partington Yvelenski: Investment.

She's a broker? Then why hide the check? What sort of investment? Black Angus cattle, like Gordon and his friends? An adult gift shop on the highway, sex aids and porno books? Worse yet, the cleaning stores are a front? Norman's mixed up with the mob . . . bookies, pimps . . . Jesus, you think you know someone and then . . .

She'd ask him tonight. She'd say, *Norman, who is Brenda Partington Yvelenski?*

And he'd say, *Why do you ask?*

And she'd say, *Because you gave her five thousand dollars.*

And he'd say, *How do you know that?*

And she'd say, *Because this afternoon, as I was about to kill myself, I found the canceled check in the gun cabinet.*

And he'd say, *You have one hell of a nerve reading my canceled checks!*

She gave Norman a little something that night. He

patted her shoulder and said, "Glad you're feeling better, San."

"Do you ever say what you mean?" she asked.

"Does anybody?" he answered.

⚜ 23 ⚜

WHEN IT DIDN'T matter any more it began to rain. It rained for two days, a heavy, steady downpour, sure to flood the second hole and close the golf course, which, a few weeks earlier, would have delighted Sandy. On the first day she stayed in bed and slept, glad that Florenzia was taking the week off to drive to South Carolina with her family. She dreamt that the man on the motorcycle was really a woman called Brenda Partington Yvelenski and that Norman had hired her to drive Sandy insane.

On the second day Sandy realized that sleeping wasn't the answer either. So she got up, dressed in old jeans and a torn shirt, tied a bandana around her head, and decided to keep busy. She would tackle the attic first.

As a child Sandy was terrified of the attic in her house, imagining all sorts of creatures up there, just waiting to do her in.

She still wasn't completely comfortable in the attic, although this one was well lit. Even so, the man on the motorcycle could be hiding up there, could have walked right in while she was out with Banushka, and as she reached the top of the stairs he would be waiting . . .

For what?

Rape . . . murder . . .

No, he's gentle . . . shy . . .

You call tossing his thing around that way gentle? He's probably violent. He'll probably strangle you first, then stab you, then . . .

Oh, grow up, Sandy!

She carried the radio up with her, turned on all the lights, and began to rummage through cartons filled with the accumulated junk of twelve years of married life, not to mention the cartons she and Norman had brought to the marriage. One was stuffed with her crinoline petticoats. She used to wear as many as five at a time to make sure that her skirt was fuller than anyone else's. How important that had been at the time. Five crinolines at once; horsehair, taffeta, net; under her felt skirt, her quilted skirt, her Lanz dresses. She'd been saving her crinolines for Jen, sure that one day she would be invited to a Fifties Party, just as Sandy had attended a series of Roaring Twenties parties when she was a teenager, dressed in Mona's flapper outfits, ropes of beads around her neck, a velvet headband across her forehead.

Somehow, saving her crinolines for Jen to wear to a party seemed foolish now. She would get rid of them. Well, most of them anyway. No harm in saving one or two.

She opened a carton marked "Sandy's School Box." She'd get rid of everything except her high school yearbook. Bucky and Jen would have a good laugh over that some day. And her Five Year Diary, with its faded blue cover, frayed at the edges. She had started it as a sophomore in high school.

She opened it to the last entry.

DEAR DARLING DIARY,

I am utterly, hopelessly in love with N. I am so much more mature now than I was last year when I thought I loved S. R. With S. R. it was all sex, sex, sex! Now, in my maturity I know that sex isn't everything. It certainly isn't love. N and I have so much in common. We want the same things out of life. I will wear his ZBT pin forever . . .

Utterly, hopelessly in love.

Had she really felt that way about Norman? Or had she just wanted to be so in love? She couldn't remember any more. She remembered loving Shep. But would it have worked out any better with him? Probably not.

Sandy, what are you saying?

The truth, for once . . . it wouldn't have worked . . . not twelve years ago and not now . . .

Sandy, I can't believe this.

Marriage to him would have meant a life very much like the one I lead with Norman.

No!

Yes, a house in the suburbs, kids, car pools.

But Sandy, what about sex?

Okay, so it would have been better but after a while, even with him, it would probably have become routine.

Routine? You sit there and call such great sex routine?

Okay . . . okay . . . so it was good, very good
. . . but God, the jealousy, the mistrust, the lies . . .
it wouldn't be worth it . . .

You don't think he'd have given up other women
for you?

Maybe . . . I don't know . . .

You don't think he runs around because it's not
good with her . . . with Rhoda?

Okay . . . so it's a nice idea . . . that he'd have
loved me so much he wouldn't have needed anyone
else . . . a nice idea but you'll pardon me for not believing it . . . I know him too well . . . on the air-
plane . . . in the restaurant . . . I think he'd be out
with girls regularly, not to mention older women . . .

Older women too?

Look at me. I'm thirty-two, for God's sake.

No, already!

Yes, already.

That's hard to believe . . . to me you're still a
girl . . .

To me too . . . but I don't want to be a girl any
more . . . I want to be a woman . . .

So be one.

How?

How, she asks . . . I should know?

Hmph!

One more question.

Go ahead.

If he should call now . . . if he should say he's
changed his mind . . . he wants to spend the rest of
his life with you and only you . . . what then?

The truth?

The truth.

I'd probably run to him.

◆❦ 24 ❧◆

HER VAGINAL ITCH returned. She was scratching in
her sleep again, waking up raw. She went back to
Gordon's office and he ran some tests. His nurse called
her two days later. "Mrs. Pressman?"

"Yes."

"Dr. Lefferts would like to see you tomorrow morning at nine."

"Why, is something wrong?"

"Doctor wants to discuss some test results with
you."

*Oh, God! Cancer. Her punishment. Her comeup-
pance. How long did she have? Six months? A year?*

"Mrs. Pressman, can you make it?"

"What? Oh, yes, I'll be there."

"Sandy," Gordon said, from across his walnut desk,
as he tapped his fingers together, "you have gonorrhea."

"What?"

"Gonorrhea."

"Oh, my God! I can't . . . I mean . . . how . . .
who . . ."

"You're not allergic to penicillin, are you?"

"No, but Gordy . . ."

"The nurse will give you the medication before you leave. You have to take it here, then wait for twenty minutes."

"Gordy, for Christ's sake, stop talking like my doctor."

"What can I say, Sandy? That I'm surprised? All right, frankly, I am, but we've been running routine gonorrhea cultures on all our sexually active patients for the last year and you'd be amazed at how many cases we've detected in that time. And by the way, your itch has nothing to do with this."

"Could I have gotten it from you, Gordy?"

"No. Not unless I got it from Myra."

"I don't think she's been with anyone lately."

"Lately, what do you mean by that?" he asked, leaning forward.

"Nothing. I think she'd have told me if she was having an affair."

"But you said *lately*. As if you knew about something."

"No. That's not what I meant at all." Oh, Sandy, you fool. First with Hubanski and now with Gordon. *Think . . . think before you speak, Sandy!* Mona had warned when she was a child.

"I haven't been with anyone but Myra," Gordon was saying, "except for that night with you."

"And I hadn't been with anyone else but Norman."

"Well, if you didn't contact it from me, then it must have been from Norman."

"I just don't know."

"Have there been others since we were together?"

She nodded. "Two . . . but mainly one . . . but I

doubt that I got it from him. The other is more like it."

"I don't follow you."

"It's complicated."

Gordon rested his elbows on his desk top and tapped his fingers together again. "In a situation like this it's pointless to try to figure out who's to blame. It's a circle. The important thing is for everyone involved to be notified and treated. I'll need the names of all of your sexual partners, Sandy . . ."

"Oh, Gordy, do we have to go through that?"

"It's the law."

Sandy hesitated. "I'd rather tell them myself. Couldn't you please let me do that?"

"You'll really tell them?"

"Yes. I promise . . . right away . . . today . . ."

"Well, I guess in this case I could make an exception."

"Thank you, Gordon."

"You're welcome, Sandy, and I want you to know that everything we discussed today is strictly confidential."

"Yes, I know."

She could still taste the penicillin mixture when she got home. Vile pink liquid. The nurse had stood over her saying, "Bottoms up, that's a good girl." And yet, something about it was funny. Funny because she'd been convinced it was cancer. And it wasn't. Who'd have thought of gonorrhea? Another exotic illness to add to her list. But a lot easier to cure than cancer. Still, which one would make Norman more angry? Cancer, probably, because that was long-term and would mess up his life. With gonorrhea you drank the gloopy pink stuff and life went on. But he'd never forgive her. Never. He'd kick her out. Unless he got it first. Unless he gave it to her. But if not, she'd fight back. Fight for the children. She'd make the judge understand that he drove her to it.

"Hello, Vincent . . . it's Sandy . . . Sandy Pressman . . . yes, fine . . . Vincent, I need to talk with you . . . it's very important . . . back to Maine? . . . no, I didn't know that . . . well, I need to talk with you *privately* . . . no, no . . . before Labor Day . . . now? . . . over the phone? . . . are you sure? . . . can I really talk freely? . . . I mean, no one's listening? . . . all right . . . Vincent, I have gonorrhea . . . the doctor just told me . . . of course I'm sure . . . and Vincent, I think it's likely that I got it from you . . . I know you didn't come but that doesn't mean you don't have it . . . how do I know where you got it? . . . all those Thursday nights of yours, probably . . . yes, Lisbeth is a possibility too . . . you should both be checked out and treated . . . and don't wait . . . you don't necessarily have to have symptoms . . . please believe me, Vincent . . . I didn't have any symptoms either . . . yes . . . yes, I will . . . you too . . ."

How she wished that Shep wasn't involved. That she didn't have to phone him now.

"Hello, Shep . . . it's Sandy . . . Shep, I need to see you . . . it's very important . . . no, not a motel . . . just a place to talk . . . oh, I don't know . . . anyplace . . . how about the Ice Cream Factory in Summit . . . fine . . . see you there at two . . ."

"A black and white soda," Sandy told the waitress.

"And a hot fudge sundae with coffee ice cream and nuts, no whipped cream," Shep said. "So how are you, Sandy?"

"Not good."

"What is it?"

"A lot of things, but mostly it's that I've just found out that I have gonorrhea." In the booth behind them four small children were jumping up and down singing, "I scream, you scream, we all scream for ice cream!"

"You have gonorrhea?" he asked.

"Yes, I saw the doctor this morning. I'm as surprised as you, Shep. I didn't have any symptoms."

"Where did you get it?"

"I don't know, possibly from you."

"Where would I have gotten it?"

Sandy didn't say anything. She just picked apart the paper napkin in front of her.

"Rhoda . . . you think I got it from Rhoda?"

Sandy shrugged.

"No, I'd bet my life on it."

"Someone else then."

"I haven't been with anyone else for at least six months."

Six months. Twice a year. Was that how he worked it?

"Six months is a long time," he said. "I'd have known by now. What about Norman? You might have picked it up from him."

"I've thought about that." Had it never occurred to him that she might have been with someone else?

The waitress served them their ice cream.

"Jesus . . . gonorrhea . . . I've never . . . even in Europe . . ."

"I'm sorry, Shep. I wish I could make it go away."

"It's not your fault, I know that." He patted her hand. "I'm just trying to figure out what to do, what to say."

"You've got to go to the doctor. He'll tell you what to do."

"Yeah, I guess, but Rhoda, she's going to hit the roof!"

"Will she leave you?"

"I hope not." He spread his hands out on the table and looked down at them. She loved his hands, rugged yet tender, nails clipped short, a spray of black hairs below each knuckle, a callus on each palm. She shuddered, remembering the way he'd caressed her. She wanted to feel his hands on her again. She had to fold her own hands in her lap to keep from reaching out, to keep from placing her hand on his.

"Look, Sandy . . ." he said, quietly, "this isn't your way of getting us back together, is it?"

He might as well have punched her in the gut. "You think I'm lying . . . that I'd make up . . ."

"I don't know what to think."

"I should have let the doctor tell you." She started to cry, fished in her bag for a Kleenex, and when she couldn't find one, used the paper napkin instead. "How could you possibly think that I would ever stoop to . . ." She blew her nose. *Remember, Sandy, a high fever . . . a raging virulent infection . . . oxygen . . . intensive care . . . okay, so I thought about it but I didn't do it . . . there is a difference . . .*

"I'm sorry," he said, "I had to be sure." He leaned over and kissed her cheek. "Thanks for telling me yourself, kid."

She nodded.

"Let's get out of here."

"Anything wrong with your ice cream?" the waitress asked as they got up.

"No, everything's fine," Shep told her.

"But you didn't eat it."

"Some other time." Shep pressed a dollar bill into the waitress's hand and Sandy could have sworn that as he did, he let his fingers brush against her breast.

Outside, before Sandy got into her car, Shep put his hands on her shoulders and looked down at her face. "I'll always love you. Think you can remember that?"

"I'll try."

"And if you ever need me . . ."

She drove home, changed her clothes, and rushed upstairs, to the attic. What to do now? Find another man? Make the best of it, like Myra? Keep busy? Yes, she'd always kept busy. First school, then marriage, then children. Busy busy busy. Until this summer. Had not being busy enough led to this . . . this strange Sandy? She attacked the cartons, tossing things into piles. She would give away all the baby clothes and the toys the children had tired of and everything she hadn't worn in two years or more. She would combine "Norman's Tufts Box" with "Sandy's School Box," saving just a few items to share with the kids someday.

Dammit! How come Lisbeth didn't get gonorrhea on her Thursday nights? Or Myra with her plumber? *Norman, I've got gonorrhea.* That's how she would say it. Simple and to the point. *And while we're at it, who is Brenda Partington Yvelenski?*

She ripped open the "Tufts" box. It was stuffed with Playbills and programs and menus. *Menus.* Who saved menus? She opened a few of them. Jesus! He'd circled what he'd had to eat. She tossed them into the trash box. Look at that, his old sweatshirt. *Pressman, '56.* She shook it out and held it up, examining it carefully. Wash it and give it to Bucky? No, throw it out, along with his track shoes, still caked with mud, and his baseball cap. He'd probably forgotten all about them by now. Besides, he expected her to sort out his junk. Junk was her job. She pulled out a tiny needlepoint pillow she'd made for him one Valentine's Day, their initials worked into a heart. She sniffed it. Musty.

She dug back into the carton and this time came up with his fraternity caricature, showing a crew-cutted Norman, all big eyes and furry brows, wearing a white lab coat. The caption read: *Dr. Frankenstein, I presume?* Why Dr. Frankenstein? Had he set out to create a monster? Had he succeeded? Was she it?

Oh, shit! She'd forgotten to pick up the barbecued chicken she'd ordered at the deli. She left the contents of the "Tufts Box" scattered on the attic floor and ran downstairs. Banushka barked, then whined, straining to get off his run when he saw her. "Okay, I'll take you with me if you promise to be a good boy." She opened all the windows in the Buick. Banushka was less likely to get car sick if he rode with his head hanging out, the wind in his face.

She drove to South Avenue, to Larry's Delicatessen, where, in addition to the chicken, she picked up a pound of cole slaw, a double portion of noodle pudding, two baked apples, and a slice of bologna for Banushka which she would give to him when they got home. No use looking for trouble. And as long as she'd brought him with her she might was well take a chance and drop in at the vet's since his office was just down the street. With a little luck she'd be able to get #4 on Norman's list out of the way now.

Sandy was surprised that there were only two other cars and a motorcycle in the spacious lot adjoining the animal hospital. Ordinarily it was packed. She parked and carried Banushka into the new brown brick building. On the side, next to the glass doors, chrome letters in satin finish spelled out *Leonard E. Krann, DVM Practice limited to Canines and Felines.* She entered the building and gave the receptionist a breezy hello, as if she didn't know coming in without an appointment was against the rules.

"Yes?" the receptionist said, giving Sandy an icy stare.

"I've brought my dog for his shots."

"Do you have an appointment?"

"No . . . but . . ."

"Without an appointment . . ." she began.

Sandy didn't wait for her to finish. "But, you see, we're moving soon and we really have to."

The receptionist shook her head and flipped through her appointment book. "We could see your dog on September twenty-fourth at one-thirty."

"But I'm here now and it makes sense. Banushka gets car sick and . . ."

Dr. Krann passed by. "Hello, Sandy."

"Hello, Dr. Krann." Funny that he called her *Sandy* while she called him *Doctor,* even though she knew Emily, his sallow-faced wife, from Giulio's and from the A&P, where they'd chat at the meat counter on Thursday mornings, even though she'd heard that the Kranns had applied for membership to The Club. "I was just passing by and hoped you could squeeze Banushka in for his shots because we're moving soon."

"You're moving?" He sounded concerned.

"Yes, to Watchung."

"Oh," he laughed. "I was afraid you meant *away.*"

Did he really care that much? Did one dog more or less make such a difference? "No, but with all there is to do . . ."

259

"Sure, I understand. I'll be with you in just a minute."

"But doctor," his receptionist protested, "we were going to leave early today."

"You go ahead, Virginia, I'll take care of this myself."

"That's very kind of you," Sandy said.

"My pleasure. Bring Banushka into the back room. I'll be with you as soon as I finish up out here."

Sandy found Dr. Krann, slim, boyish, and usually quite shy, very attractive. At first she'd been bothered by his left eye, which wandered, and she'd had trouble looking directly at him. But now, having learned to concentrate on his right eye, she was at ease with him. She carried Banushka, who was already tense and shaking, into an examining room and sat down, holding him on her lap. "Poor little fellow." She stroked his soft fur and talked to him reassuringly. "It's all right. Soon your ordeal will be over for another year and when we get home I have something yummy for you." Banushka looked up at her, cocking his head to one side.

"Well, here we are." Dr. Krann walked into the room, washed up at the sink in the corner, dried his hands with a paper towel, and approached the examining table.

Sandy hated to set Banushka down on that cold slab of metal. Dr. Krann smiled at her. Sandy smiled back. "Nice dog," he said.

"Yes." *You'd never guess from my seemingly calm exterior that I'm in big trouble, would you, Dr. Krann? That I have to go home and tell my husband that I have gonorrhea?*

"Could you hold him still, Sandy."

"Oh, sure." Sandy had to look the other way as Dr.

Krann prepared Banushka's injections. She'd never been able to look when the kids were getting their baby shots either. But the pediatrician had had a nurse to hold them still.

"There we go, that wasn't so bad, was it?" Dr. Krann asked Banushka.

Sandy let out a deep breath. The palms of her hands were covered with sweat.

"Have you had a nice summer?" Dr. Krann asked.

"Yes, how about you?"

"Emily and I were in Europe for two weeks. We just got back."

"Oh, that must have been exciting. I've always wanted to go."

"It's something everyone should do once. There's a lot of history there."

"So I've heard. Well, thanks very much," Sandy said, opening her purse. She pulled out her checkbook. "How much do I owe you?"

"Twenty-eight."

He held Banushka as she wrote out the check. Not only was she sweating but her hands were shaking too. She felt a lump in her throat and thought for a minute that she might start crying. *Hang on . . . hang on . . .* "I really appreciate this," she said, trying to keep her voice from breaking. "And next time I'll phone ahead for an appointment."

"Are you all right?" he asked, his right eye looking directly at her, his left jumping from the wall to the door and back again.

"Yes, of course, why?"

"Nothing . . ."

"I'm just not a very good doggie nurse."

"If you wait a minute, I'll grab my helmet and walk you to your car."

"That's not necessary . . ."

"It's okay. I'm finished for the day." He returned, carrying a stars and stripes helmet. No! Sandy thought. Not Leonard Krann, DVM, with a practice limited to Canines and Felines, with a wife who has problem hair, with two small screaming, snot-nosed children. Not Lenny Krann, future Club Member. No!

He saw her to her car, jumped on his motorcycle, revved up the motor, and took off, waving to her as he did.

My God! Could it be?

No! Steve had told her stars and stripes helmets were very big last year. The moon landing and all that.

Still . . .

25

She had the table set and the food attractively arranged on a platter when Norman came home. "You didn't cook again?" he asked.

"I was very busy and it was so hot."

"Carry-out food two nights in a row?"

"Last night I wasn't feeling well. Besides, what's the difference?"

"I counted on pot roast tonight. I'd really like to get back on schedule, Sandy."

"All right, as soon as the kids come home I'll try. I did take Banushka to the vet though."

"What did he say?"

"He said Banushka is a beautiful dog . . . very strong and healthy . . . he could be a show dog he's so perfect . . ."

"Really?"

"Not exactly in those words."

"Well, at least you managed to accomplish one thing today."

"Yes, at least I did."

She waited until after dinner, until they were both

seated in the den, Norman reading the paper, Sandy with her needlepoint spread out on her lap, the TV tuned in to some variety show, a summer replacement, before saying what she had to say. "Norm, I'd like to talk to you."

"Go ahead."

"Will you put down the paper, please, this is important . . ."

"I can read and listen at the same time."

"Norman, I've got gonorrhea."

"Uh huh . . ." He turned the page.

She raised her voice. "I said I've got gonorrhea!"

"What are you talking about?" Now he put the paper down and looked across the room at her.

"I'm talking about gonorrhea . . . the clap . . . you must have read about it in one of your *AMA Journals*."

"I know all about gonorrhea."

"Well, I'm telling you that I've got it."

"You've got gonorrhea?"

"Yes!"

"Says who?"

"Says Gordon, who the hell do you think?"

"It must be a mistake. They must have switched slides or something."

"No!"

"Sandy, if this is your idea of a joke."

"Would I joke about something this serious?"

"Where would you have gotten gonorrhea?"

"From you." Liar, liar, from Vincent X. Moseley, most likely, if Shep was telling the truth and if Rhoda doesn't play around and if Gordon really hasn't been with anyone else and if Myra hasn't lately and if *you* didn't.

264

"The hell you did! I haven't been with another woman since before I met you."

"How about a man? You can get it from them too."

"Are you calling me a fag?"

"I'm just stating the facts." *Almost.*

"If you've got gonorrhea, you got it from somebody else," he said, raising *his* voice as her words sank in.

"And I say that *you* got it from somebody else and gave it to me." Better to accuse than admit.

He stood up and paced the floor, smashing his right fist into his left palm. "I can prove that I haven't been with anyone."

"How, how can you prove that?"

He turned abruptly and pointed at her. On the TV screen John Davidson was singing to a woman named Loretta. "One of us is lying and I know it's not me! Not that I haven't had the chance. Just last weekend when you were away . . ."

"Last weekend, well, I'd certainly like to hear about that."

"Not one, but two, get it, two women at The Club propositioned me." He waggled two fingers in her face.

"Who . . . who were they?"

"You'll never know. I didn't take them up on it because I consider marriage a contract, not like you, you fucking bitch! I should have known. You've probably been screwing around for years."

"And what about you? You and Brenda Partington Yvelenski!"

He turned white. "What do you know about her?"

"Plenty."

"How did you find out?"

"That doesn't matter."

"It matters to me."

The audience was applauding, John Davidson was smiling his beautiful, dimpled smile.

"You've been in my Tufts box?"

"Yes." What did that have to do with it?

"What right did you have to go into my Tufts box?" The TV camera cut to an Alka-Seltzer commercial.

"I was sorting out your junk. And what right did you have to give her five thousand dollars without discussing it with me?"

"You never missed it."

"That's not the point."

"I suppose you read the letters?"

What letters?

"Answer me!"

She just looked at him.

"Answer me, I said!"

"Yes, the answer is yes." *But not to that question.*

"Then you know all there is to know." He walked across the room and switched off the TV.

I don't know anything, she wanted to say but she was already in too deep to back off.

"So you know that I couldn't have given you gonorrhea . . . so that leaves you . . . so who was it, Sandy . . . who'd you spread your legs for?"

She didn't answer.

"Tell me," he shouted, lifting her out of the chair by the shoulders. "Tell me, you bitch!" he said, shaking her. He was losing control now. She couldn't remember ever having seen Norman out of control. She found his anger frightening, but at the same time exciting. Exciting because she was the cause of it.

"Cunt!" He smacked her across the face, catching the corner of her mouth. Her hand automatically went to the place, holding it, trying to ease the pain. She tasted blood. "Who was it?"

"It doesn't matter," she said, as tears came to her eyes.

"Aha! So you admit it, you've been screwing around."

"Yes, I admit it! I've been with somebody else."

"I ought to beat the shit out of you."

"You touch me again and you'll live to regret it."

"Who was he?"

"I don't have to tell you. I don't have to tell you anything." She turned and ran, ran upstairs, and then upstairs again, to the attic, locking the door behind her.

Norman followed, yelling, "Goddamned whore. Goddamned fucking whore." And when he reached the door to the attic and found it locked, he kicked it, shouting, "Come out of there! Come out right now!"

"Go away," Sandy hollered. "Go away and leave me alone!" She heard Norman clomp back down the stairs. And then it was quiet. What was he doing? Would he get the gun, shoot the lock off the attic door, then shoot her? Or himself? Or both of them? *Murder-Suicide*

Local Businessman Shoots Wife, Self
Norman Pressman, owner of Pressman's Dry Cleaning Stores, shot and killed his wife, Sondra Schaedel Pressman, last night, before taking his own life. Friends and relatives described Mr. Pressman as a quiet man. "In fact, phlegmatic," said Mrs. Pressman's sister, Myra Lefferts, of Short Hills, the owner of a showplace with eight and one half baths . . .

One of them was supposed to leave. Sandy knew that. She'd read enough books, seen enough movies.

She could hear Myra advising her. Pack your bags and come over here. We'll call a good lawyer, the best in the state. We'll take the bastard for everything!

But Myra, the children. What am I going to do about them? They'll be back soon.

For the time being you'll stay with me. Then we'll help you find a place of your own and you'll start a new life. Nobody has to take what you just took. Forget what I told you two weeks ago. Get out now!

But I want to end the marriage on my own terms, when I'm ready.

If you're not ready after this, then you'll never be ready and you deserve what you get.

Are you saying I'm a masochist?

I'm saying you're a meshugunah!

She thought she heard the front door slam. She ran to the window and looked down. There was Norman, walking Banushka, as if it were just any other night. She went to the "Tufts Box," her heart beating so loud she could hear it.

She turned the box upside down, dumping the rest of its contents all over the floor. Tiny color slides spilled out of dozens of Kodak boxes. She swallowed hard, then sifted through four years of junk until she found the packet of letters, eight of them, all in blue envelopes, addressed to Norman at the Plainfield plant, in purple ink. The return address read B.P.Y. Newburyport, Massachusetts. She checked the postmarks. Yes, they were in order, beginning in October, 1969, not even a year ago, and going through May, 1970. She turned them over in her hand. Did she even want to know?

Yes.

Yes, she certainly did!

October 18

Dear Norman,

So many years have gone by since we last saw each other yet I feel sure that you will remember me as I remember you. I made a lot of mistakes, Norman, and I know how deeply I must have hurt you. I don't expect you to forgive me or to understand. I loved you, not Stash. How can I explain? Let me try. I guess what happened was that I saw my life with you and I got scared. You had everything so well thought out and I didn't want to think about the future at all. I wanted to live only for the moment. So I rebelled and ran away with Stash, who didn't have a thought in his head. Does any of this make sense to you? I hope so.

Stash and I had three children in four years. He made some money in the used car business but then gambled it away. I finally left him, two years ago, and went to California. I worked as a waitress most of the time. Stash has never sent a penny to me or the kids. I've heard that he's in New Mexico now, involved in some land deal. But I'm not complaining. I've never been one to complain, as you know.

I came back east six months ago and am hoping to open a small restaurant in Newbury-port. Remember the weekend we spent here? I guess that's why I've always wanted to come back. That weekend with you was the happiest of my life. But enough looking back. You can't look back, can you? You have to go forward. And that's what I'm trying to do, with a little help from my friends. To be blunt, I'm asking you for a loan of up to $5000. I will pay you back with interest, of course, I hope within two years. Less if things go well.

On a more personal note, what happened to us, Norman? You were going to be a great biologist and save the world. Instead you clean people's clothes. (You see, I've kept up with you!) Not that I am knocking your chosen profession. I certainly haven't accomplished what I set out to do either. Now, instead of becoming a great actress or writer, I am happy if I can manage to feed my family. But please do not feel sorry for me. I am strong and determined. At least I haven't changed that way.

With love and affection always,
Brenda Partington Yvelenski

My God! Was she writing about Norman, *her* Norman? A great biologist? Saving the world? When? How? By the time Sandy had met him he was a senior business major. He'd never even mentioned biology to her.

November 9

Dear Norman,

Thank you for your kind letter. I can understand that you want more information before committing yourself to an investment in my restaurant. It will be small, serving only 20-30 at a time. It is located on the main street, next to the bank. I plan to decorate with butcher block tables, wicker chairs, local artists' work, and plenty of plants. We will have a limited menu. (Remember how we used to save menus, circling what we'd had to eat?) I am a fine cook and my children are wonderful, willing helpers. I hope to hire two or three waiters. We won't have a liquor license at first, but customers will be encouraged to bring their own wine.

Norman, on a more personal note, I'm glad you're happily married and enjoying your two children. I'm sure Sandy is exactly the wife you always wanted. Even during that long, cold winter when we loved so intensely I had my doubts about us. You were already so sure of what you wanted out of life and I wanted, needed, to be free. Strange how things work out.

> With love and the happiest of memories,
> Brenda

Exactly the wife he'd always wanted? Not lately, Brenda!

November 24

Dear Norman,

Thanks so much for your letter and check. The $5000 is more than appreciated. My parents have come through as well and are lending me $2000 and my cousin, Irene, who married a stockbroker in Spokane, is lending me $2500, as is my brother, Rog, who is a butcher in Providence. Now I can go to the bank and make all the arrangements. I hope to open by Valentine's Day which I think will be a fitting holiday considering all the love that has gone into this project, not the least of all, yours.

On a more personal note, thank you for the picture of Sandy and the children. They look just right for you. I wish you had included a picture of yourself, as well. Norman, if it matters at all, please know that I have never loved anyone the way I loved you. And please know that I will always love you and if ever things aren't going well with you . . . I hope you know what I am trying to say.

> With all my love and gratitude,
> Bren

The love of her life? Norman? God, had Brenda been the love of *his* life too? Had he married *her* the way she had married him? For safety . . . for comfort . . . for convenience. Were she and Norman really alike after all?

> December 16

A CHRISTMAS WISH TO YOU AND YOURS
A NEW YEAR FULL OF BRIGHTNESS

> Brenda Partington Yvelenski

> Andrew, Robin, and Yvette

All of this was printed on a color photo, showing three beautiful children and Brenda herself, a chunky woman of about thirty-five with a pretty, round face, framed by long dark hair. Beneath the photo she had added,

Thinking of you on this day . . . Remembering the holiday season we spent together. Was it really so long ago? It seems like yesterday to me.

> Love always,
> B

> January 5

Dear Norman,

I am going to be in New York on the 12th to shop for supplies for the restaurant. You can't beat the wholesalers prices there. I hope I can see you then. I want so much to thank you in person. I'll be at the H.J. Motor Lodge in mid-Manhattan. Please call me.

My love and devotion,
Bren

Had he gone? January 12, they'd been back from Jamaica ten days. Norman was still tan, thanks to his new sunlamp, and he had no herpes on his lips. Jesus, if he'd gone . . . if he'd . . .

January 18

Dearest Norman,

It was just wonderful seeing you again. You are every bit as attractive as you were way back when. I enjoyed our lunch so much. I only wish it could have been more. You know what I mean. Yes, I can understand your feelings about Sandy and I think it is admirable of you to choose to remain faithful to her. I certainly have no desire to break up your happy marriage. I guess I just wanted to renew our relationship on a "special occasions" basis. However, I will respect your wishes and will not contact you again except to let you know where to reach me. I am already on a crash diet and plan to lose 25 pounds before summer.

Much love, always
Brenda

Admirable intentions. How like Norman. Maybe if he had let go this time, given in to his emotions just

once, she could have told him about Shep. Maybe
then he would have understood and they could have
worked things out together.

Sandy, you're supposed to feel proud that he cares
so much he wouldn't you-know-what with another
woman . . .

Maybe, but I'd rather know he's human . . .

Sandy, I can't believe this. Any other woman would
get down on her knees and kiss the ground he walks
on.

So sue me . . .

February 9

Announcing the opening of Brenda's Bistro
Main Street
Newburyport, Mass.

Serving dinner from six to nine
Reservations, please

Brenda Partington Yvelenski, Owner/Chef

(With a little help from her friends)

And finally . . .

May 10

Dear Norman,

I've been so busy I haven't had a chance to
write. Business at the Bistro is excellent and we
are looking forward to summer, our heaviest tour-
ist season. Also, I have met a very nice man, Ken
Sweeney, who has a house here. He is semi-
retired, with business ties in Boston. He is
slightly older (61) but we really enjoy each other's

company. I am enclosing a check in the amount of $2750. I plan to pay off your loan by November. Again, thanks so much for your help, your support, your confidence in me. I will never forget you.

Affectionately,
Bren

How easy it should be to hate this overconfident, independent woman! How easy to hate this Brenda, who wanted to renew her relationship with Norman on a "special occasions" basis.

Sandy, you sound jealous.

I'm pissed, not jealous.

You could have fooled me!

Oh, yes, she wanted to hate Brenda Partington Yvelenski. But it wasn't so easy after all. Brenda sounded too decent, too human, and more love poured out of her letters than Sandy and Norman had shared in twelve years of marriage. That hurt more than anything else. She had a sudden desire to call Brenda, to ask her what Norman had *really* been like way back then. Because she could see now that there must have been another Norman. A Norman who dreamed of becoming a biologist . . . of saving the world. A Norman who loved intensely. Could that Norman still be locked inside the Norman she knew, just as another Sandy was inside her, struggling to get out?

Her Norman had opted for his parents' way of life . . . was becoming his father just as she was following in Mona's footsteps. Oh, God, do we all turn into our parents in the end?

Norman was banging on the attic door again, calling, "Sandy, come down, come to bed."

"Just leave me alone."

"You can't stay up there all night. Come down. I won't hurt you, I promise."

"Go away!"

"Sandy, please . . ."

"No!"

Sandy turned out all but one of the attic lights and crawled into Bucky's Snoopy sleeping bag. She slept fitfully, thinking about this man who was her husband. This man whom she hardly knew.

🐝 26 🐝

IN THE MORNING Norman was gone. To work? To his lawyer's office? To Reno? She didn't know. She checked his closet. All of his things were in order. She ran a hot tub, looking at herself in the mirror for the first time since last night's main event. Her lip was swollen. She should have put ice on it then. Now it was too late. She sank into the tub, trying to soak away the pain.

What was she supposed to do about her life?

Where were the rules when you needed them?

Norman came home from work carrying a pizza. A peace offering? "I didn't think you'd want to cook tonight."

Absolutely right.

"And I didn't think you'd feel like going out either."

Right again.

"I went to the doctor this afternoon. He had to massage my prostate to get a culture. You have no idea how uncomfortable it is for a male to have his prostate massaged."

Try having a baby some day.

"He didn't see any sign of gonorrhea but given the circumstances felt I should take the medication anyway . . . just in case . . . to be safe. I'll turn on the oven." He studied the knobs. "Which one—bake, broil, preheat, or time-bake?"

She almost laughed. "Bake, three-fifty."

"You don't look bad."

Thanks very much.

He shoved the pizza into the oven, closed the door, and, still facing it, said, "I've thought it over carefully and I've decided to let you stay. There's no point in messing up the kids' lives. I assume that you've learned your lesson and that it won't happen again." He paused. "Say something, will you?"

"I don't know if I want to stay," she said. "I don't know what our lives will be like if I do."

"I don't know either and I don't know if I'll ever be able to trust you again . . ."

She stood up. "Well, then . . ." She started to walk toward the door.

"Sandy . . . wait . . . don't go . . . please . . ." he said, turning away from the oven at last. "I need you . . . and I'm willing to try . . . I'll make every effort to trust you . . . if you promise . . ."

How like Bucky he seemed now. How like a little boy. Did he really need her or was he just saying it?

"And I'm willing to get a double bed for the new house."

"A double bed?" Now she could see how scared he really was. Scared that she'd actually leave him. For the first time in years she wanted to put her arms around him. To comfort him.

"Yes. You've always wanted one, haven't you?"

"But Norm, you . . ."

"I said I'm willing to try and I'm sorry if I hurt you

278

last night." He looked at the floor, not at her. "But you have to remember that you hurt me first."

Okay. She could understand that. Could try to, anyway. "You should have told me about Brenda. I read her letters last night."

"Reread them, you mean."

"No, I read them for the first time."

"But you said . . ."

She shook her head. "I found the canceled check . . . that's how I knew."

"What were you doing in the gun cabinet?"

"Dusting."

"Come on, Sandy."

"All right . . . I was thinking about shooting myself."

"Because of the gonorrhea?"

"Because of us . . . me, you . . . I don't know . . ."

"Sandy, what would that have solved?"

"For me, everything, but, as you can see, I decided against it."

He let out a deep sigh. "I don't know what you want from me, San. You once said *love*. Well, I love you. I love you the only way I know how. I'm sorry if it's not enough for you." His voice caught.

She began to cry, softly. "Can we make it work? Can we, Norm?"

"I don't know. I think if you'll be reasonable this time, we can. I think if you stop thinking, stop questioning everything, and just settle back and relax, we can. If you accept me the way I am, yes. Otherwise, I just don't know, but I find the idea of divorce repulsive."

Divorce.

"Tomorrow's our anniversary. You don't throw twelve years of your life away just like that," he said, snapping his fingers. "I think we should turn over a new leaf. Maybe I shouldn't have pushed you so hard this summer. Maybe I should have let you sit home alone day after day. I thought I was doing what was best for you. I've always tried to do what's best for you."

That's news to me.

"So what do you say, San?" he asked, nuzzling her.

"The pizza's burning."

27

"HAPPY ANNIVERSARY!"

Myra had arranged a family dinner at The Club to help them celebrate. Twelve years. Sandy looked around the table as they toasted her and Norman, thinking, *What am I doing here?*

Myra sat opposite Sandy in faded bluejeans, a T-shirt, and a sleek new haircut, her San Francisco look. "And Sandy," she'd said earlier, when they'd gone to the Ladies Room by themselves, "Gordy and I smoked our first grass out there. Everyone at the convention had it and it was great. I'm telling you, we've never enjoyed each other so much . . ."

I know, Sandy wanted to say, *I saw pictures.*

Gordon sat next to Myra. He looked slightly embarrassed. From the intimate details of *her* life, Sandy wondered, or his own?

Connie sat next to Gordon, and Kate, next to her, each of them twenty-five pounds lighter, with an adorable new nose and acting *vivacious,* just like their mother. The wonders of plastic surgery!

Mona, next to Sandy.

Enid, next to Norm.

Myra was saying, "And Gordy and I flew to Aspen on our way back from San Francisco and we bought a fabulous condominium and we're all going to learn to ski next winter."

"Wonderful," Norman said. "I've always wanted to ski."

Not you, Sandy thought. Them.

"Let's hope nobody breaks a leg," Mona said.

"Oh, Grandma, you always think the worst about everything!"

"Somebody has to."

"And . . ." Myra went on, "that's not all. We're thinking of going into boating next summer. We've been looking at yachts all week. They're so cute. Just like little houses, with three bedrooms and two baths and double ovens. What size are we looking at, Gordy, fifty feet?"

"Something like that."

"We're thinking about boating out to the Hamptons or up to the Cape . . . and did you hear that Gordy's taking a partner next month so he won't have to work so hard . . . and we're going to have more time together . . ." She leaned over and kissed him. Gordon blushed. "And you're all invited on our yacht next summer."

"Thank you, but I prefer land," Enid said.

"Yes, we hear you're going to Florida," Gordon said to her.

"Maybe. My son thinks I should retire." Enid gave Norman a martyred look. "But I don't know."

"You've worked hard for a long time, Mom," Norman said.

"Oh, I'm sure you'll love it there, Mrs. Pressman," Myra said. "Gordy's parents have been there for years and they're very happy."

"It's full of old people," Enid said, "waiting to die."

"No, that's not so at all," Myra told her. "There are a lot of retired people but they're not necessarily old."

"And who knows," Mona said, "maybe you'll meet a nice man."

"I don't see you with one," Enid shot back.

"But I'm not in Florida," Mona said, winking at Sandy, letting her know that she and Morris Minster were still going strong.

Enid turned to Mona. "Never mind Florida . . . I suppose you hear they sold the house to a realtor . . . practically gave it away . . . and the railing on the stairway alone is worth a small fortune . . . imported . . . I tell you, Mona . . . it's one disappointment after the other . . ."

"Be happy they're well, that's what counts."

Enid sighed. "Who's to say? If I had it to do over again I would do it a lot differently, I'll tell you that."

"So who wouldn't?" Mona asked.

Yes, Sandy thought. Who wouldn't? I might be sharing my anniversary dinners with Shep, and Norman might be sharing his with Brenda, no matter what our parents had to say about it. No . . . wait . . . that's unfair . . . I can't go on blaming Mona forever . . . I'm the one who married Norman . . . nobody held a knife to my throat . . . stop thinking, Sandy . . . it hurts too much to think . . .

"Sandy, you're not touching your food," Mona said.

"Who can blame her?" Enid asked. "You should only try cutting this drek they call roast beef, and cold soup just like last time."

"What happened to your mouth, Aunt Sandy?" Kate said. "It looks swollen."

"Another herpes, San?" Myra asked.

"No, it's . . ." She had applied her makeup carefully, hoping that no one would notice.

"We didn't want you to know," Norman said, "but Sandy had a little accident two days ago. She fell down the stairs."

Very good, Norman. Very imaginative.

"Sandy, sweetheart!" Mona looked concerned.

"I didn't fall down the whole flight," she told them, trying to laugh it off. "Just the bottom three. I tripped."

"You went to the doctor?" Mona asked.

"Yes, of course."

"You're sure you're all right?"

"Yes. Fine." She caught Gordon looking at her, skeptically, and repeated, "I'm fine, really."

Enid offered an after-dinner toast. "May the next thirteen years be just as happy."

"Twelve," Sandy said.

"So be happy an extra year."

"How about a little something for our anniversary, San?"

"You already gave me a gold bracelet."

"But you haven't given me anything yet."

"I didn't know what to get."

"I'll settle for a little something. Remember our wedding night, San?"

"Very well."

"And our honeymoon?"

"Uh huh."

"We were really hot stuff then, weren't we?"

"I guess."

He rolled on top of her. "Got your diaphragm in?"

"No."

"I'll get it for you." He padded off to the bathroom and returned with the blue plastic case.

"Norman, why didn't you ever tell me you wanted to be a biologist?"

"I was just a kid then. By the time I'd met you I'd changed my mind . . ."

"I wish you'd told me anyway . . . about that and about Brenda . . ."

"It was a long time ago."

"You must have been very hurt when she ran off."

"I don't want to talk about it."

"Sometimes you have to talk about things even if they do hurt."

"Look, there was no way I was going to marry Brenda."

"Why not?"

"Because she was too . . . too . . ."

"Too what?"

"Too different."

"Because she was a shiksa?"

"She was a shiksa, she was a townie, and if you want to know the truth, I sent her the five thousand dollars because I've always felt guilty."

"She's the one who ran off."

"And when she did I was relieved. I knew I'd never marry her."

"But you loved her."

"What's love, anyway?"

"It's a feeling."

"I told you, I was a kid then. None of it matters now."

"What was it like when you saw her in New York?"

"I didn't sleep with her. You already know that."

"But you wanted to?"

"I thought about it."

"Maybe you should have."

"Maybe."

"Norman, why did you marry me?"

"Why does anybody get married?"

"I'm asking you."

"Because you were the right girl for me, the girl I wanted to spend the rest of my life with."

"And now?"

"I like things the way they are. That is, the way they were, until recently."

"We don't really know each other, Norm. Doesn't that scare you?"

"Sometimes."

"We should get to know each other better."

"How?"

"I'm not sure. I think we have to get to know ourselves, first."

"Okay."

"Okay, what?"

"I'm ready for you, San." He ran his hand down her body.

She inserted her diaphragm.

She came twice.

Well, why not? Who was it helping when she didn't come? Not Norman. Not herself. Not the marriage.

After, instead of rolling into his own bed he stayed close to her and asked, "Was it good with the other guy?"

"It was okay."

"So who was he, San?"

"You don't know him."

"Was it *as* good with him?"

"Different."

"You always come twice with me."

"Yes."

"Did you with him?"

"No." *How about a five-course meal, kid?*

"I want you to know that I understand why it happened," he said and she could feel his relief. "I really do. You married me when you were just a girl. You'd never slept with anyone else and you were curious. I guess I'm glad you got it out of your system now so long as it never happens again. Because that would be the end. I couldn't tolerate it happening again."

"Norm . . ." She took his hand.

"Uh huh."

"If I shave off my pubic hair do you think you might, you know?"

"Did *he* do that to you?"

"Yes."

"And you liked it?"

"Yes."

"And he didn't gag?"

"No."

"I see, but if you shave won't that make it feel like whiskers?"

"I don't know. I think you have to develop a taste for it, Norm, like lobster."

"Maybe so . . . maybe so . . ."

"And without hair to get caught in your throat."

"Yes, I see what you mean."

"Didn't you and Brenda . . ."

"No."

"Oh."

"Tell you what, shave it off tomorrow and we'll give it a try."

"Fair enough."

"Night, San, glad we got it all worked out."

"Night, Norm, glad we got started."

28

THE NEXT MORNING Norman got up and sprayed the bedroom with Lysol. He showered and shaved, kissed Sandy's cheek, and left for work. Sandy lay in bed thinking, about Norman, about herself, about the marriage, until she heard the sound of the motorcycle. Was he back? Was he? She hurried to the window in her nightgown. Yes, there he was. In his usual place. When he saw her in the window he dropped his jeans around his ankles and began. In the middle of his act she called, "Who are you? Take off your helmet for a change."

He stopped.

"Are you Dr. Krann?" she asked.

He pulled up his jeans.

"I want to know who you are!"

He ran to his bike, jumped on it, and took off.

Damn! She'd probably never know now. Whoever he was she had the feeling he wouldn't be back. Just as well, she told herself. The kids were coming home from camp today. They'd be moving in a few weeks. She'd be busy again. Much too busy to think about him or anyone else.

Enter the world of the rich and the powerful, where people stop at nothing to gain even more wealth and power.

———————

Become enmeshed in the glamour, the greed, the fatal secrets and the torrid love affairs of those who control the government, the economy, every walk of life.

———————

These are the people that intrigue millions—the lives that never escape public attention.

Bestselling Novels from